If you have a lust for life,
a sense of risk,
or a wild imagination—
nothing is impossible.
Charles de Belmont
had all three . . .

In 1940, in Nazi-run France, the penniless young son of a village whore began his odyssey of ambition . . .

Within a decade, Charles de Belmont was one of the richest financiers in the world. He'd loved the most beautiful, the choicest women. And controlled the most powerful—and dangerous—men.

He'd learned to play

THE ODDS

THE ODDS

Eddie Constantine

A DELL BOOK

Published by
Dell Publishing Co., Inc.
1 Dag Hammarskjold Plaza
New York, New York 10017

Dell ® TM 681510, Dell Publishing Co., Inc.

ISBN: 0-440-16602-0

Printed in Canada

First printing—November 1978

THE ODDS

Part One

MAKING THE ODDS
Europe, 1939–1948

I

Young men from the French village were fighting in the dry riverbed, throwing stones that the torrent brought down from the Alps every spring with the melting snow. A youth in a red shirt was struck on the head, and he fell with blood on his face the color of his shirt. Two of those in black shirts were already out of action, one nursing a leg and the other a broken arm. But slowly the blackshirts were driving the red shirts up the dry torrent—there were ten of them and only four of the enemy. A final volley of stones sent the red shirts scrambling away, leaving their bleeding comrade. The blackshirts rushed at him and kicked him until he was unconscious. Then they marched away down the riverbed, singing one of the songs the Action Française had made so popular that summer before World War II.

A young man tall for his age and too handsome for his clothes stood watching them from his hiding place in a small cave above the river. Stringy and loose, Charles Gruex sprawled on the stone. His patched

pants and shirt and old sandals seemed like a bad
joke, as if he were a prince playing a poor young
man. His hair was fine and very fair, and his large
eyes blazed with the shifting blues and greens of fired
copper. He had been dreaming in his cave, counting
his escape money of nearly twenty *mille* francs, half
of what he needed. So he had seen the whole fight
from the beginning.

He had sometimes thought of joining the red shirts,
but they were too few and they had to lose. He had
thought of joining the blackshirts, but they had to
win, and he did not want to be a camp follower. The
whole world seemed to have gone mad, trying to
force everybody to take sides. Yet there was only one
way to go—his own way.

When the blackshirts had marched off, Charles
climbed down to the body of the red shirt lying on
the stones. He recognized the young man immediately. It was Marc from the village. There was little
of his skin which was not cut or bruised, but as
Charles felt his limbs, he could find no broken bones.
The blackshirts had been wearing sandals. In boots,
they might have killed him.

Charles walked over to the solitary clump of oak,
where the only spring for miles around bubbled out
salt water. He took off his old blue shirt, soaked it,
and then squeezed the water out over Marc's face until he became alive again.

On the way home Marc asked Charles why he
wanted to save him.

"You're not political, Charles. You're not for Hitler, not for us. Why did you help me?"

"I couldn't leave you lying on the stones, Marc."

"They'll think you one of us now. Oh, my leg—"

The two young men stopped and watched the

night bright with stars. There was a huge peace as large as the sky, and in the coolness the only warmth was the touching of their thin bodies. Charles's eyes burned, his fair hair gleamed, almost luminous in the dark.

"Hang onto me," Charles said. "I'll get you home."

"Will you join us?"

"No," Charles said, "I won't. If you'd won and left one of them there, I'd have done the same thing for him."

"You're very noble," Marc said, hobbling along with his arm round Charles's shoulder.

"Not at all. I may ask you to help me one day and you won't be able to refuse. If I was part of a mob kicking you, who the hell would remember me?"

"You're very cynical," Marc said. "I think there's something else disturbing you."

Charles felt his body stiffen in fear of Marc's words. The arm on his shoulder weighed a ton. He knew what Marc would say. It was always the same. It would be about his mother, the village whore.

"You feel out of it, Charles—unable to join—different. You even look different—taller than us, fairer. You feel you have to stand apart."

"You mean, my mother—" Charles tried to keep his voice steady, but he heard it tremble in his mouth. "You mean because I haven't got a father—"

The lights of the village were near now and the dogs began barking as if thieves were coming in the dark.

"You should join us, Charles; we're all comrades in the Party; it doesn't matter where you come from. In fact, to be a proletarian—"

Charles pushed away Marc's arm that hung so heavily on his neck.

"It's right up the road from here," he said. "You can make it on your own. I'm going home."

"But Charles—"

"Don't thank me, Marc. Remember me."

He didn't want to come to the farmhouse by way of the barn, for fear of what he would find there. But it drew him to the rays of light that came out of the cracks in the wooden door. Inside, he would see the oil lamp burning, the bodies lying on the hay. And he knew he had to look.

So he found himself standing at the peephole in the barn door. He could see his mother lying on the straw, her dress spread under her body. A sailor was on top of her moving between her legs bent into two white triangles.

"You're taking your time," she was saying.

"You're not helping much."

"OK, *chéri*—I'll help."

She began to move her buttocks from side to side, rolling her thighs and squeezing them against the sailor's straining hips. Suddenly she crooked all her fingers and dug them into the cleft of his bell-bottomed trousers, pulling him painfully into her. He groaned and came, and she groaned twice to show some sort of pleasure. Sometimes she got extra for that.

"That was marvelous, *chéri*," she said.

Charles Gruex felt anger making him sick. But stronger than his anger was his curiosity. He was watching his mother, who had given birth to him out of that body. He was seeing her sex—her sex with a stranger, a stranger like his father. He shivered and ⸴ed at the door.

⸴ sat up on the straw, her big breasts falling onto

her knees, then jerking upright as she held her dress above her and began to pull it down over her head and shoulders. The sailor felt her breasts for the last time, but she turned her back on him and stood up, pulling the dress down over the swell of her hips and brushing away the bits of dry grass.

"You like sailors," the man said.

"Yes," the woman said. "I've a son by a sailor."

"Like me?"

"No, not like you. He wanted to marry me."

"I bet he sailed away. Sailors always do."

"He sailed away," she said. "It was the end of the war. He never wrote. Maybe he was killed. I don't know. He was from the north. Did you ever go to a place called Scapa Flow?"

"It's in Scotland," the sailor said. "Near Loch Ness, where the monster comes from."

"We had all kinds of ships in Toulon during the war," the woman said. "British, Italian, American. There were sailors everywhere, and all our boys were away at the front. The girls from the villages would go down to see them. Just for a dance and some fun, but—things happen—"

The boy's ears burned at the door. They were talking about him. Had she no shame? It was worse than the act of sex—animals did that. His mother was telling his shame to a stranger, that he was a bastard.

He lowered his head and waited to charge before he vomited.

Inside the barn, the sailor took from his pocket a few French notes, crumpled into a ball. He slid a *mille* off the top, then his hand went into his pocket again and came out with a coin.

"Buy something for the kid," he said.

Charles came through the barn doorway in a low

rush. He butted the sailor in the stomach, knocking the wind and the sense out of him. The sailor fell, and Charles was on his chest, tearing at the man's face with his fingernails until his mother dragged him back.

"Don't, Charles, he'll call the *flics!* We'll go to jail. They'll think we set it up."

"I'll kill him!"

"Please—"

The rage washed out of the young man. He looked at the blood on his fingernails and the bleeding face of the sailor lying unconscious on the straw.

"*Merde,*" he said.

He felt in the sailor's pocket and took out the ball of money. There were sixteen *mille* notes and some change. Enough to escape on along with his hoard in the cave.

"You can't steal it, Charles."

"Why not?"

Charles stood over his mother, lean and tall and alien, a blond, thin avenger from another country—almost from another world. His eyes glittered like a beast's.

"You earn it, *mille* by *mille,* on your back slowly. I earn it in one night, like that. I'm going."

"I only do it for you, my son."

"Then give it to me."

The tall young man held out his hand. There was a force in him, an air of command that allowed no resistance. His mother put her hand down the neck of her dress and took out the *mille* she had made and gave it to her son.

"You leave me nothing," she said.

"What have you left me?"

Charles raised his hand as if he were going to slap

her. She crouched, her elbow in front of her face.
They had changed their roles. How many times had
he thrown up an arm to ward off her knuckles sting-
ing against his cheek? How many times had the
punishment been followed by wet kisses in his
mother's arms?

He dropped his hand and walked over to the barn
door.

"I'm leaving after I've seen Granma."

"Where to?"

"I don't know. As long as it's not here."

"You'll run away and leave us to the police?"

Charles looked at the sailor, who was beginning to
move and moan.

"He won't talk. He'd be too ashamed. Robbed by
the son of a whore like me?"

Charles took one of the coins he had taken from
the sailor and threw it across the barn. It hit the
sailor's face. The man groaned again.

"I'm giving it back," Charles said.

He walked out of the barn. Already the pale light
of dawn was picking out the bleached, dry hills behind the farmhouse. There were more stones than
blades of grass in the fields. The udders of the cows
had dried up; the corn withered on the stalk out
there in the sun and the dry wind. There was no farm-
ing in the village—just surviving.

As the young man crossed the farmyard, the sow
grunted at him. He looked over the edge of the sty, at
her white unlovely mass. Only three of her piglets
were still alive lying around her. She had eaten most
of her litter because there was nothing else to eat.

In the farmhouse, his old grandmother was at the
scrubbed table, feeding her husband in his
wheelchair. Bread and watered milk—it was all he

could take in. Charles looked at the face of the old
woman who had raised him, and he saw skin cracked
into a thousand lines by overwork in the sun. His
grandmother turned away and spooned more soup
into the slack lips of her old husband, who dribbled
down the front of his black jacket. Charles flinched at
the sight of him—that limp weight to lift, that sour
smell of age when a man couldn't look after himself
anymore.

The young man took out a *mille* note and put it
on the table.

"Get some coffee in town," he said. "And some of
the sweet biscuits Grandpa likes."

The old woman looked at the money.

"Where did you get it?"

"Take it. Don't ask me."

The old woman picked up the *mille* note and
tucked it into her apron.

"Your *maman* gave it you."

"I took it. I'm going, Granma. For ever."

He stood by the kitchen door, fair and straight, not
yet stooped by long labor on the stones, not coarsened
by dust and sun. He was a stranger, not part of the
place and the ground. All he had was a name,
Charles Gruex.

"We need you," the old woman said. She wiped the
mess off the face of the old man who was nodding
and grumbling. "This was a good farm once. If your
uncle hadn't been killed in the Great War—"

"There are nothing but stones here. I won't kill
myself on them, break my back like him—"

Charles looked fiercely at the paralyzed old man as
if he were ready to pounce on him for being a victim
to the barren earth. He would never end that way.
Never, never.

"They all go," the old woman said. "All the young ones. Soon there will only be the stones in the village. And us—who will bury us?"

The young man came forward. He wanted to kiss his grandmother, but he could not, in case a feeling for her helplessness made him stay. So he stared at her with glittering eyes as if he hated her. His voice was hoarse.

"You'll never see me here again. I can't take it here."

"You'll always be Charles Gruex."

"Not even that! I'll start again."

"You'll always be Charles Gruex."

As the old woman spoke her flat words like a judgment, the young man felt his blood rushing to his face. His anger, his shame, his impotence, his pity would condemn him always to this harsh life on the stones if he did not run out of the door, run to the steep path winding over the hills toward the west, where people said there was a sea called the Atlantic which millions had crossed to begin their lives again.

He put his head down for the second time that early morning and charged out of the kitchen, hurling himself forward to the cave above the dry riverbed. He would get the rest of his money and get away. Already new names whirled in his head—names of glory and greatness.

Charles the Bold, Charlemagne, Charles Martel . . .

All was possible if he could leave these killing stones before the war of the Blackshirts came over the mountains from Italy to murder all the young men who had not got away.

II

The young Charles had the plump girl hanging onto the rails of the brass bed, shouting at him as he took her from the back on all fours like a ram with a she-goat.

"You're hurting me—you're raping me!"

The fingernails of one of his hands scratched at her hanging nipples while his other hand rubbed at the opening of the cleft between her legs where her soft triangle of hair pointed the way. As he came, she shook and shuddered and lowered her face on the pillow in submission. He bit her softly on the nape of the neck, then he pulled out of her and lay on his back beside her, kneeling on the bed, with her rump in the air and her face down by his cheek. His lean body stretched the whole length of the bed. A yellow light filtered through the closed shutters of the dock-side hotel in Bordeaux.

"I couldn't rape you," he said. "I bought you."

"You could do it softly," the girl said. "Most of the

men do it softly. But you do it as if you had to hurt—
Was your mother a whore—?"

Charles gave her raised buttocks a ringing slap with
the back of his hand. Then as she raised her face
toward him, he slapped her cheek back on the pillow.

"Don't say that," he said. "Never say that. My
mother was a lady. I buried her—"

She might as well be buried. He never wanted to
see her or the village again. He was better off as
Charles de Belmont, a young man without a past,
born in his own image at the age of twenty-one.

The girl on the bed began to cry, "Is that why you
always go with whores?"

"No," Charles said, "I want to."

"If you're so fine, you should go with ladies."

As she stretched out on her belly, Charles took her
hand and trapped it between his legs.

"Whores do what you tell them. Ladies don't always."

"You're very young," the girl said, "to know so
much."

Outside the hotel, tanks and army trucks were
thundering on the cobbled streets. They lurched aim-
lessly, blundering and blind, along the boulevards
toward the docks. They did not know where to go or
where to stop. Beyond Bordeaux, there was only the
Atlantic or the Pyrenees to cross. Paris had fallen to
Hitler's panzers. The French government had fallen.
The grand old Marshal Pétain of Verdun was talking
of an armistice. The last of the French armor and aircraft and warships were milling around the western
and southern ports, waiting for orders from the General Staff that never came, looking for a way out that
they could not take. On the BBC from London, an
obscure general called Charles de Gaulle was broad-

casting that the Free French would fight on from overseas and the French colonies. But what was a new general and an old marshal in the scale of orders? Bordeaux was chaos at the end of the road.

"You're not in the army or the navy," the girl said. "What are you in?"

"I'm in the Free French," Charles laughed. "The French who are free to fuck off from this shitty mess."

"They're all fucking off without their uniforms," the girl said. "I had another client this morning—in the room next to this one—"

"Oh, that's what woke me up," Charles said. "All that bumping and groaning—"

The girl laughed. Charles saw that she was pretty for her trade, and plump too. Her best feature was her wet red lips that invited one to come in.

"He liked being whipped like those army guys do," she said. "I had to beat him with his baton a few times to make him hard. He was generous though, five *milles*. Skinny like you, too. He had another passport and a gray suit. He was ditching his colonel's uniform and going over the Spanish border. He didn't want to be interned in a prison camp for the rest of the war."

Charles watched the girl's red lips move, listening to what she was telling him, feeling desire again in his loins. He took her by the back of her head and forced her face down to his groin.

"Do your work," he said. "I want to think."

He swelled and reared under her fingers. As the tip slipped in and out of the soft rub of her lips, as her falling hair teased the skin of his belly and thighs, Charles worked out the odds. He could walk out of the hotel in half an hour, a French colonel! In the chaos of Bordeaux, anyone could command if he

wore the right gold braid on his cap and shoulders!
France had fallen, but somewhere across the Channel
a lone voice was crying, *Vive la France!* There was
loot in Bordeaux and Charles knew where some of it
was—industrial diamonds stored in the glass factories
where he had worked earlier in the year. There were
destroyers in the harbor, a chance to get to England.
France was no more; French society was finished. For
a young man with a false name, no papers or passport, it was time to risk it—to leap forward—

He felt a surging and a swelling in his groin. He
forced the girl's mouth against the hair of his crotch,
so that he came deep in the soft curve of her throat,
driving on and on and on—

He walked out of the hotel into the street in his
loose uniform and held up a hand. The first army
truck stopped. The driver and the corporal were so
delighted to receive firm orders that they almost
smiled as they saluted. Charles found himself in the
passenger seat, directing the two men to the glass factory on the outskirts of the city. Wherever there was a
jam of trucks or refugees on the road, Charles laid his
hand on the butt of his revolver in its holster at his
belt, and spoke in a clipped decisive voice that he
had assumed with the colonel's uniform. The clogged
streets opened ahead like the waters of the Red Sea
in front of Moses and the Israelites.

At the glass factory, work had stopped. Most of the
men and the office staff had gone home. The rest of
the workers were grouped round the radios, listening
to old Marshal Pétain's voice announcing the terms
of the new French government's surrender to Hitler.
The war was over for France. The nation had given
up, although Britain still fought on under Churchill.

Four of the workers in their faded blue cotton

clothes were playing *boules* in a patch of dust by the factory gate. The oldest stood and considered the group of metal balls clustering around the white mark twenty paces away. He held a ball in his hand, judging what he should do.

Charles went up to him. His new uniform made him confident enough to break all the rules, including the most sacred rule of all: Never tell a man what to do when he is playing *boules*.

"Smash them," Charles said. "Then go softly with your second *boule*."

The aged worker in his denims looked at the young colonel.

"Why don't you fight the fucking war," he said, "instead of running away?"

He ran forward and lobbed his metal ball underhand—a perfect pitch that landed by the mark and scattered the cluster of *boules* around it in whirls of dust.

"Right," Charles said. "Right. Now go softly."

He waved his own two men forward with the point of his pistol. He led them at a run at the guards by the factory gate. The first of the security men threw up his hands without a fight; the second pulled an old pistol on them. He was so close that Charles could shoot it out of his hand, leaving the man looking stupidly at his smashed fingers, while the three attackers ran into the main building.

The factory manager sat weeping at his desk. Tears glistened in snails trails down his pale pasty cheeks. Behind him a tricolor stood on its pole in the corner of the office—the red and white and blue of the flag of France. He did not seem surprised when Charles burst in with his two men. He was too lost in his own grief.

"You have come to tell me we have surrendered our nation," he said. "France, my country—"

"No," Charles said. "I have come to tell you we will win the war. General de Gaulle has gone to England to fight on. We will join him. We are the Free French. Those who stay here are traitors and slaves."

"We will resist here too," the manager said. "In our own way. What do you want from me?"

"The keys of your safe. All your industrial diamonds. General de Gaulle needs funds for the struggle. England will give him nothing he cannot pay for."

"How do you know of the diamonds?"

Calculation changed the manager's look from self-pity to suspicion. He stared at the young man in the colonel's uniform who had been a workman in that factory only three months before. The peaked cap changed the contours of Charles's face, adding authority to the strong line of nose and chin. The manager did not know him.

"That is my business," Charles said. "I have my orders. Are you a Frenchman or a traitor?"

The manager rose to his feet, insulted.

"You don't have to ask me that! I fought at Verdun for two years under Pétain, when he was our hero. We stopped the *Boche;* we saved France! And now my marshal has sold us out. I trust your general will not betray you."

"Be sure of that," Charles said. "De Gaulle will never betray France."

The manager opened the safe. Inside it were twenty bags of industrial diamonds, crammed together in the steel vault. Worth a few million dollars on the open market, Charles supposed.

"I wish I had more to give you," the manager said. "I would give you my life."

"Come with us," Charles said.

"I have a wife and two boys to see through the bad years to come," the manager said. "If only I were free—"

"You will be free again," Charles said. "I can promise you that—in the name of General de Gaulle."

Charles and his two men drove back again through the morass of pushcarts, refugees and soldiers, old Citroëns, armored personnel carriers, tanks, and self-propelled guns. There was enough matériel to fight several wars on the road, and it was all to be given to the Nazi war machine. It took Charles's truck three hours to reach the docks. There, in the long evening, seven destroyers at anchor were lounging like whales on the surface of the deep. Only one of the dark shapes spouted smoke out of its funnels, waiting to sail without a destination.

Charles took over a naval launch and rode out with his diamonds and his men to the destroyer with the smoke rising above it. He climbed aboard up a swinging rope ladder, and demanded to be taken to the captain, a man in his forties who looked at him with curiosity.

"Colonel Charles de Belmont," Charles said, knowing that his bluff would be called. "I have orders."

"Orders from whom, *mon colonel?*" The two words were said mockingly.

"Orders from General de Gaulle," Charles said. "He sent me back over here."

"Did he promote you from lieutenant to colonel in one day, *mon colonel?*"

"That's not your business," Charles snapped at the

captain. "What General de Gaulle does is his business. Yes, I was promoted very quickly because of services to the General during his escape to England. I am bringing with me industrial diamonds to finance the Free French forces abroad. I am a colonel, you are a captain. I order you to sail directly to England. Do you want to fight the *Boche* with me or surrender like Pétain? I don't have to remind you of your duty."

The captain looked at the young colonel. He did not believe him, and yet—what was there to believe? France had fallen, had surrendered to the Nazis! At least this was an order from someone who claimed to be a superior officer. Now his ship could fight on.

The captain saluted.

"Yes, *mon colonel*," he said without mockery. "At your service."

La Belle Hélène fought its way up the Bay of Biscay across to Southampton. The destroyer had just enough coal to make the voyage. Twice, German *Stukas* dived to drop their bombs on the ship, but they fell wide, making waterspouts to port and stern of the destroyer.

Charles stood on the bridge with the captain, watching the sailors fire gray smokeballs from their cannon at the airplanes. They missed their targets. War seemed a game of a splash against a puff, where nobody ever died and everyone rushed around at the orders of a young man who could hardly remember the name he had chosen for a future he didn't know. Only when a Messerschmitt flew a strafing run and tracer bullets chipped the turrets and whined along the deck, did Charles see a sailor near him fall, bright blood bubbling from his lungs as he choked to death.

War was still a game, everything was a game—the trouble was, people believed it.

At Southampton, Charles insisted on being taken immediately to the port commodore, who arranged for him to speak on the telephone to General de Gaulle himself. Charles reported to the General what he had done.

"I have a million dollars' worth of industrial diamonds," he said, omitting any mention of two of the bags he kept for himself. "I also have a destroyer called *La Belle Hélène* and its crew."

"Take command of the Free French navy at Southampton," the General replied. "Require that you are treated with full military honors, Colonel de Belmont. Then report to me in London within twenty-four hours."

"Yes, *mon général*."

So Charles was treated as his rank seemed to deserve. A naval band played when he arrived to dine with the admiral in command of the Home Fleet at Southampton. His uncertain aristocratic French and his ignorance of military affairs was met by the uncertainty and ignorance of the British naval officers, who knew next to nothing of France or its language. He won admiration for his youth and his daring escape.

"We would promote our own chaps just as quickly," the admiral said, "if we could find men like you."

A military pass took Charles de Belmont in a private first-class cabin on the train to London with his two men, who guarded the diamonds in the compartment. Charles did not bother to explain to them why two of the diamond bags were missing, hidden in a safe-deposit box in the vaults of the Midland

Bank in Southampton. He was a colonel; he did not have to explain; he knew it was unlikely that either of them would inform against him to General de Gaulle. Anyway, he was due to receive something when he was giving away so much.

The General's office in a Kensington Square house was a clutter of files and boxes, but the tall man with the hooked nose and sad, calculating eyes dominated the room as though the mess were his wish. He wore the uniform of a French general, even keeping his gold-braided peaked cap on indoors. As Charles saluted, he could see the reason that the General remained standing and dressed in full uniform. There was something ungainly about his body and narrow skull that the shoulder knots and braided *képi* changed into the brooding and immense presence of a commander of men.

"Colonel de Belmont reporting, *mon général*," Charles said. "My men are giving eighteen bags of industrial diamonds to your aides-de-camp. Worth more than a million pounds, I believe."

De Gaulle peered at the young man through his thick spectacles, judged him in an instant, then took off his glasses to hold his great nose even higher in the air.

"See to them," he said, waving a hand toward the only aide who stood in the room. It was the gesture of a king accepting a small gift he did not need. "Tell the Anglo-Saxon War Office we have them. We will put them up as security against a list of war matériel which I will supply within twenty-four hours. That is all."

The aide saluted and marched out of the room, leaving Charles alone with the General, who was even taller than he was—a dark outline more than two meters high, looming above the young imposter in his colonel's uniform that did not quite fit.

"Colonel de Belmont," General de Gaulle said, "tell me exactly who you are."

If Charles thought for a moment of lying about his rank, he had only to look at the hard search of the General's half-blind stare to dismiss a lie as useless.

"I am no colonel," he said, hoping that his run of luck would see him through. "I am a patriotic Frenchman! I knew you would need money and ships. I brought them to you here."

"That is an honorable admission," the General said. "I could have you shot for wearing a uniform to which you have no right at all."

"It was abandoned by a real colonel," Charles said. "He took it off to escape over the Spanish border. I thought I might use it properly in your cause, *mon général.*"

"I knew you were a fraud," the General said. "I had the army list checked. Were you ever in the French army?"

"My parents were planters in Africa," Charles lied. "I returned to fight for France. When I arrived in Bordeaux, I heard you on the BBC. So I came here at once to serve you—with something useful I picked up along the way."

"A man of action," the General said. "A man of quick decision." He put his hand on Charles's shoulder as heavily as a lump of plaster falling from the ceiling. "You will be sent north to be trained as an agent. If you last the course, you will go back to France as my direct representative. You will be able to prove again what you have already suggested—that you are a young man of energy and authority."

"Yes, *mon général*," Charles said.

The General did not smile, because his manner was Olympian. Yet a hint of pleasure or malice glinted at the corners of his hooded eyes.

"As for your rank," the General said, "you are dismissed with my thanks—*mon capitaine*."

III

He learned to kill with the best and the worst of them. Some were aristocrats and some were criminals, but all were joined in the quick act of butchery. Noisy killing was easy—the cross-sight on the sniper's rifle or the stutter of the sten gun before it jammed. Quiet killing was harder—the loop of piano wire around the throat with the knee in the small of the enemy's back, the steel arrow driven from the steel bow, the two thumbs pressing on the artery by the backbone. Explosives were touchy, but soon Charles was carrying *plastique* like putty in his pocket, ready to stuff it into any crack under a bridge or a car, then walk away unrolling the detonator wire, and pouf— the bits and pieces would somersault into the air. Most dangerous was the reflex killing, the changing of a young man into a wild beast, so that a tap on his back set off a chop to the hidden enemy's neck, a footfall was answered by a flying scissors kick to the groin, a whisper by a slashing leap to choke off the voice. Killing became an instinct for Charles. He was good at it.

They changed his body as they changed his reactions. Every day he had to cover twenty miles over the Scotch mountains. The last day he had to run or climb for nearly twenty-four hours with sixty pounds on his back. Those who dropped out were sent back to their units. His lean body became a grid of sinews like wires, and muscles like chains. He could see in the summer night like a cat; he could hear like a hunting animal the soft movements of the dark. When his training was finished, he was a thing who could survive in the wild.

His mind was also changed as he was learning his second language—English. The British taught him how to dupe enemy intelligence and cover his tracks. He was naturally a good learner and a good liar. All his childhood he had hidden the boy he really was— now he had to hide the identity of the man he pretended to be.

As a joke on himself, he chose the code name of Bâtard, the Bastard. And he learned his new false identity so completely that Jean-Luc Augremont's family history and dossier were more real to him than the fading memories of his own youth. He would make no mistakes after three days and nights of interrogation without sleep or food or water. He was not taught to endure torture. They hoped the Gestapo would not catch him.

On one solitary survival test in the mountains, he saw a woman driving a tractor in a rocky field. She was plowing the poor earth poorly, making a mess of it. A scarf was knotted around her red hair. The wind had tanned her cheeks and had raised freckles around her small nose. She smiled to see him and shared her lunch with him—salmon, scones, and cold tea. She said her name was Catherine and that her father was the keeper on the big estate of the Earl of Kirtlemuir. She and Charles arranged to meet for his leave at the end of his course. There had been something instant between them on that windy, hot day—a recognition that was almost desperate. They had to mate—there was no time for courting; there was a war on.

They spent three days in Edinburgh in a hotel. They hardly left their room. Incredibly, Catherine was a virgin at twenty-one, and Charles was moved and disturbed by the discovery. He took her brutally and painfully the first time. Her blood stained the sheets and she had to wash them in cold water in the basin behind the blackout curtains. But he was softened by her open love for him, her cheerfulness in her pain, her wanting to try again and again until the hurt changed to delight and—on the third night— to a weeping ecstasy.

He always raped his whores in hatred and need. Now his first violation of Catherine was at her asking. Later he became almost gentle as sexual fatigue unstrung his nerves and dulled his lust. He found himself tracing the soft curve of her breasts with wandering fingers, following each faint blue vein as it wound upward to the pale pink nipple at the tip. Sometimes he would use his fingernails as a fine comb on the red bush of hair that hid her mound of Venus below the soft arc of her belly. He loved her, he said, and he briefly believed that he did, and she said she would always love him. A woman always loved her first man, he thought.

"I am not who I said I was," Catherine told him on their last night together. "My name is Catherine; I am the daughter of the Earl, not his keeper."

"Then why were you driving a tractor?"

"You know how people like me are meant to be—duty and all that. We think we should do our bit to win the war too."

"That's why Hitler didn't invade England—he'd have to fight people like you."

Catherine smiled and took his hand to cup her girlish breast.

"Then why did you come with me here?"

"I wanted to. If I didn't—I might be an old maid before the war was over." She squeezed his hand hard over her breast. "I love you, Jean-Luc."

Charles smiled. "I am also not what I said I was. I gave you my cover story. They're sending me to France with a false identity. Jean-Luc Augremont—I've only been called that for nine months."

"And your real name? I must know who you really are." Her green eyes were full of tears and larger than eyes had a right to be, in a face that was small and freckled and soft-mouthed and all Charles wanted a face to be, in that room in Edinburgh.

"My real name," he said, "is Captain Charles de Belmont. But that is an official secret. As your people say, walls have ears. You won't tell anyone, will you?"

"No one. And your family?"

"Planters in Africa."

"Charles, will you write to me?"

"From Occupied France? There's no way."

"Then I'll wait; I'll wait till the war is over."

"Don't, Catherine. That's too much. A dear, passionate girl like you—"

"Charles, I love you. Please don't leave me."

"I must. Promise you won't cry when I go?"

"People like me," Catherine said, "aren't allowed to cry when their men go."

But cry she did when he went, lean and tall and light on his feet, his blond hair short under his peaked cap, his thin smile staying in her mind long after the train had left the smoky black station as empty as her heart was.

During the next three years Charles, alias Bâtard, became the most wanted man in Provence. The French resistance fighters struck at the Fascists over the Alps. All the efforts of the Vichy Gestapo—they were called the *Fifis*—could not track down Bâtard. He was as lethal as a shrew, which has to kill and eat three times its own weight in meat each day, or else die of the acids in its stomach. He was as elusive as a snake in the scrublands and a rat in the back streets, striking and burrowing secret information back to London through the pirate transmitters of the resistance fighters. The price on his head was a hundred thousand francs, more than the total cost to bring him up as a child in the village which he never visited.

He was well protected. One of the heads of the local *Maquis* was Marc, the young man he had saved in the riverbed after the beating by the Blackshirt Fascists. Marc and his comrades were trained in Marxist discipline, in underground work, in secrecy and cells. They were dedicated to the death for a cause that was their lives. And Marc remembered Charles. Once he lost three of his better men to get him out of a trap set by the *Fifis*.

"You didn't have to do that, Marc," Charles said afterward. "I could have got out alone—or I wouldn't have."

"The individual is useless, the mass is strong. Don't you trust your comrades?" Marc asked.

"Only myself," Charles said. "But thanks for the dead comrades."

The *Fifis* caught Marc in a special raid after the Normandy landings, while the British armies were already battling around Caen and the American tanks had broken through toward the south and the west. Marc was tortured horribly and slowly, but on the third day his warped body still had the guts to crash through a fourth-floor window and end its agony on the paved stones below.

A day later, Bâtard received instructions from London. Marc had been betrayed by Louis Durac, also known as Lilas. Bâtard was ordered to execute the informer at once.

The leaves of the walnut tree were shiny bright above the two young men lying in the shade, drinking a bottle of *vin gris* and eating bread and *jambon de Bayonne*. It was a feast, a lull in war. The wine flushed their faces and liberated their tongues. They chatted easily and indiscreetly. Louis Durac talked of his rich father's business in antiques and his vineyards around his château, while Charles told of his father's African adventures and plantations. The two young men were a world away from war.

"And after it's over," Charles said, "after France is free, what then?"

"Ah," Louis said, "an education, I suppose. We're barbarians. We went to war, not university. I have a lot to catch up—and forget."

"And inherit," Charles said. "A lot to inherit."

"Will you go back to Africa?"

"No," Charles said. "To Scotland, maybe! When I was training, I met a girl—"

"You never told me."

"I haven't been in touch with her for three years. I

had to disappear and become Bâtard and Jean-Luc Augremont. Officially, I was dead."

"And now you're alive again, you can be born as anyone."

"I know that," Charles said.

He rose and held out his hand to his friend to help him to his feet.

"I'm going to have a piss," Louis said.

As his friend opened his fly and turned his back, Charles took his revolver out of his pocket and put its muzzle on the back of Louis's neck.

"I have been ordered to execute you," he said. "You gave Marc to the *Fifis*."

The stream of piss stopped short in shock, then flowed again as Louis regained control of his thoughts.

"That's a lie. You know that, Charles. You know me."

"It's an order from London. Bâtard always obeys orders."

"You're not a bastard. I know you're not."

Louis turned around coolly, buttoning himself up. His full mouth smiled; his brown eyes were frank and wide.

"It's a lie," he said, "a Communist trick. They're trying to take over after the war by getting us to execute each other. Would I betray Marc? Would I betray you?"

"Yes," Charles said flatly.

He lowered the muzzle of his revolver.

"I won't execute you, Louis. The war is nearly over. There is no point now. But I don't believe you. You gave Marc up, and you might give me up. How did they get you? Through your father?"

Louis was silent for a moment, then he saw the muzzle of the revolver rise.

"They got me through my father," he said. "They said he was a Jew."

"Is he?"

"He always told me he wasn't."

Suddenly Louis began to tremble and plead like a small boy in the body of a young man.

"Don't think badly of me. The *Fifis* have my father. They've confiscated everything, even the château. We only had it for ten years and now we have nothing. They say they'll send him to Auschwitz if I don't cooperate. I haven't done anything—just a couple of names—a place where they might be—mostly lies—"

"Bullshit," Charles said.

He pointed his revolver at Louis's belly. Louis fell on his knees and began to sob, dry sobs that shook his body like a cough. Charles stood over him for an instant, watching him. He did not pull the trigger. He walked away, leaving Louis kneeling under the starry leaves of the walnut tree.

Three days later, on a liaison trip to Paris, Charles was betrayed to the Gestapo.

IV

He could take the kicking in the ribs and the slapping in his face and even the hanging by his thumbs with curious ease. He found there was a pain barrier. When he broke through it, he felt detached from his own body, watching its torture as if he were the S.S. officer who sat behind the desk in the plain white room, a man as fair and tall and lean as he was—almost his double, but in the wrong uniform and on the wrong side, if there were any sides left in the chaos at the end of a world war.

During these trips of his mind from his body, Charles was able to think of what he should say, before the lack of sleep made his mind stupid, before the torturers damaged his limbs beyond repair. He still had a long life to live, he thought. He hadn't begun playing the odds.

They were fixing the clamps of the electric-shock machine onto his balls when he smiled with his bruised lips at the S.S. officer and spoke in English.

"OK! I'll have that cigarette now and I'll talk."

The S.S. officer looked at him in surprise. Then he smiled and told his men to release Charles. He put a cigarette in his captive's mouth and lit it and had him placed in a chair at his desk. Charles could no longer walk.

He studied the dark bruises that swelled over Charles's face. "Were you at Oxford or Cambridge before the war?" the S.S. officer said in perfect English. "I can't really tell by looking at you, but perhaps you were a bit young for that."

"I was first year Trinity," Charles said. That was part of the cover story of Jean-Luc Augremont. "If you hadn't started this bloody war, I'd be a professor by now. Would you tell your people to leave us alone? I have things to say to you in private—"

The S.S. officer told his men to handcuff Charles and leave the room. After they had gone, he poured a schnapps for Charles and held it to his lips.

"I must say," he said, "I have always admired the British code of honor."

"I'm French," Charles said. "I was educated in Britain for one year. My name is Captain Charles de Belmont." His plan required him to take the identity he would use after the war. The schnapps was a reviving fire in his throat.

"It's still the British code of honor," the S.S. officer said. "You resist torture one day, to give your men time to get away. Then on the second day, you talk a little, your name and rank and a few details. And on the third day, you tell quite a lot, but nothing which will really hurt your remaining men. Then you shut up, not a word. That's honor, a sensible sort of honor."

"I'll tell you all you want," Charles said. "But

haven't you realized—all the people I know in Provence are safely behind the Allied lines?"

"That's more like French honor," the S.S. officer said. "That's either cowardice or martyrdom. Either a Pétain or a Joan of Arc. No balance to it."

"And even my contact in Paris," Charles said, "he's no good to you. Paris is falling. The underground is already in the open. The *Maquis* is fighting you in the streets."

"We can take you with us. Don't worry, we can play our little games with you all the way to the last bunker in Berlin."

"You've lost the war," Charles said. "Why don't you admit it? What's your name?"

"*Obersturmbannführer* Kurt von Appel."

"And when the war is over, sir? I was just saying that to the man who betrayed me. They're making ropes to hang people like you all over Europe."

Kurt von Appel was silent for a while before speaking.

"We haven't lost yet."

"Oh yes," Charles said. "And you know it."

The S.S. officer looked at Charles, then his voice became harsh.

"You have something to tell me in private?"

"Yes. A proposition."

"Captain de Belmont, I only want information. About you. About your associates in Paris and London."

"I can be of help to you in Switzerland," Charles said. "I have contacts there. When you've lost the war, I can get you and your associates and your assets out through Switzerland to South America. Think it over."

Kurt von Appel was silent.

"Why should I trust you?"

"You have no alternative."

"Why you in particular?"

"I am trusted by British and French intelligence, that's why. They will need me, even when the war is over."

"You say you would be our contact in Switzerland?"

"Yes. I would get you out and your money, too."

"You would betray us and keep the money."

"No. That's not in my interest."

"Why, Captain?"

"Because there will be enough of your people left to execute me if I betray you. You have looted all Europe. You have hundreds of millions stacked away in the caves of Bavaria—gold bullion, art treasures, bearer bonds. I want a piece of that. If I betray any one of you, there will be nothing left for me. I want a lot of money, and you are clever enough not to give it to me in one lump." Charles tossed his head to one side, spitting out the cigarette butt. "I won't be cheap, but I'll be effective."

The S.S. officer took out two more cigarettes from his platinum case. He put them both in his mouth and lit them with one flame from his gold Cartier lighter. To Charles, the gesture meant an agreement. The second cigarette was placed in his mouth.

Outside the shuttered windows, machine guns stuttered in the distance.

"Listen," Charles said. "Paris is rising against you. The American tanks and General Leclerc are already at Versailles."

"Those are firing squads," the S.S. officer said. "They are for idiots who want to throw their lives away."

"But you don't," Charles said. "Take my offer. There won't be time for another one or a better one."

Kurt von Appel came and sat on the desk beside Charles and swung his left boot backwards and forwards. He studied the gleam of the black leather.

"I admire you," he said. "To think up a scheme like that under torture."

"I'm at my best, hanging from a hook by my thumbs."

"What would you want for these services?"

"Ten percent of all money or bonds passed through Switzerland in my name. Twenty percent if I pass a man through with his assets to South America."

"For a man I could kill this minute, you drive a hard bargain, Captain. Five and ten percent. That's all."

"Ten and twenty—take it or leave it. To a man who will be hanged in less than a year, it's a fair price."

Kurt von Appel laughed.

"You have it all—British cool, French gall. And if I and my friends accept?"

"You release me and provide me with money and a pass to the Swiss border. My address in Geneva will be *Poste Restante* Box 3001. I will wait by the lake to hear from you—while I recover from your rest cure here."

Kurt von Appel laughed again.

"After all, what do I have to lose?"

There was a burst of rifle fire close to the windows. Then a grenade exploded and a voice screamed and cursed in German.

"Nothing!" Charles said.

The *Maquis* attacked Charles as he left in the S.S. car down the Right Bank toward the east. Two young men in civilian clothes with red armbands on their sleeves ran out towards them, firing with sten guns. Three of the bullets smashed the car windows, cutting Charles slightly and nicking von Appel in the arm. The motorcycle outriders pulled up and killed the two young men with their Luger automatics. The S.S. officer was right, Charles thought. The young men, the best young men, the brave young men were throwing their lives away just as the Allied armies were about to enter Paris, all to prove to the Free French and the Americans that they also fought.

"You're leaving just in time," Charles said, as the car drove on. "Anyway, don't worry. I'll keep a bank account warm for you in Geneva."

Refugees again began to clog the road, fleeing in the other direction. There were always refugees in front of advancing armies. Only this time it was not a temporary panic by the defeated French; it was a panic by the French who had counted on a permanent defeat.

"Collabos," Charles said. He wanted to spit, but his lips were too swollen and he had no saliva to spare.

"I despise them as much as you do, Captain. But one has to have traitors entirely dependent upon oneself to govern a defeated country. We had a very simple technique which you should not forget. We put most of your policemen in jail, and we made your criminals policemen. They already know each other and it worked very well."

"Cynicism will get you everywhere," Charles said.

"It got us to the Channel and the Volga—don't underestimate its power. Cynicism—and Herr Hitler."

"A madman," Charles said. "I prefer gamblers, those who calculate the odds. So much for me, so much less for you, my friend, my enemy—and the rest is left in the pot for later."

"I think you will manage our money very well."

"I am sure!" Charles smiled.

It took him six months to recover fully from his ordeal. Two scars on his legs would always remain. He would show them off in bed as proof of his courage—war wounds had a great effect on women. He sat in the cafés of Geneva, measuring out the Allied advance into Germany through hundreds of coffee cups. He acquired some Swiss government bonds and the respect of the staff of the Hotel d'Angleterre, where he stayed and tipped well. Once he went around Lake Geneva to the Villa Diodati, where Lord Byron had stayed with the Shelleys and where *Frankenstein* had been invented and started. Charles knew that a little literary knowledge was necessary for a man of the world.

News reached him from Paris that the Communists wanted to put him on trial, if he could be found. He was accused of betraying Marc and of failing to execute Louis Durac. He was also accused of being a Gestapo agent, which explained his escape from S.S. headquarters in Paris. His many exploits as Bâtard were forgotten in the envy that ruled Paris after the liberation.

General de Gaulle, however, forgot neither friend nor enemy. He remembered the gift of the destroyer and the diamonds after the fall of France, and he had the name of Captain Charles de Belmont struck off the list of those to be prosecuted for war crimes. When a small bald man came to Charles at the Hotel d'Angleterre just as Berlin was falling to the Red Army and the Germans were about to surrender, Charles knew that British intelligence had found him. Their best agents were always so obvious. They were the most nondescript men, people who never showed in a crowd and stuck out on their own.

Charles had his explanation prepared. He began by pulling up his left trouser leg to show his war wounds.

"When the S.S. finished working me over," he explained, "Paris was falling. They decided I was important; they wanted to take me back with them to Berlin. I was in such a bad way and the car was so full, they dumped me out near Berne. They left me for dead, but a farmer found me, and I ended up in a hospital in Geneva. You can check the records—they've been treating me for a long time."

"Why didn't you contact us?" the agent asked.

"I had a breakdown. The war was nearly over. I was a physical and mental wreck. I'd done my bit as Bâtard, don't you think?"

"Oh yes," the agent said. "You've got three medals waiting for you including the Croix de Guerre and one from us. We thought it might be posthumous. Still, we're glad you're alive, old chap."

"I'm not moving," Charles said. "I'm staying right here, reading the newspapers, letting you finish off the war. I might even become a Swiss citizen."

"Could I ask what you're doing for money?" The agent's voice was casual, his eyes sharp.

"My family knew enough to put some away in a safe place," Charles said. "What they had is here and I can use it."

"I see," the agent said. "It's not the sort of thing one can check on—Swiss banks and all that." He stood up, pulling his old brown felt hat over his eyes.

"I'll report back to London. With your record, I don't think they'll do anything. Not if—"

"Not if I do some things for you here."

"There'll be a lot of people coming through. Particularly Nazis trying to get away. All sorts from the Balkans, quislings, S.S. types, traitors. And a lot of loot. We've only got a few chaps here. We'll need you."

"I'll do all I can," Charles said, "for old time's sake. But don't ask too much of me. I'm a civilian now. My war days are over."

"As long as you'll help."

"You can count on it."

British intelligence informed French intelligence. A Gaullist agent made Charles the same proposition. So when Kurt von Appel and his friends and the bullion and the art treasures began moving to Geneva, Charles was in a good position. If he had any trouble with the Nazis over payment or threats, he could give a name to the British or the French agents. He was soon known to be dangerous, but strictly a man of his word. He always delivered, if the price was paid. Charles wrote in his private code in his diary: *In Geneva after the Second World War, the only honest man is a triple agent.*

Gaia, the Contessa Frescaviolli, was a precious liaison. Luckily, she had an apartment on the same floor as Charles. They met often in the elevator and in no time she was in his apartment having cocktails. She was a magnificent creature from an aristocratic Italian family. She taught him good manners and he fell quite in love with her. He was soon at ease in any drawing room or dinner party in Geneva. They spoke French at breakfast with the croissants and the *grandes crèmes*. At lunch they spoke Italian with the

tomato salads and Ricasoli Chianti. English was no
problem and it ended always with fierce lovemaking,
Charles forgetting all the niceties he learned to the
delight of Gaia.

Sometimes Charles thought of Catherine in the
Scotch highlands. He wanted to write to her; he
wanted to send for her. But it would be too involv-
ing. If he did, she would tell her father and expect
marriage. The Earl would then check into his background and find nothing but obscurity. Although
Catherine might be strong enough to insist on the
marriage, Charles did not feel secure enough to want
that. The odds were still against him.

His position in Geneva was precarious. One day he
would have to leave before the Nazis or the Allied
agents decided to get rid of him. It was no place for
Catherine to come. And anyway, although his pride
made him hope that she had waited for him, although he told himself that she was the only girl he
had ever loved, his reason told him that she would
not wait forever. She would presume that he had died
in Occupied France, since she had never heard from
him again.

So he was not surprised to read in an old *Times,*
dated November 3, 1946, of the forthcoming marriage
between Lady Catherine MacGowrie-Scott, the only
daughter of the Earl of Kirtlemuir, and Charles
Adam-Villiers of the Foreign Office. At least she had
taken someone of the same name in memory of her
Charles the first.

Among his calculated affairs in his three years in
Geneva, Natasha was the most fantastic and disturbing. He met her at a reception given by an art

collector who stacked his Picassos and Mondrians and Soutines in bank vaults, knowing that some of them had been stolen during the war and might be reclaimed by their owners. Charles had arranged to sell him a pair of Matisses—white-faced girls with orange lips in pink dresses standing out against the bright square of the Mediterranean sky like two flags of joy. The price had been low, the source unmentioned except for a remark from Charles that perhaps the pictures should be left to age a bit like young wine.

In return, the art collector introduced Charles to Natasha, a white-faced woman of thirty-five with blond hair piled on her head and strange eyes that changed color from gray to emerald to light green with her moods.

"I am Princess Natasha of All the Russias," she told Charles. "You probably know my story. My older sister and I were not killed by the Bolsheviks with my father and mother and the rest of the family in that cellar. We were too small. The commissar let us escape. You will call me Princess Natasha or Your Royal Highness, if you please."

Charles did, but he could not help wondering whether he was dealing with a madwoman or a case of possession. Her memory was extraordinary. If she had not spent her first seven years in the court of the Czars, she must have read every book of memoirs about that period. She could quote dogs' names and describe her nannies and her father's ministers. She was word perfect.

Sometimes he wondered if she did not have a hypnotic gift. When she spoke of her past, her eyes would widen with the shifting colors of her memories—light green for the little girl rolling her hoop in her frilly summer dress along the paved stones of the palace at

St. Petersburg—emerald for the autumn of their hopes when the family escaped—and haunted grays for the winter of the news of the massacre in the bloody cellar while she and her sister were spirited away to the White Armies in the Ukraine.

"We took jewels with us, but we gave away fortunes to survive. A Fabergé pendant for a rail pass, a diamond tiara for some milk and honey—if they knew who we were. We were at their mercy, and men enjoy women who are at their mercy."

In bed, with Charles, she was imperious, telling him to come into her slowly, to move up her slowly, to arouse her slowly, while she built up her passion into the racking surges and spasms of her comings, time after time after time in a matter of minutes, while she scratched her lover's shoulders with her nails like a drowning woman, crying out Russian words that he did not understand.

"I should never give myself to a commoner like you," she told Charles. "I know you are not what you seem to be. You probably picked that *de Belmont* out of the gutter you were born in. Nobody is who he seems to be in Geneva."

"Are you?" Charles asked.

"Do you doubt me or will you serve me?"

It was a difficult question. If she really was one of the few survivors of the Czar's family, her claim was as strong as Anastasia's to part of the imperial fortune still blocked in foreign banks. If she was deluded or a fraud, there was a lifetime to be spent in lawsuits and intelligence work and gathering affidavits. These were not her attractions to Charles. As a peasant boy with no pedigree, at last he could sleep with a princess! He could drive his terrible stake of flesh into her and make her cling to him like a torturer and savior. He could fulfill all his fantasies of lust and power, covering her soft body and impaling her at his will. If she ordered him at first, she begged him at the end, to stab her slowly and stir her to her troubled ease.

"I won't serve you," Charles said finally, "but I want to believe your story."

"Then you must serve me. I am Princess Natasha of All the Russias."

"I serve myself," Charles said.

He wanted to believe she was a true princess. If she lived in a dream and a fantasy, he wanted to dream as well, and satisfy his childish yearning for the most distant and unlikely woman of them all. Once a young man had everything society had to offer, it could not lure him anymore. The greatest temptation the privileged had to offer was to try to make an outsider want to join them. Yet Charles wanted to stay outside all things so that he could use them. As the lover of the Czar's daughter, who could ever offer him more? To him, position was a stronger aphrodisiac than power.

For a week he did not see Natasha. Then a man who called himself a psychiatrist came to see him at the Hotel d'Angleterre. His name was Dr. Rudegirt, a small man with the face of an intense ferret, sharp-nosed and gingery.

"You have been interfering with a patient of mine," he said to Charles. "Ruth Hochstein. She has the delusion that she is the Princess Natasha of All the Russias. She stopped a course of therapy with me, but I am happy to say that she has returned to complete it."

"Am I the cause of her stopping?"

"Yes. She told me you were Ivan the Terrible, masquerading with a blond wig and no beard, under the assumed name of Charles de Belmont."

Charles laughed until he choked and his ribs hurt.

"It is no laughing matter," the angry psychiatrist said. "It is criminal to interfere with a patient under analysis. You encouraged her delusion in order to have an affair with her."

"I believed her," Charles said. "That's all."

"It suited you to believe her."

"That's true," Charles said. "We usually believe what suits us." He smiled at the man. "Does it suit you to believe you are a psychiatrist?"

"I *am* a psychiatrist! I shall complain to the police about you!"

The little man was dancing with fury as Charles put a lock on his arm and put him through the door.

"I believe in the Princess Natasha of All the Russias. And I shall complain to the police that she has been kidnapped by a deluded psychiatrist who wants her fortune for his fees."

He didn't see the psychiatrist or Natasha again.

Wintertime, Charles traveled long distances alone on his skis. He did not care for the packed slopes where the rich occasionally went, followed by the many who believed that some mysterious fortune would brush off on them if they sat in the places of the wealthy. Davos, Gstaad, St. Moritz, these were too obvious a hunting ground for Charles. His preference and business led him to the solitary mountains and downhill runs near the Swiss border close to Germany and Austria. He could make his contacts there in deserted cabins which only the shepherds used in summer. He would brief his picked mountain men, who would cross the border and guide back into

Switzerland the ex-Nazis hidden in the Black Forest and near the lakes by Salzburg. Once Charles had to send twenty men as a human ski train to carry back the hoard of an *obersturmführer* who had a taste for Breughels and Patinirs as well as for killing off Dutch Resistance. Charles's men were well paid and as silent as he. In the high Alps, breath was worth more than speech.

Charles enjoyed matching himself against the cold and the snows. There was not only the obvious delight of the rare downslopes, rushing and slinking between the pines and leaping the snowbanks. He almost preferred the marathon slogs uphill, sidling with his skis along the ridges, hour after hour of little progress in his white lost world of time to plot and plan, the frost nipping at his cheeks and his mind. Then there was the danger—the hole in the snow, the hidden crevasse, the tumble down, and the slow dragging out with the hooked telescopic pole he carried for emergencies. His only help then lay in himself, and that was what he wanted.

On one winter night in a cabin near the Austrian border, the killers came for him. He was dozing in the dark in his sleeping bag, the intense cold on his face making the warmth around his body a contrast of delight. As the ice on the door cracked open, he woke in an instant, reverting back to the wild animal he had been trained to be in Scotland. He was rolling in his sleeping bag across the floor, ripping it open, as the first man pushed into the room. He was striking at the intruder's groin with his right fist before the man had time to level his automatic. He was scything down the second killer with a flying scissors kick while he still was standing in the doorway. He was standing above the two men, kicking and chopping them into unconsciousness before they could get to their feet again. Then he tied them with the rope in his knapsack and left them to freeze into cooperation before morning.

The interrogation did not take long. The two killers knew that they would die if Charles did not free them soon. Frostbite had already begun to blacken their cheeks and fingers and feet. They were professionals, veterans from the Foreign Legion who now murdered privately for hire rather than publicly. Their employer was a Herr Gerstein in Zurich, who had offered them five thousand dollars for the job. They did not know whom he represented—the French, the British, the ex-Nazis, or merely competitors in the human smuggling trade. They had been told that Charles was dangerous and ruthless, but he left them a knife when he went off on his skis with their weapons. If their frozen hands could use the knife, they would cut themselves free. If not . . . ?

His time in Geneva had run out. He went to his bank and asked the manager to transfer his funds to Rio de Janeiro through the numbered accounts and the private Brazilian bank which he had used so often for his clients. There was about half a million dollars on deposit from his percentages as a courier and middleman for the Nazi refugees. He looked forward to going to Rio. It was the last place to make a real fortune, and Brazil was a country where to be white and European was enough to put a person in the highest caste of society. A multiracial society meant that whiter people floated to the top like cream, or scum.

So Charles finished his European education and left for the new world under another false name on a flight that only landed at Lisbon and the Azores before it reached Rio. He could not risk extradition at London airport or Paris, if his old associates were after him. The odds that had been against him since his birth would now begin to work for him.

Part Two

PLAYING THE ODDS

Brazil, 1948–1957

I

It was only ten days before Carnival. Charles went up to the black girls in Carioca, fifteen minutes away on the packed trams they called the *bondgis*, where purple and scarlet creepers could do nothing to hide the tin roofs and burned clay walls of the slums. Danger stood on the corners there with the gangs and *pistoleiros*, but it was worth it for the naked girls behind the shutters, writhing to the sambas and the rhumbas and the rhythms of the night pulsating with hand drums and maracas. In the sweaty dark of the little rooms, there were quick animal embraces to be had, the bodies of the lean girls still moving as they lay beneath him to the beat of the music of the night, the harsh wire of the hair between their thighs scratching at his violent thrust inside them, the sucking muscles of their stomachs making him come in moments, then massaging back his desire to come again more slowly in their crawling delights. They laughed lazily at his pleasure, then took him to the little local clubs, where the men in tattered pants and the girls in print dresses of flame and flowers shook their shoulders and their breasts, strutting and jerking to the stomp of the music that brought some kind of forgetfulness after the hunger and slavery of the day.

Carnival, masks and brocades, wigs and flounces, empresses and angels, Lucifers and pirates, all mixed in an orgy of humanity, a volcano of crowds. An ebony Gabriel swung Marie Antoinette in a kick of golden petticoats. A fire-eater blew out spears of flame at Death with his chalked skull skipping to the rhumbas. On each hood of a procession of Cadillacs and Rolls-Royces, a model flaunted a new dress from Coco Chanel or Dior, slim-hipped and plucked hairless beneath a blond wig, only the muscles under the silk stockings giving away the Drag Drive. Near them in a battle of champions, two fat monsters shimmied and jellied to the bands hour after hour—the King of the Gays and the Queen of the Queens—until the Queen dropped in a mound of veiled chiffons and the King quivered in a victory dance in his lilac tent suit.

Charles knew that in Carnival no one had an identity and pursuit was impossible; the pickpockets worked at will. So he taped his fifteen hundred-dollar bills inside the pale blue britches of his Grandee's costume. It was the last of his traveling money. The transfer of his half million dollars from Geneva to the Brazilian bank would be completed after Carnival was over. He planned to open accounts in many different places. Money was safest when well spread. He would not leave his assets in one private bank in Rio. They might know of his deals with the Nazis and could inform on him.

Charles, the young Grandee in pale blue and gold, strolled out into the chanting and dancing hordes along the Copacabana. They were ringing the floats which were brighter than tropical gardens with hundreds of Carmen Mirandas growing bananas and orchids out of their hats. There was a ferment everywhere. Excitement ran from hands to hips as the crowd conga'd in a serpent a mile long through the streets leading up from the sea. Charles joined the back of this huge snake, catching Jezebel by the waist, a yellow girl in a slit scarlet dress that slid back from her smooth taut skin. The tops of her buttocks rolled lazily, then became firm in his grip as she felt him kneading her flesh down from her waist. She turned slowly and smiled at him, longing for the dance to be over.

Down the hill toward the human snake, the Undertakers came. Four giant black men with gold stovepipe hats and white tailcoats and scarlet bow ties carrying a luminous coffin on their shoulders. It glowed with fluorescent lights, swamp green and neon purple. These Undertakers all began dancing together to the beat of the conga, stepping out beside Charles so that the shadow of the box on their shoulders fell across his white wig and the beauty spot stuck to his cheek as part of his Grandee disguise. Tall as cypresses shaking in the wind, they blocked Charles's escape.

On the other side, a Terror Squad drove up in a black Buick. The doors opened as the silver grill of the car touched the flank of the human snake of dancers. Four men stepped out in a parody of fear. They wore gray fedora hats pulled down over their foreheads and white silk masks, slit at the eyeholes like the hoods of the Ku Klux Klan. Their jackets were Chicago style, broad-striped and pinched at the waist with padded shoulders. On their sleeves, swastika armbands. On their legs, the black britches and boots of the Nazi stormtroopers. The tommyguns in their hands were real enough, and if their masks had not been painted with great grinning Mae West mouths to show they were in the Carnival, the conga snake would have split up into a screaming mob, running from the Black Guards of President Vargas, who was said to settle scores with his Terror Squads.

Charles was caught between the Undertakers and the Squad. In front of him, the sultry Jezebel. Behind him, the tail of the conga. He tried to watch his enemies on either flank, dropping his hands from Jezebel's hips, ready to chop at the gun or the blackjack waiting to hit him. He swung around to face the leading Undertaker, who now stepped free of his coffin pole to clench both hands together in a huge fist of fury above his stovepipe hat. Then a tommygun barrel struck at his neck from behind, paralyzing his shoulders. Charles dropped, clawing at the silk mask with the painted red smile, ripping it off to see as he fell into darkness—the blue stare of Kurt von Appel.

The conga snake wriggled on up the hill, but its tail was broken. Jezebel turned to see the Undertakers opening the lid of their green and purple coffin. They laid away her Grandee, limp and broken-limbed. She screamed, but her scream was a whisper in the wild cries of joy and the shrieking brass trumpets of the Carnival.

The Undertakers took the body away, racing along with the coffin held high above the dancing crowds. The Terror Squad turned back to the black Buick, three of them still wearing their painted smiles on their masks, the fourth covering his pale face with his fedora hat. They fired their tommyguns into the air like firecrackers to show it was all play.

It was a nightmare of pain. He fainted time after time as his ribs cracked, his cheeks split open, his balls crushed by a boot. When his body was thrown out of the car at midnight into a dry ditch beyond Cachias, the cool dust on his face was sweeter than water. The two shots fired into his back at close range drove his body even deeper into the dust as if he were diving into the earth. He sensed the flash of approaching headlights as the cold muzzle of the pistol was put to his neck, then somewhere the scrabble of boots and the roar of a car engine and nothing at all—

The ants covered him, crawling around the dark scabs of blood, lifting the crust away, crumb by crumb, to take back to their ant heaps. He moaned and moved his arms, dragging himself forward by the elbows. The ants hurried off, falling back into the dust. Slowly, inch by inch, he dragged himself by his fingernails and knees and forearms to the little trickle of muddy water at the end of the ditch. He wriggled like a seal with its back broken by a fur hunter's club, putting his cheek and half his mouth under the green scum on the surface of the water. He drank and spit and drank again. For half an hour he lay there, letting the blood set hard again on the wounds that had cracked open as he moved. He was not dead yet. He had to get away.

All that day, the sun burned him, making him faint every few minutes, only to be aroused by a torment of flies. He would not let his beaten and bruised body betray him. First he worked the fingers of his left hand, then the fingers of the right hand, then his wrists and his feet. His neck would not move. His back was caked stiff with a shell of dried blood. Both bullets fired into his back had passed straight through him, missing his lungs and coming out through his ribs. He was lucky—he knew that—the Nazis were stupid. They should have nicked the ends of their bullets, making dumdums that would have split in his flesh and blown him apart.

By noon, he was crouching with his back against the side of the ditch, trying to stand. By three o'clock, he was stumbling toward the small round hut a few meters away, when he collapsed.

The noise of his fall brought out an old man with a shock of white hair, limping toward him. With the last of their forces, the cripple and the aged African reached the hut. Then Charles fell into a babbling fever and did not know what he said or did.

Days, weeks, years later, he woke on a soaked blanket on the mud floor, his mind quite clear. There was a glob of white paste in his mouth. He could see the old man blinking at him through red eyes, trying to feed him from a wooden bowl with a wooden spoon.

"Senhor," the old man said in a singsong kind of English. "Ah—good—you live now."

Charles gave him a weak smile and began to chew on the paste. It was like semolina, a flour from a crushed root. He looked down at his chest, which was bound with poultices of squashed leaves and bandages of creepers. His legs were shrunken, the skin fallen in against the bones.

"You saved me. Thank you!"

"Black guards," the old man said. "They think—you—dead—"

The old man rose and went over to the heap of pale blue rags on the mud floor of the hut. He came back with fifteen hundred-dollar bills.

"Here," he said.

Charles looked at the old man, nearly blind, only just able to talk, his face and skin withered away into the dust that would take him back soon.

"Why are you so honest?"

"Me slave in big house," the old man said. "My name Garcia Smit'. Now me old man, me free man, no good to work."

Slowly Charles moved his hand up the leaf bandages on his chest to the fifteen green bills. He pushed five of them toward the old man, who stared at them as if they were green scorpions.

"Go ahead," Charles said.

"No."

"Take them. You won't starve now. You can bury yourself well." Charles tried to grin, but he was too exhausted.

He fell asleep again.

Two months later, when he was in fairly good shape, he went off on the bus to Rio, passing through the murderous suburb of Cachias where the Senator's killers lounged in the streets. He changed buses to get to the port where the freighters unloaded the luxury goods and machines for the making of the new Brazil. He walked along the warehouses and offices, looking for the names of the ships' brokers and agents. At the sign *LEVY, EPSTEIN, SOLOMON et Cie,* he went into the building. He sat in the waiting room until one of the partners would see him—a sallow, wiry man with bad eyes watering behind rimless glasses as they peered at the fair, tall man with scars healing on his cheeks.

Charles said, "Your people are looking for the Nazis who got away." He took a piece of paper from the pocket of his old cotton shirt. "I have written here the name of a bank which is owned by them. I helped them escape from Geneva. Here are their names. The first is *Obersturmbannführer* Kurt von Appel, who was personally responsible for the deaths of three hundred French Jews. If you watch the bank, you will see all of them draw money from time to time. Their other address in Rio is a penthouse at the end of the Copacabana. They use it as a clearing station for new arrivals—and for beer parties when they remember the good old days." Solomon put on his glasses and studied the paper.

"Why are you doing this for us?"

"I have my reasons," said Charles.

Solomon thought for a moment. "You will want money from us." His tone did not accuse Charles. It merely accepted that this was so.

Charles rose to his feet.

"I want nothing, for now," he said. "Just deal with them for me."

"We will do that, but we prefer to pay. We are used to paying for information. We do not like debts."

"Don't pay me now," Charles said. "One day I will ask for it."

"We won't forget you," Solomon said. "With five million of us killed, how can we forget?"

For the next two months, Charles stayed away from Rio, letting the Israeli agents eliminate his enemies. A bomb wrecked the private bank; several bodies were found in the penthouse; a couple of leading, newly arrived German businessmen vanished.

Charles was living in a small inn up in the hills near the great *fazenda* and *haras* of the Guinleys, where a hundred thousand head of cattle roamed the grass and their stallions bred foals for the races. He got a job as stableboy, taking care of six horses every day. He watched the strings of racehorses as they exercised, getting to know their form, and he made friends with the stableboys, and played polo with them in the evening, learning Portuguese and getting drunk with them. One day he heard of a colt called Rondon, who had been held back for a big coup. The horse had run four times out of the money. He was sharpened up until he could show his tail to the rest of the two-year-olds in the *haras*. Charles had a bet on the colt when he went back to Rio.

The odds on Rondon were thirty-five to one. He still had seven hundred and fifty dollars. He changed it into *cruzeiros* and put it all on Rondon's nose. There was no chance of the colt losing except to the odds-on favorite, Capataz Sertão. But Carlos "the Whip" Cervantes was riding the favorite and he had put a hundred thousand *cruzeiros* himself on Rondon!

Charles was in the crowd with the stableboys as the runners came up to the starting gate. The silks a bright patchwork on the backs of the crouched, monkeylike jockeys, the racehorses straining and kicking their hind legs at the gate until they were off. Rondon broke badly on the six-furlong sprint. Cervantes was out front looking back at the field, while the crowd on the rails screamed him forward.

Eight lengths ahead with two furlongs to go, Cervantes began pulling back his horse, but the roar of fury from the crowd made him loosen the reins again. Behind him, Rondon had found an opening in the pack. He was closing on the leader, still five lengths in front. Cervantes leaned forward and urged the favorite on, his elbows flying as he *reined in his horse.* The crowd was screaming murder at him—jockeys had been killed for less by this mob. Rondon's rider was flailing his whip—two lengths, one length, half-a-length, a head behind, as he hugged the rails. Then Cervantes pulled Capataz Sertão to his left nearing the post, swerving into Rondon so that the two horses collided and were running as a pair, the jockeys' stirrups locked, their whips lashing at each other. The race over, the crowd was seething and roaring. The first bottles crashed onto the track. Then the crackle of pistol shots and the banging at the judge's box as they waited for the result.

Charles did not move his mouth, but his stomach was sick. He passed his bet ticket through his fingers over and over in his shirt pocket. The stableboys had only said that Cervantes was fixed, not the judges. The crowd had its money on Capataz Sertão, the favorite. The judges would not want a riot on their hands. That would be a police matter.

The board came up with a surge, showing Capataz Sertão had won by a short head from Rondon. Cervantes could not pull it in time. The judges did not dare throw the race.

He got very drunk that night on bad rum and the last of his *cruzeiros.* His clothes were acrid and filthy from the ammonia of his defeat. He did not want to think. He had gambled and lost. It was a sure thing, but what was a sure thing in a country like Brazil? He had one clean shirt left and a couple of dollars. It was not much. He walked out of the little inn in the hills, leaving his dirty laundry behind him.

He was on the bus to the docks where he meant to humble his pride and call for payment from Solomon and his partners, when he saw the back page of the newspaper which a man beside him was reading as they both hung on to the luggage racks of the jolting vehicle.

Judges Reverse Decision. Rondon Wins!

The clever Cervantes had blocked his rival and was disqualified. All winning tickets would be honored only if they were presented at the course on that day's meeting.

Charles felt in his clean shirt for his ticket and it was not there. He remembered that he had left it in his dirty shirt to be laundered at the inn in the hills above Rio. Again the sickness started in his stomach and the sweat pricked his groin. A streak of bad luck could run on and on until no one could believe in luck anymore. He pushed to the front of the bus and jumped out.

It took him fifteen minutes to find a cab in that poor district. Traffic jams clogged the streets all the way through the Carioca on the road to the hills. The old DeSoto boiled over on a steep climb and water had to be found for its engine. It was four o'clock when they arrived at the inn. The racecourse closed at six!

The cab driver began to shout and scream as Charles ran into the inn. He had not been paid; he would not wait.

"My shirt!" Charles shouted at the maid. "My dirty shirt—where is it?"

Mutely the maid pointed to a small room. It was full of filthy clothes, heaps of rank-smelling pants, and foul sheets and torn shirts, smeared with dirt and yellow with piss and sweat. Nausea bubbled in Charles's mouth as he stumbled over the piles of wash and began to search. At the door, the maid was watching and sneering, while the cab driver cursed and swore that he would put a knife in the white dog who would not pay.

At ten past five, Charles found his filthy shirt at the bottom of a heap of rags. In its breast pocket, a crumpled piece of cardboard numbered with violet ink.

"There," he shouted to the driver, "twenty thousand dollars! If we get to the racetrack before six!"

"Son of a whore—" the cab driver was saying when he was knocked unconscious by a fierce blow to the throat.

Charles took the keys of the cab from the man's hand. The maid stared at him in silence and then began to scream as he ran out of the door of the inn. The old DeSoto had been abused for too long to make much speed, but the cars were all going the other way as the crowds began to leave the Hippodrome before the last race. With steam spurting from the radiator and the gears grinding, Charles came to the main gate at five minutes to six. Two policemen came at him as he abandoned the cab and ran into the gate. Four more security guards took after him, pulling out their guns as he vaulted the turnstile and dashed through the thinning crowds. As he reached the pay window, the cashier brought the shutter down on his wrist, shoved under the glass with his winning ticket in his fingers.

"Rondon! I win! Rondon!"

II

"Early Matisse. Very simple, but you can see the whole Riviera in it."

As Charles spoke, he was watching the beautiful girl standing with her mother in his gallery in the hills above Rio. She was tall and frail, slightly stooping under the weight of her long black hair like a serpent on her head. Her eyes seemed to have drowned her face, pools of dark blue which spread light violet smudges down into her cheeks—the marks of ancient blood or late nights. Her mouth was sensual and drooping in the fine bones of her face, as if God had split a plum open and had squashed it for her lips. Her little breasts pushed at her white lace blouse, and her long legs wore the white silk stockings and brown shoes that were one of the signs of a Brazilian aristocrat.

Her mother standing beside her seemed to have had nothing to do with her birth. She was a plump, artificial blonde, only rescued from plainness by the ruin of a handsome face and the same dark blue eyes, filled in at the lids by fat.

"You are looking at my daughter," the mother said, "as if you know her, Senhor de Belmont."

"She reminds me of a painting—"

The girl turned away from the Matisse to look at him. Her eyes were open and inquiring. He could tell what she thought of him. She did not blush or turn her head aside; she just considered him.

"What sort of painting?" the mother asked.

"One of those *fin-de-siècle* paintings. Lovely society ladies which Aubrey Beardsley drew. They float around in long gowns, all eyes and hollow cheeks, and listen to Oscar Wilde being witty. There was something haunted about them."

"And decadent," the girl said. "Why don't you be frank? They were decadent."

"You're not," Charles said. "Really, I mean it. You're—"

He searched for the right word. "Unearthly! That's what I think of you. Unearthly!"

The girl smiled with her full bruised lips.

"What do you think of that as a compliment, Mama? You have an unearthly daughter."

The mother promptly changed the subject.

"Isabel, perhaps we should look at another picture."

Nothing personal was discussed that day.

The Portalena women bought the Matisse and a charming beach scene by Boudin, of girls walking with their parasols and men with straw hats on the promenade at Deauville at the turn of the century. Isabel Portalena asked Charles to get her some Beardsley drawings to see. She wanted to examine her rivals in his imagination. Charles promised that he would do what he could for her, although he knew that his sources in Geneva dealt in the art looted by the Nazis, and the Nazis had never looted England. When the Portalenas invited him to a party three days later, he was not surprised.

He had been on the guest list of most of the rich families who lived in their modern palaces on the hills above Rio. He used the money he won on Rondon to set himself up in the art business. It was a well-calculated move, since he knew where to get cheap masterworks in Switzerland that would sell in South America. It was bad manners in Rio society to make too many inquiries about a wealthy man's origins and possessions. All that mattered was a man had what he had and showed everyone that he had it. Charles fascinated the women he met with his withdrawn charm and the hint of ruthlessness in his lean mocking face with its compelling blue eyes and slight scars on one cheek. The men liked him as well because he would joke and gamble with the best of them at bridge and poker and at the racetrack. He was known to never bet when on a losing streak, and to be dangerous when the cards were falling his way or if he had researched a horse.

"You're a winner, Charles," was a comment frequently made.

It was common for Brazilian families to have French, English, German, and American names. Most of the wealthy people had European connections, financial and social. If a slight mauve tint beneath the pallor of the women hinted at that racial mixture which was the force and promise of Brazil, a common explanation was an Indian princess in their distant ancestry—there was something chic in that. The Portalenas were one of the few families who could boast of being among the founding Portuguese conquerors. They had served Lisbon and Madrid and the Empire of Brazil for four centuries, but their blood was running thin. Perhaps it was time for a new conqueror in the family.

"You remind me of a piece of art too," Isabel told Charles, taking him aside at the party in their house. "Not a painting. One of those beautiful early Crusaders who used to massacre people and destroy whole civilizations—and then be made a saint for it."

"You think I'm dangerous?"

"Yes—and blessed in your way."

Isabel stayed with Charles to the point of being rude to her other guests. He knew she was playing up to him with her eyes. She would hide them for a moment, then reveal their glittering depths until he felt drawn into their mysteries. Her long fingernails fluttered on his arm, rustling on the white sleeve of his dinner jacket. When her father came to scold her for neglecting the other guests, she knew how to soothe his complaints and introduced him to Charles. Portalena was tall and gaunt and soft-mouthed. Isabel might have been molded from him. The three of them talked of the pictures which hung in the house, the water lilies and haystacks of Monet; the feathery woods of Corot were placed like a peaceful dream between the old family portraits of Brazilian admirals and generals covered with medals and gold braid.

"It's good to talk to a man who knows about art," the elder Portalena said. He gestured toward the hundred guests who stood in the huge hall of the house, wreathed in bright silk and cigarette smoke as they chattered to hear themselves and not to each other. "In there, they only boast about how many tens of thousands of head of cattle they have—or when will Mercedes or Hispano-Suiza make a decent sports car again."

"Talking with Charles"—here Isabel gave her man the full brilliance of her eyes—"is like talking with one of the family."

The Portalenas appeared to accept her choice of him. In a discreet way, they seemed to want him to marry her. In a month, her father had called Charles into his study for a serious talk.

"The bloom here of girls is earlier, Charles. Not that they are not beautiful in middle age, but they are at their best young. It is a hothouse here—we force our plants ahead." He looked at Charles. "I should tell you, Isabel has a fortune in her own right from her dead grandfather. He had holdings in Diamantina right in the middle of the diamond mountain. They used to say of him that he could smell a diamond through a brick wall and find one lost in the Amazon."

"I've been lucky with diamonds before." Charles smiled.

The old gentleman chose to ignore his comment. He continued, "There is one thing—perhaps—I should tell you. If you are interested, that is."

"How could a man not be interested in such beauty?"

"And fortune." The gaunt father's voice was dry. "I should ask you a little about yourself, although here such things are often ignored."

"I am an only child," Charles said. "My parents are dead. I did well in the war—I have three medals to prove it. I came here to make my fortune. That is all."

"Your fortune by work, not by marriage?"

"Yes," Charles replied.

"We have herds of cattle, coffee plantations, a shoe factory and a chemical business, the last of the diamond diggings, a few million acres of jungle and rock in the interior—I need a son-in-law to help me with all this. Is there anything which attracts you?"

"Only Isabel," Charles answered. "She haunts me."

He forgot to ask what Portalena had to tell him, and he was never told.

Isabel had crept into his dreams. Her eyes brooded over his life, the kisses of her pulpy mouth wiped away his will, her small breasts quivered with his need when she pressed herself against him. He knew he could not have her without marrying her. The Portalenas were an ancient Catholic family. There was no question that the honor of their only daughter was the honor of them all.

So Charles was married to Isabel Portalena by the Cardinal himself in the Cathedral of Rio de Janeiro. The Vice-President came to the ceremony, so did the governors of five states, thirteen generals, four admirals, two air marshals, seventy-one high-ranking officers, three hundred and seven cousins, several hundred wives, more than a thousand children, various people thought to be important or useful, and one schoolteacher who had to be asked because she had married the only radical black sheep in the family. Isabel's intent eyes seemed to bring Charles back to earth as he moved with her down the aisle after their exchange of vows and rings. He felt as if he were floating with a wraith in white lace, so light she was on his arm, so transfigured by the yellow candle flames and incense smoking and organs sounding like choirs of angels.

Charles wanted to travel with his wife. He was

uneasy about going back to Europe yet. The war had not been forgotten; there was rationing in England and austerity everywhere. He decided to take her to the United States where the Portalenas had still more cousins. When the family had owned half of the coffee plantations around São Paulo, they shipped the beans to Savannah and New Orleans. Having no trust in agents, they sent their own blood to sell the coffee in the Deep South some generations back.

"Your family isn't a Mafia," Charles said to Isabel. "It's a monopoly."

They visited Isabel's cousin Edward, who lived south of Savannah on St. Simon's Island. In front of the great white classical house, the oak walk stretched for half a mile and the gigantic trunks of the ancient trees climbed like the pillars of Rio's Cathedral until their branches met in a vault halfway to heaven. Spanish moss drifted from the leaves like spirals of incense, but they did not shred away in the damp air. The old slave cabins of the house were still being used by the black families who worked in the rice fields laid out in vast squares for miles around. There they stood, up to their waists in mud and water, patient as storks while they picked the crop in clouds of mosquitoes and flies. Ten gardeners kept the banks of camellias and azaleas blazing beside the black waters of the cypress gardens on the edge of the swamp. House servants trimmed the lawn around the plantation until it was as smooth as a bowling green, while the oak floors and ebony curve of the grand staircase in the domed hall shone with the polish of centuries of maids. Black butlers in white gloves hovered in every corner. Charles had only to lift his finger for a mint julep to find the glass put in his hand.

"You know how to look after yourself," he said.

"The *war* looked after us," Cousin Edward said. He was as tall as old Portalena, but his paunch swelled the waist of his plaid cotton jackets and white shirts, which he changed four times a day. "Coffee, rice, and cotton—how could we go wrong? And now that fat-head General Marshall has a plan; we'll send it all to Europe for free and Uncle Sam will pick up the check." He held up the frosted julep glass with the green mint curling over the rim. "Here's to war—as long as it ruins everyone except us."

In the four-poster bed in the Azure Room, where peacock-blue drapes fluttered in the night breeze, Charles explored Isabel. She was his slow discovery, his pleasure, his sensual drug. When she undid her coil of hair, it fell below her waist like a black wedding veil. When she lay back on the sheets, it framed the pallor of her body. The hollows under her thin neck, the mauve of her little nipples, the dimple of her navel, and the black down that curled softly at the cleft between her legs was dark and shocking against the cream of her flesh.

In his quiet moods, Charles would lie on one elbow for hours and trace the bones of her body, his wandering fingers feeling the two arcs of her pelvis that rose above her flat, soft belly. Then he would feel gently between her legs, searching at the mouth of her cleft, rubbing her until she sighed and arched and pressed herself gratefully into the palm of his hand.

"Thank you," she whispered.

Then he would come into her and move lazily above her, watching her face below him change from melancholy to quick nervous smiling. He would tease himself and her, holding them both on the edge of orgasm until her anguished pleasure dissolved in a shuddering delight. And he would come in the warm gush of her coming, as her squashed lips opened in the perfect happiness of satisfied desire.

In his rough moods, he would take her casually, almost raping her in his hurry. Sometimes she would be almost as wild as he was, as though she was starving to break out from her languor into a fierce lust. Sometimes she would endure his thrust into her with limp flesh and a sad sweet smile on her bruised mouth. This would make him drive even deeper into her, maddened at her pity and her detachment. When it was over she would say, "Thank you," in a voice that came from very deep.

He often asked her if she wanted to move on, to the bright lights, perhaps to New York, where they could see *Oklahoma* and *Carousel*. They could visit Miami Beach or the old mansions of Charleston, or even the boardwalk at Atlantic City. But as the months passed on St. Simon's Island, she kept refusing to move.

"We'll never get to know each other really well again," she said. "I want you to concentrate on me—study me so well in the quiet here that I will always be in your mind. You'll close your eyes twenty years ahead, and you'll see Isabel de Belmont, your wife.

"Things will drive us apart. Business, travel, something. So know me now—forever. I love you, Charles."

They liked taking boat rides through the cypress gardens with Tom, the black boatman, using a pole in the stern of a gray flat-bottom. They would lie on the purple cushions in each other's arms, watching the wet tar of the waters stained by the cypress bark, gliding silently between the specters of trees rising darkly to blot out the blue skies of Georgia. They seemed to be slipping down an underground river with a ghost as their guide, taking them deeper, deeper—until they would round a clump of coal-black branches to see the fire of the azaleas on the sunny banks with purple bougainvillaea pouring its riches down to earth and magnolias holding out their white opulence to flag them back to the land of the living.

"We must leave," Charles said after three months.

"But we're happy here."

"We've stayed too long."

"My cousins don't mind."

"It's not that. I feel you withdrawing from me. As if you're slipping away every day, even when I hold you in my arms."

"I love you, Charles. I want to be part of you forever."

Cousin Edward and his wife Cindy Lewellen Portalena gave a farewell party for Charles and Isabel before they left for New Orleans. They invited the prominent Georgia people in those parts, the old families who had sailed over with Oglethorpe's soldiers when he licked the Spanish at Bloody Marsh. Some of the war rich also came—the businessmen who were beginning to make a new South on munitions contracts and federal highways and dams, arranged by their senators in Washington. Part of the pork barrel was being sliced in Dixie at last.

Charles looked across the room full of large men in creased white suits and their ample women in pastel dresses and sequined gowns. Most of them slouched in their bodies, ill-at-ease. They could not relax like the Brazilians. They had to be working with their hands, taking cigarettes or drinks or food, or touching each other.

Isabel was the center of a group of men, all talking to her with molasses in their voices. She was listening to them with a faint smile on her lips, the circles around her dark blue eyes now indigo in the evening light. She did not speak. Her shoulders were bent forward. She began to sway and fall as Charles ran to catch her. She woke a few minutes later on their bed to find him putting a cold towel on her forehead.

"Will you be well enough to travel?"

"Yes," she said, "it's nothing. Let's go now. This place is stifling me. It's too far from—what I need."

She became weaker in the old hotel where they stayed in the Vieux Carré of New Orleans. She would lie on the veranda of their suite, looking through the iron grills toward the tropical palms in the enclosed garden, while the sounds of the city murmured in the hot air. She would eat little and drink fruit juice all day, her pallor almost a sickness in the bright light. She developed asthma, which made her breathing difficult. Charles brought doctors to examine her, recommended by her cousin Hebe, one of the top Democratic bosses in Louisiana. They prescribed tonics and injections so that her arms became pockmarked with the thrusts of the needles. She made love to Charles rarely now, but at those times she clung to him, trying to engulf him in the clutch of her coiling legs.

"Thank you. Oh, thank you. I love you."

One day she felt better, and Charles took her down to the old coffeehouse on the docks, where they sat at marble counters and ate fresh-fried doughnuts, dipping them into the thick brown Brazilian coffee that the Portalenas shipped there. Huge silver bowls, chained to the mahogany of the wall mirrors, were full of a light powdery sugar for dusting the doughnuts. Charles poured a little into his palm and tasted it with his tongue. It was dry and sweet like the memory of a lost pleasure. He sneezed, puffing the white dust into the air. Then he saw the look of terror in Isabel's eyes, and he knew her secret.

"Show me," he said and took her back to the hotel.

She kept the white powder in two compacts. He tasted it and sniffed a little. His nose began to grow cold. In a few minutes, excitement spurted in his veins. He saw her standing naked against the light, a drooping shadow with the curves of shoulder and breast and buttock waiting for him. He put his arm around her, but she knelt and unbuckled his belt and began to lick his groin with the split plum of her mouth.

"I always wanted you to do that," he said.

He was so swollen now that she could hardly hold the tip of him in her mouth. She put her hand to the crawling skin that needed to plunge into her. She rubbed some of the white powder onto the quivering tip.

"What are you doing?"

The cocaine began to sink into the tender skin, chilling it.

"Before that wears off, you will have made love to me all night. You will want me—you will take me—you will not have me."

He put her on the bed with his blood on fire and he opened her legs and forced himself into her to find her already wet and hot and straining against him. There was a cold burning nothingness in his groin, a parched and freezing heat that couldn't be satisfied. Hour after hour they made love in a torment; their tongues were like dry winds over the fever of their bodies; their fingers fierce in their plucking at nipples and folds of flesh and the secret places of all desire.

Isabel became unconscious before dawn when Charles found himself still raging. But the urge in his loins was so strong that he came inside her in the morning, as if he were making love to a pale dead body who was his wife.

He woke in the late afternoon to hear water running in the bathroom. He walked across to find her wearing her flowered satin housecoat with its left sleeve rolled up. She was injecting cocaine into her veins.

"You're an addict," he said.

"The pain . . . I have to have it."

"What pain?"

"Oh nothing—just the pain—"

"You're not ill. It's that damned drug."

"Yes, maybe—but I have to have it."

"I'll get you cured."

"Don't try. You can't. I swear to you—it's too late."

Charles took the hypodermic, the needle, the capsules, and the powder, and put them in a paper bag.

"Don't get rid of them," she said. "Join me."

"I don't like habits I can't control. Where did you get it?"

"It's easy in Brazil. Lots of people are on it. It comes from Peru. All the Indians there chew coca leaves. How else could they survive, barefoot and starving in the high Andes, without their coca? It stops the pain. I tell you, it stops the pain."

"But you're *happy* with me."

Tears filled Isabel's dark blue eyes. She begged him with the tremble of her soft bruised mouth.

"Charles, you have made me happier than I ever thought I could be. I never believed I would have the time to live—to meet you—to love you—"

Charles threw the paper bag away in a bayou where it could not be found. But he could not stop her from getting new supplies. He even suspected that the doctors sent by Cousin Hebe were bringing her the cocaine. So he went to see the Democratic boss in his old office, stale with the smell of leather bindings on his law books and the cigars of the party regulars. Hebe himself was a dapper little man, wearing a yellowish suit that might have been white before time and the sun had pissed on it.

"Eh, Charlie," Hebe said in his bayou patois, "I think you not so damn clever to try to stop Isabel. *Ça manque d'esprit.*"

"I love her! I don't want to lose her."

"Listen, Charlie, we have damn fine hunt Sunday. At my bayou, down 'long the levee. Come, *mon vieux,* forget her for a day. You see her all de time."

"I can't leave her. She's ill."

"She can rest all day, all night. She wants you to have a fine time. You ask her."

He asked her and she did.

He had never seen such a hunt. The bosses and their guests and the hound dogs were driven out in black limousines along the flat levees of the Mississippi delta. They were transferred into three motor launches at a Creole fishing village. The whole population came after them in a fleet of dinghies and shrimp boats until the brown waters were alive with the patois chatter and the red bandannas of the fishermen. Aboard the launches, the bosses gave everyone a pump gun with ten cartridge belts, a Colt revolver, and a bottle of sour-mash whiskey. Then the engines were started and took them to a bayou in the swamps. The Creole fleet behind them filtered off into the waterways of the bayou, gradually encircling it in a great net of boats and people. At the mouth of the net facing the sea, the bosses and their guests waited with their guns. Between the launches, long steel-meshed catch nets were slung to gather anything that swam with fins or legs.

The drive began! Down the waterways the Creole boats came, whooping and yelling. The ducks rose by thousands, filling the sky with their wings. They raced over the mangroves into the barrage of the pump guns. The waiting hunters did not even have to aim. They rested the butts of their weapons on their thighs and pumped cartridges into the whirring air. The dark waters were bombed with falling birds. The hound dogs went wild, plunging over the rails of the launches to retrieve the carcasses. Pink flamingoes took off and were massacred in flight, falling like flaming streamers. Egrets exploded in puffs of white down, a heron had its beak shot away and flew on headless before it plunged into the swamp. Yet for all the birds that skidded out of the sky, there were ten thousand more winging out safely to sea, from the sanctuary that men broke only once a year.

"Damn fine hunt," Hebe shouted to Charles, pumping off his shotgun till it smoked hot in his hand. "Damn finest."

The Creole boats came further down the waterways, chasing the land and sea creatures toward the launches, which now chugged forward gathering in the steel nets. On the surface of the water the bodies of the ducks were joined by snakes and turtles and alligators, fleeing the shouts behind them. They met the nets advancing toward them and were caught in their meshes. Raccoons took to the water, their babies hanging onto their tails. A bobcat spit and snarled and paddled on. A small brown bear waded out and was shot down. The nets swept in all the swimming creatures, knots of water moccasins coiling around the sawtooth jaws of the alligators, while land crabs and catfish snapped and jerked in the wires.

"Haul in," Hebe shouted. "Haul in!"

The winches turned and dragged in the bulging steel nets. Shouting and swigging at their bottles of sour mash, the men drew their Colts. As the nets swung out of the waters over the stern, they began blazing away at anything that was moving. The loads spilled onto the deck. A bobcat sprang, choking with fury, and was cut down by a volley. Bullets whined off the scales of the alligators, then pierced holes that dripped dark blood. One of the bosses was hit in the arm by a stray shot. He poured whiskey over the wound and knotted a bandanna around it. The shouting, raging mob was drunk with blood and booze. They emptied their Colts until they had no bullets left. Nothing moved on the deck now. It was a *damn* fine hunt!

The whole fleet sailed over to a sandy hook on the levee. They dumped their catch near the great fires already blazing there. The village women were ready with the iron pots and spits. They seized the duck and turtles, the crabs and the catfish, and they stripped them all down to meat. Over the charcoal, the game was turned and the fish boiled in the pots. Cayenne pepper was hot in the air. The men sang Creole songs of the delta. The whiskey was the melody in their throats. The mass murder was over.

Charles woke to a cold dawn on the sand. Around him drunken bodies in the yellow flush of a new day. He remembered Isabel lying alone in the hotel, so he dunked his head in the foul water and rinsed some around in his dry mouth and staggered over to the levee. He passed an old brick church, raised above the swamp ground on piles. The graves were also raised among the cypress trees, marble family vaults on stone crutches, crumbling with moss and time. He thought he could smell the sweet stink of rotting flesh, and he ran toward the levee with fear in his heart.

A car stopped for him at last and took him to the Vieux Carré. Isabel was lying naked on her bed, breathing deeply, straining the air into her lungs. He held her upright, shaking her shoulders, her long hair knotting around his wrists. She opened her eyes, heavy-lidded and slit.

He raged at her, calling her a degenerate, a fool, a slut. She fell forward onto his cheek, her body against his, her small breasts brushing his shirt.

"Hold me," she murmured. "Please hold me."

She moaned and moved in his arms. Suddenly her ribs shook in a spasm. There was a rattle in her throat. Her breasts heaved hard and high, then sagged back. She slumped down, unconscious, as she had been once before, when she had eluded him on the night of the cocaine.

Only this time, she grew cold. She was not breathing. Charles was holding a dead woman who was his wife.

III

The autopsy gave the cause of death as a cardiac arrest or heart failure. Advanced leukemia was also diagnosed. Isabel had been a dying woman all the months of her marriage. Drug addiction was not mentioned as a contributory cause of her death.

Her father sent over a private Constellation from Brazil to take her body and her husband back to Rio de Janeiro. He met Charles at the airport. He had arranged with customs that the coffin be carried by four undertakers directly into a hearse from the belly of the airplane.

There had been Carnival once in Rio, Charles remembered. There had also been undertakers and a coffin there. He thought they were going to take his life. Now the undertakers were taking her away in their black limousine, encrusted with heavy silver decorations like Death's wedding cake.

Charles drove with old Portalena to a hotel on the Copacabana. He refused to stay at the family's house in the hills. He was bitter and suspicious. He sat down with the old man in his anonymous living room and began the inquisition.

"Did you know she was dying? Did you know before the marriage?"

"Yes," Portalena said. He opened his hands in an appeal for sympathy. "We have known of the leukemia and her bad heart for years."

"You should have told me."

"One time I nearly did, but we talked of other things."

"You didn't want to tell me."

"*She* didn't want to. She wanted to be happy with you and forget about death. Can't you understand?"

"I can understand I was tricked."

"Tricked?" Old Portalena's eyes were almost as large as his daughter's for a moment, dark blue and haunted with their pain. "Yes, you were tricked. But death tricked you, not us."

"You said nothing."

"I wanted my child to be happy. She *was* happy with you. I thank you for it. And I ask you to understand, if you can."

There was magnificence in the old man's appeal. Charles could see that, but his rage had been building since the catastrophe in New Orleans—his rage that she had kept it from him, his guilt that he had perhaps forced her death.

"I understand, all right. You had a dying daughter who you wanted taken care of."

"You loved her and wanted to marry her," Portalena said. "She loved you. Nothing was fixed."

"What about the drugs?" Charles could see the mouth of Portalena wince. "You knew she was on cocaine. Did you supply her?"

"Yes." Again the old man looked for sympathy in

Charles's cold, thin face and could find nothing. "Her pain was so great. The cocaine gave her peace—and the strength to love you and be with you."

"And if the woman *you* loved," Charles said, "turned out to be a dying addict? With her father giving her cocaine? What would you feel? I suppose the family knew too. That's why we spent all those months with Cousin Edward and Hebe. They were pushing for you, waiting to bury her."

The old Portalena's shoulders slumped. The hollows in his face were like yellow-black bruises. If Charles had beat him, he could not have looked worse.

"You are right," he said. "God forgive us. We deceived you because we loved our Isabel. If you loved her too, you would forgive us."

Charles walked over to the window of the hotel. He looked down at the lights of the jammed cars on the highway below and the neon signs of the cabarets scattered as far as the Casablanca near the Sugarloaf Mountain. Yes, the Casablanca cabaret was their favorite. He thought of the nights, sitting close to Isabel, listening to a French singer singing fabulous Edith Piaf songs, which told the same tragic stories he was living himself.

He turned from the window to look at the old Portalena.

"I will not be at the funeral," he said. "You bury her. She's yours."

"Your bitterness will pass," the old man said. "I understand it."

"I don't want your understanding, Portalena. I was cheated, that's all. Take your daughter back and leave me alone."

Portalena rose. He hesitated, then he spoke.

"Charles, I am grateful for what you have done for Isabel."

"Yes, I know," Charles said, and turned his back.

All of Isabel's money went to Charles in her will. It came to nearly three million dollars' worth of real estate and holdings in Diamantina, where the yellow diamonds of Brazil were found. There were also mineral rights to a river off the Amazon, where the diamond pirates were known to dive. They were the men with glazed coppery skins, armored against mosquitoes. Charles had met them in the Carioca bars, spending millions of *cruzeiros* on rum and women before going back to their foul toil on the murderous muddy waters. One of them had slapped down a pouch made of crocodile skin on the bar, pouring out the valuable pebbles in front of Charles.

"Two hundred thousand dollars," he said. "My share and my partner's. Fever got him so I got his."

Charles did not touch Isabel's money. He left it at her bank and appointed a business agent. He sold the last of his paintings and closed his gallery in the hills. He found himself with eighty thousand dollars. Twice he went up to the Carioca and the black girls. But when he went into their steamy rooms where they were moving naked to the sambas of the night, he walked out again. He swore at Isabel, who had screwed him up and would not let him loose. He wanted only her and she was dead.

He had to forget her. He had never been into the interior, the dry insane *sertão* where the bandits and the prophets slaughtered and preached the end of the world, or the burning Mato Grosso with its scrub alive with snakes, or the jungles of the Amazon where the rubber trees bled away the lives of men, and the

Indians still existed with their hidden lives and poisoned arrows. He chartered a Tiger Moth and took off for Manáos, the deed to the diamond river in his pocket. Somewhere near the Aripuanã River, his luck ran out in an electrical storm. It sucked in his biplane and spit it out onto the treetops of the tropical forest. Charles's parachute opened a little above the branches and he found himself jerked to a stop, hanging on his harness between heaven and earth, shocked and bruised, but alive.

He couldn't undo the buckles of his harness. They were jammed. He swung his body desperately, hoping to jerk the cords free from the branches. After an hour of twisting and rolling through the air, he got nowhere. The parachute was stuck firmly. His shoulders felt as if they were being pulled from his body by the webbing of the harness. He had been hung out to rot in the tropical forest.

He must have passed out for some hours. He awoke to the sound of birds or voices. Looking down, he saw a group of naked brown people on the ground below his feet. They were watching him and quarreling in their shrill voices. One of the Indians lifted his bow and aimed a long arrow. He fired, and it struck the buckle of the parachute harness. The arrow broke in half and fell back at the Indian's feet. He looked at it in terror, then at the man hanging from the parachute. He began to raise his arms and chant. The other Indians raised their arms and chanted with him. Above them Charles flew, a new god trapped in his machine.

That night the whole tribe met to worship their new god. They lit a fire beneath, so that its rising smoke made him choke, but it chased away the mosquitoes that were eating him alive. Medicine men danced, their bodies daubed with stripes of white and red, rattling their gourds, screaming at the great spirit to tell them what to do. The warrior Indians had taken *epena*, sucking the vegetable drug into their noses through a hollow cane. They were hallucinating, writhing and rolling on the ground, seeing visions of the god that had come from the sky. The Indian women squatted by the fire, giving their babies the breast, while the older children waited in wonder. Above their heads, Charles hung, his shoulder joints wrenching in their sockets, his skin cracking from the hot smoke and his lungs burning. He might not have been a god, but he was suffering like a martyr. He gave a great groan and fainted again.

He woke to the touch of a hundred fingers. He had been cut down and stripped naked. Indian women were squatting in a ring around him, pinching his white skin, giggling at his bush of pubic hair. For their bodies were hairless, smooth-skinned under their arms and beneath their legs. The string they wore around their swelling bellies was an ornament like the three sticks stuck below their lips and the wooden pin through their nostrils.

For two days, he was hand-fed on banana pap. A medicine man worked on his back and spine, pushing the joints of his shoulders back into place. Mud and chewed herbs cured his raw skin. When he recovered, he was led naked to a meeting of the elders. There he was put to a test. He stood opposite the largest of the warriors, who gave him a heavy blow in the chest. Charles chopped once with the edge of his right hand to the man's neck, hit the nerve, and stopped the flow of blood to the man's brain. He watched the man fall. When the next warrior took his place, Charles ducked his blow, knocked him down, then struck a third one to the ground with a left hook to the jaw. That was all. The elders were pleased.

Two nights later, the village of cane-and-leaf huts was attacked by another Indian tribe. Charles reverted to the savage fighter he was once trained to be. As an Indian struck at him with a spear, he swayed to one side and kicked his enemy in the little pouch that held up his balls on the string around his waist. He was hit in the arm by a poisoned arrow, but one of the Indian girls wrenched the point out of his arm and bit deeply and sucked the blood and *curare* out of the wound before the poison could spread. Raging at the pain, Charles fought to kill. He strangled two of the attackers with a liana creeper knotted around their throats. He left three more with broken bones, their forearms and shinbones snapping under the swings and kicks of his anger. The attackers fled, leaving Charles's Indians screaming the triumph of the new god, who had brought defeat to their enemies.

Two of his tribe had been killed. A feast was held to bury them and celebrate the victory. The two bodies were burned and the charred bones were powdered to dust, which was then mixed with banana pap and eaten by their families to quiet the spirits of the dead. The hearts and livers of the dead enemies were roasted and served to the warriors. Charles thought that disgust would stop him from swallowing, but he found himself eating it like any other meat.

The hunters had also caught some monkeys and a jaguar and five agoutis, the small wild pigs of the jungle. The tribe gorged itself on their flesh, then the men took out their hollow canes to sniff *epena*. It was not white like cocaine, but a brownish powder.

Charles sniffed it once, twice, three times, then lay on his back, naked, near the fire.

Isabel came to him as he closed his eyes. She was hanging naked in the smoke, her eyes flooding until their dark blue waters swamped her pale body and put out the fire so that she vanished in billows of smoke. He jerked and moaned. The Indian girls were around him, plucking at their god and rubbing him, pressing all the holes and folds of their bodies onto his fingers and toes, filling his mouth with their breasts and the smooth lips of their clefts, plunging him into their bodies, squatting, swelling, rearing, falling beneath him, their buttocks quivering, their legs knotting around him like lianas, until he was lost, lost in an orgy of beasts that the drugs made longer than time, until the last throb of desire was sucked from him and the ghost of Isabel set him free.

Charles woke, drained of his hate. Around him the Indians were lying in heaps of flesh. He could try to escape now but the murderous jungles stretched for thousands of miles around the Amazon basin.

So he trained his Indians in the arts of killing he had learned in the highlands when he was a boy. He was naked himself now, except for the pouch on the string that kept his balls from being scratched on thorns. His skin had fallen in on his ribs and buttocks, but his body was again the wire and sinew of his war years. He taught them how to chop and kick and garrote. He made their bows shorter and stronger, their arrows sharper and straighter. He showed them how to back each other up in attack, half shooting while the other half charged, instead of rushing in a mob at the enemy. In a short time he had fifty mean jungle-combat specialists. He had learned enough of their language to persuade them to come to the river with him on a looting trip. They would return rich, he told them. He did not say he would not return with them.

The seven canoes were the hollowed trunks of trees that raced down the brown waters of the Aripuanã. They would come in to the assault on the river villages in a cloud of poisoned arrows. But Charles had issued his men shields of bark that took in the arrows like a dart board. Then his Indians would attack, sending their naked enemies fleeing to the jungle in minutes, leaving a few dead and wounded behind them. After that, they would fill their canoes with manioc and monkey meat and palm nuts, while the village women prepared a meal. They would take some of the girls along with them down the river, to use among them when they tied up at night. Charles stopped them from killing the girls when they had finished with their bodies.

Charles and his men must have gone more than two hundred miles down the Aripuanã before they came to the first of the huts of the *seringueiros*. It was a log cabin with a thatched roof built on piles by the muddy waters. As Charles led the Indians toward it at dusk, he saw civilization at last—empty cans of beans, broken bottles, a rusted knife, newspaper covered with shit. On the little platform before the door, the dark balls of boiled latex were piled, the *borracha*, bled daily from the rubber trees by the *seringueiro* on his endless rounds. None of them lived for long—the jungle saw to that.

There was the sound of singing from the hut. Charles paused at the doorway. There he saw an object lying on a stained hammock, swollen with beriberi, surrounded with black vomit. It was hardly human, greenish and bearded and babbling. The naked-bodied Indians slipped past him at the doorway and killed the *seringueiro* with their spears. They shouted with pleasure to see the sacks of dried fish and beans and flour. To them, the dead man's old rifle and twenty fishhooks were a treasure.

Charles led his Indians on, although they now wanted to turn back. They found three more cabins of the rubber slaves. They killed none of them, taking only food for their journey. Finally they discovered a *seringal*, a fortified trading post that stopped the rubber slaves from escaping. Charles had decided to attack it at dawn to guarantee his escape up the Amazon to the airstrip at Manáos.

As the mists rose out of the hot swamps by the trading post, the Indians drifted in, dark ghosts in the smoking air. They killed quickly and silently as Charles had taught them, winding lianas around the throats of the boss's killers, then strangling them with a knee in the backbone. There was a slave tied to a whipping post, unconscious, with his back lashed to raw meat—flies laying their eggs in his wounds. They freed him and moved silently to the store, where the drunken slaves were sleeping off their debauch with the Indian prostitutes. It was the custom each time they brought in their balls of rubber from the jungle; they were given rum and girls for one night of lechery. Charles's men found one girl kidnapped from their tribe. They began to kill, and he could not stop them.

When the killing was over, Charles let the Indians choose the best of the loot—rifles and hammocks, dried fish, knives, and bright shirts. They were to fight their way home in their canoes, the richest tribe on the Aripuanã. The rest of the stores Charles gave to the Indian prostitutes and the rubber slaves who still survived. He told them to escape—they would have a few days before the soldiers came to kill anyone there who was innocent or guilty. Charles took the bags of gold dust and diamond pebbles that he found in the *seringal.* He also took a shotgun and the old motor launch rusting by the jetty. He took the Indian girl-child along with him.

Before he left the *seringal,* he set it on fire. The whole compound burned, sending a black pillar of smoke into the air, burning also the bodies of the dead. Charles set off on the launch, now loaded with cans of gasoline, his Indian girl-child preparing dried fish and flour cakes in the bow of the boat.

The engine pushed him slowly along with the current. He could not make more than fifteen miles a day. The mosquitoes settled on him like a hood of insects. To drive them away, he chain-smoked the cheroots rolled for him by the Indian girl.

When he saw the lights of the city in the interior ahead of him in the night, he put the Indian girl ashore. He did not want her to end as a slave whore again. He gave her all she needed in clothes and food, also a bag of gold. He told her to buy an Indian husband and forget her tribe. She kissed his feet when he left her.

Early that morning, Charles broke open the rusting bottom of the launch with an ax and swam to shore, pushing a raft holding the bags of diamonds and gold. The launch sank with the evidence of the raid on the *seringal.* He hid his loot on the riverbank and staggered into Manáos to tell a fine tale of horror and adventure. They believed him, for jungle survivor stories in Manáos were like fishing stories in Florida—you believed all you were not told.

When he was asked for the truth later, Charles could only say, "I lived, didn't I?"

The bulldozers and cranes gouged the earth and swung it away, while the cement mixers turning on the trucks filled holes in the ground with the foundations of a new capital. Concrete towers and cubes were rising. God was sent underground to His cathedral, the heavens cut off by Plexiglas. Men ruled the new earth making a future city in the wilderness. Brasília was being built where President Kubitschek's plane had landed—an instant ruin for later archaeologists or a superhuman promise that Brazil would conquer the continent as the North Americans had conquered their own.

"Greed," Charles would always say. "Greed is what will make Brasília work. That's why I'm here."

After his escape from the jungle, Charles was sure nothing worse could ever happen to him. He borrowed two million dollars on the security of Isabel's fortune, and bought marginal lands a little ahead of the politicians and the promoters. As jungle, it was worth a dollar an acre. When the first dirt road reached the area, it was worth five dollars an acre. Charles sold out. He did not want the problems of developing the land—the shantytowns, the Indian killers, the bribes to officials, and the dealing with contractors. If he had done that, his marginal land would be worth fifty dollars an acre in a few years. But after the jungle, he could not waste his life on struggling against nature and men.

Charles had made two million dollars after repaying his loan from the bank. He lived in a *supercuadra* in the first block of condominiums built in Brasília. He traded in building lots like poker hands, bluffing and sweetening the pot till he found a new client who wanted to buy into the game. He would show his cards and let the newcomer buy his hand. And then he would bid again.

Inflation was his ally. The President couldn't pay the bills for the new capital city, so he printed money to finance it. Prices would rise up to thirty percent in one week. Charles's fortune grew to billions of *cruzeiros* on paper, but soon he dealt only in dollars with the Americans who were coming to the new city, sniffing a fresh fortune to be made on another frontier. Brasília was sold and resold twice each year. In three years of dealing there, Charles once owned the same apartment block four times, and each time he doubled his profit.

The city was unlivable, harsh white lines that hurt the eye and red mud skirting the sidewalks. But on the borders of the federal capital a fun avenue grew. In those garish nightclubs and pizza palaces and hamburger heavens, the speculators and government officials would drink away the steamy nights and show off their flashy women and Lanvin suits. In one of the clubs called El Jockey, Charles was sitting alone one night waiting for a banker who would change his *cruzeiros* into dollars. Suddenly he saw a face he remembered and he forgot his business. The woman had red hair and a pale face, her lips parted in wonder or desire. Her green eyes were staring at him as if he had risen from the grave. Catherine, the Earl's daughter from Scotland, now married to the block of wood by her side.

Charles rose and went across to their table. He bowed slightly and took Catherine's hand and kissed it.

"Charles de Belmont," he said to her husband. "I was a friend of your wife during the war."

The English diplomat's eyes were glassy. Charles could not tell from his expression whether Catherine had told him that she had had a love affair before her marriage.

"Really?" The diplomat inclined his thin neck toward his wife. "You know Mr. de Belmont, Catherine?"

"Yes," she said. Suddenly a hot red color burned her cheeks as the wind had done that day in the fields when he had found her driving her tractor. "I thought you were dead, Charles. I never heard a word—" She stopped talking, confused.

"I went underground in Occupied France," Charles said. Then he lied. "And after the war, I had to stay underground. I had strict orders to tell nobody I was alive."

"Intelligence," her husband said. "Which branch?"

"Intelligence," Charles said, "is not asking me which branch."

The two men looked at each other in open hatred. The diplomat rose to his feet.

"We must be going, dear. We have a reception. . . ."

"Yes."

Catherine rose and held out her hand to Charles.

"We"— she paused as she emphasized the word— "would like to see you again. You must meet my children."

"Of course," Charles said.

Of course, they met alone. At first, Catherine Adam-Villiers held herself back. She had loved Charles too much. She had a private shrine to their passion. She used to worship in secret at the altar of the young French hero, killed in the war, who would have brought perfect love to her life. He was a mature man now, in the prime of his vigor, as lean and hard as ever, but wealthy and seductive and experienced, a man with a contempt for society and his own safety. He shocked her, but she could not resist him. She talked of her love for her two children, her respect for her husband, her wish never to cause him pain or scandal—and she found herself naked on Charles's circular divan.

He saw her shyness, her arms crossed over her breasts. So he knelt between her legs and began to lick her lower belly, his tongue searching through her fine red hair for the opening into her and the rose-tip of delight that would make her quiver. She had known him as a young rapist, but now he was wiser and more detached, finding his pleasure in a woman greater if she had pleasure from him. Force was not the way to approach old lovers. They needed tenderness and guile. And under the pressing caress of his tongue, she unclasped her hands from over her nipples, still as pink and small as they had always been, and she dug her fingers into his hair and pulled his face into her as her breasts swelled and she said, "I love you, I love you, I will always love you."

When she lay back on the bed in her orgasm and smiled her secret smile of satisfied desire, she might have never left the bed in the Edinburgh hotel for his *supercuadra* in Brazil. Time had stopped because of her love for him.

"It's better now," she said. "I'm not a shy virgin any more. And you Charles, are the most delicate and virile man in the world."

"I love you better as a woman," Charles said, because those were the words she wanted to hear, and he wanted to please her. The truth was—she was more sensual, a better lover, but he could no longer feel that desperate eagerness to have her, that sharp regret that the war was taking him away from her body too soon.

"I don't know if you really love me better," she said. She smiled and held his head between her small breasts that showed no signs of her being a mother. "I don't want you to be kind to me. I know you must have had a terrible life in the war and afterward. You never speak of it. What brought you here to Brazil?"

"I wanted to make a fortune."

"We were posted here, Charles and I."

"Your husband and I have the same name."

"It's lucky, if I say your name in the night."

"Do you say it?"

"When I am happy, I say your name—or his."

"Does he make you happy . . . ?"

"From time to time—"

"Even now?"

Catherine looked at her lover, grinning and sure of his hold over her.

"Especially now," she lied. "You've aroused me for him."

Charles slapped her cheek lightly, playfully. She was shocked for a moment. Then she saw him beginning to laugh, and she laughed with him.

"You don't believe me, Charles."

"No, I don't."

"Well," Catherine admitted, "I don't always believe myself."

After six months, she was free for a weekend with him. Her husband had been recalled to London for a conference over a new posting at home. Her two children, at the ages of eleven and nine, were at their English boarding schools. British parents usually showed their love for their children by sending them away. Catherine was at last a woman on her own as she had not been since her marriage.

"Where shall I take you?"

"To a place which I will always remember and love all my life!"

He knew of an old monastery and *fazenda* in the mountains near Paraguay, a secret retreat. The building had been founded by the old Jesuit orders expelled long ago from their communes in Central America. A hotel group had bought the place, intending to convert it into a stop for air package tours because a waterfall plunged spectacularly down from a cliff nearby. But the tours were still in the future, so the monastery was kept as an occasional conference center and secret hideaway for political meetings. Charles hired the whole of it for his lost weekend.

Barefoot boys wearing bright silk shirts danced and swayed as they served iced punches to Charles and Catherine in the garden of the old cloisters, perfumed with oleander flowers and gardenias and orchids hanging from the *jacaranda* trees.

"You are so extravagant, Charles."

"That's what women like best, extravagance."

"You think we're all whores?"

"I used to. Now I know that women have to possess a man. And the best way is to ruin him."

Catherine laughed.

"What keeps you in Brazil? I've heard you're a multimillionaire."

"Not really," he lied.

"Come to England. You liked it there. And—we're going back."

"I only know England at war."

"These are probably the last of the good years there," Catherine said. "With just enough virtues of old England left—and some of the new fairness. Everyone has enough to eat for the first time and go to school for free and are looked after when they're sick and have pensions. It's never been like that before. Yet people haven't quite forgotten the old system. They're not too greedy. They still have their manners."

"What would I do there?"

"Love me—you wouldn't have time for anything else."

They both burst out laughing and went in to dine on a whole suckling pig, roasted in honey, and imported Chateau Haut-Brion thirty years old.

Afterward, he took her to the waterfall. A single stream arched over the top of a cliff and fell two thousand feet into a boiling cauldron. Over the seething waters, the sun just beginning to set was shredded into broken rainbows, purple and red mists, green and orange hazes hanging in the air.

Charles turned to Catherine and began to undo the buttons of her dress. Her fingers moved at his shirt and waist. They stripped each other, their bare skin flinching at the cold invisible drops of mist, quivering with strange desire. They felt one another until she was hanging, panting on his arm, and he was rearing in her hand. He thrust inside her, bending at the knees, then jerking her upward on tiptoe, his arms locked behind her back. Her arms were around his shoulders, her neck arched, her mouth moaning. Then he threw his weight to the side and their linked bodies dived into the cold-boiling waters a few feet below.

There was a shock of ice, harsh fists, painfully cold, battering at the fire in their veins. He tightened his legs and arms around her under the whirling foam that hurled them up and down and over and over, thrashing and twisting their locked bodies. Catherine could not breathe. She knew she would choke and die with the hot blood hammering in her belly and lungs and ears, the chill, drowning waters slapping and sluicing her flesh that had no weight or shape. The rush of her love was part of the rush of tumbling waters. He shuddered and drove deep inside her and split her in two, and she drew him against her in racking spasms, and she opened her mouth to breathe death from the whirlpool. But the force of the cauldron had thrown them up to the foam on the surface and air flooded into her lungs, ecstasy in the ragged mists of strange light and the thunder of the fall.

"You have to risk it all," Charles told her later, "if you want to remember it always."

It was at a reception in the Palacio Itamaraty that Catherine's husband detected her affair. The Ministry of Foreign Affairs in Brasília did not usually invite foreign businessmen like Charles de Belmont to their diplomatic gatherings. He disliked these parties—the formal clothes and stuffed shirts bored him. But he wanted to arrange another meeting with Catherine, and he knew she would be there. For once he forgot his rule about affairs with married women.

Charles Adam-Villiers had just turned to introduce his wife to His Excellency, the Ambassador from Costa Rica, when he saw her sad face break into a wonderful smile. Her lips parted in joy, her eyes glinted their delight. He followed her look and saw that Charles de Belmont had just come into the room. He was holding up a hand to Catherine, doing no more. He could see Catherine's rapture and her husband's accusing stare at her side. The secret was out.

Later that evening, the two men met.

"They tell me—you—play bridge," Charles Adam-Villiers said. He flicked his words at his rival as if he were slapping him on the cheek with a pair of gloves.

"It depends on the company," Charles said. "Whom do you play with?"

"My usual partner—the Count di Broglioso-Schifani. However, the stakes might be too high for you."

"Ten dollars a point?"

"No! We start at fifty dollars a point. We go to a hundred."

"You must have a fortune to lose."

"Do you?"

The insolence of the Englishman was not concealed. He had to humiliate his rival. He had chosen his best weapon and Charles could not back down.

"I don't have a partner."

"Shall I find you one?"

The triumph of the diplomat showed on his smug mouth, fat and loose after too many receptions. Charles grinned, his mouth thin and twisting as a coral snake.

"Does your wife play?" he asked.

He looked at the Englishman who was staring at him. There was a silence between the two of them.

"I think that perhaps—if we are only men—"

"Is there a rule against women playing bridge?" Charles's voice was very brittle.

The Englishman just managed to keep cool. His eyes narrowed.

"If you want my wife as your partner, I'm sure she will accept."

"Perhaps you should ask her?"

The Englishman turned and held up a hand. He knew Catherine would be watching, sick with worry, as they talked on the other side of the room. He clicked his fingers and she hurried over to him like a dog.

"We are having a bridge game, Catherine. I am playing with Pufti Broglioso. This gentleman wants you to be his partner."

"But I can't!" Catherine was pleading to her lover. "They're international standard. I'm a bad club player. You and I, we've never even played together!"

"Play with me, Mrs. Adam-Villiers," Charles said. "It would be an honor and a pleasure."

"You'll be ruined."

Charles smiled at her in his amusement. There was a big risk; the odds were against him. He felt excited and young.

"I couldn't be ruined," he said, "in better company."

"I presume you will be responsible for your partner's debts," Catherine's husband said.

"I'll pay your wife's debts," Charles said. "Think of us as one."

Charles lost a hundred and sixty thousand dollars in the first two rubbers of the game, as he had guaranteed the debts of Catherine and himself at fifty dollars a point. The two of them went down by seven hundred points in the first rubber and nine hundred points in the second. Under the strain, Catherine could not be expected to play well. She failed to make an easy bid of Three No-Trump by letting her husband and the Italian count play out their long suit of diamonds.

The cards were not falling particularly well for either side. It was a matter of the diplomat and the Count seeming to know exactly what the other held. Almost uncannily they made their contracts each time, one spade here, three clubs there. They seemed to have second sight at each other's hand—and Charles only believed in firsthand information.

As they played the opening two games of the third rubber, Charles began to check on the usual ways of cheating. There were no mirrors in the room. The card table was too wide for foot signals—he had tried to touch Catherine's ankle with his foot but she was too far away. He watched the Count and the diplomat for any repeated actions—a finger scratching a cheek, a sniff of the nostrils, the raising of an eyebrow, the rubbing of a chin in thought. The Count did move frequently, but without a plan in it. The Englishman never moved his face at all, except for a patronizing smile of triumph on his mouth. He and his partner took the first two hands with bids of Two Diamonds and One No-Trump. Again they made exactly contract they called with no tricks to spare.

The third hand Charles could hardly lose. He was dealt seven spades to the Ace King Queen, the Ace King of Clubs, the Ace of Diamonds, and the Queen of Hearts. He called Two Spades. Getting back No Bid from Catherine, he settled for Three No-Trump. At that moment, he saw the Count's little finger move slightly along the back of the cards he held in his playing hand. The finger stopped on the back of the fifth card from the right. Then he closed up his thirteen cards and spread them out again.

He's got five spades to the Jack, Charles thought.

*He's telling his partner. If Catherine has nothing, I'll
lose this game too. They'll double.*

They doubled. Charles did not walk into the trap
of redoubling. Catherine had no honor cards in her
hand and no spades. Charles lost two of his spades to
the Count's Jack and Ten, and he went one down.
The diplomat smiled at the Count.

"My deal," he said.

During the next hand, Charles worked out the signals between his opponents. When they had won another rubber by eight hundred and fifty points, he
could read their hands as well as his own. They arranged their cards from left to right in the order—
spades, diamonds, clubs, hearts. A little finger moved
across to indicate the number of cards in each suit.
Then the cards were closed up and spread out again.
The little finger started moving again slightly up and
down along the backs of the cards. At the top it
meant an Ace, a little lower a King, then down a
fraction a Queen or a Jack. It was a clever system and
almost undetectable.

"You owe us two hundred and forty-five thousand
dollars," Charles Adam-Villiers said. "Would you like
another rubber?"

Catherine's face was white.

"Please—no," she whispered.

Charles took a checkbook out of his pocket. He began making out a check for the full amount. Then he
stopped.

"OK," he said. "One last rubber. But may I suggest
real money? Five hundred dollars a point."

There was silence in the room. The other players
looked at Charles as if he were insane.

"I agree," the Count said at last. "However, I think
you're being foolish."

"I won't play," Catherine said. She rose from her chair, but she was so weak and trembling that she had to sit again.

"You will," Charles said, "if your husband agrees to play."

"I agree."

Charles was dealt another strong hand in hearts, six to the Ace Queen Jack. Although Catherine did not bid well, too scared to say more than No Bid, Charles could read the strength of his opponents' hands. They had only three hearts between them. Their King of Hearts had no cover. It would fall to his Ace. He had two other Kings in other suits sitting above the Queens in the diplomat's hand. He had a good chance of game. He called Four Hearts, was doubled, and he redoubled.

When Catherine laid her cards on the table as dummy, they were exactly the cards he had foretold from knowing his own hand and reading the signals of his opponents. She had a long run of low hearts and a vital Ace and a King.

He played quickly, putting down his cards as if he were reading the game from a book. The tricks came to him precisely as he had calculated. He could not go wrong. He took the last trick and the game.

"Four hearts doubled and redoubled. Four hundred and eighty points at five hundred dollars a point. Two hundred and forty thousand dollars. Good I didn't complete the check. We're even."

"You haven't won the rubber yet," the Count said.

"You were lucky that time," the diplomat said.

Charles said, "Luck has nothing to do with it."

There was no luck in the rest of the rubber. Knowing his own hand and seeing what the moving fingers told him of his opponents' hands, Charles could deduce what Catherine held in her thirteen cards. The Count and the diplomat made Two Clubs in the second game, then they lost to Charles playing out a little slam in hearts, again doubled and redoubled. At five hundred dollars a point, they now owed him over half a million dollars.

"Would you give me a little time to pay?" the Count said thickly. He could hardly get the words past the tightness of his mouth.

"Of course, is one month OK?" Charles asked. He looked across at Catherine, who was staring at her husband. Her lover had ruined her and her husband. Charles did not want that. His winnings from the Count were enough for the night's work. He meant to take his final revenge on Charles Adam-Villiers—an intolerable act of mercy.

"I cannot pay it all at once," the diplomat said. "It will take some time while I liquidate an estate—"

"You owe me nothing," Charles said. "You owe it to your wife. I give her your debt to me."

"But you are responsible for her debts. We agreed to that."

"I did not say I was responsible for her winnings. The Count pays me. You pay her."

The color came back into Catherine's face. She caught Charles's eye and tried to smile. He stood up.

"I'll probably see you in England," he said. "I hear you're going there."

"Yes, that would be a pleasure," the diplomat said. He was trying to keep cool, but his ruin and his rescue were too much of a shock to him. He was humiliated in front of his wife. He had to be pleasant to the man he hated.

Charles walked to the door and turned there.

"Good night," he said. "Thank you all for a lovely

evening. And—maybe we can play again sometime, soon?"

Before Charles left Brazil, he wrote to Isabel's father sending him a power of attorney over all of Isabel's fortune left in the bank in Rio. His letter was short.

> *Dear Portalena,*
> *I am returning Isabel's fortune to you. I have used it to make my own, just as you used me to make Isabel happy before her death. But I never wanted her money, and I do not intend to possess it without possessing her.*
>
> *Sincerely yours,*
> *Charles de Belmont*

He knew it was an act of arrogance, not of generosity. But he could think of no better way of proving that his honor was greater than even her family's pride.

Part Three

ODDS ON
Europe, 1958–1967

I

"You wish to be invited where it matters during the Season?" The tall woman examined Charles with a professional stare. She might have been appraising him for auction. He looked back at her coolly, noticing the lines around her neck which makeup could never conceal, the sharp nose, and the eyes that glittered too brightly from adrenalin drops or greed.

"Yes, Lady Coresby-Doone. I understand you can arrange that."

The Lady gave her gracious smile. "Of course, I know all the right sort of people to know."

"So I am told," Charles said.

Charles wanted a shortcut. He knew she was the most efficient fixer in London. Money could buy any invitation through her, as long as the man was presentable and had money. Charles was a most presentable man with a lot of cash.

"How exactly would you like—our *arrangement*—"

Charles took out a stack of bank notes and pushed them toward her.

The Lady smiled, her eyes fixed on the pile of stapled five-pound notes. She picked them up, riffed through them with a painted nail, and put them in her handbag, closing its snap with a noise like a pistol shot.

"Exactly what do you want?"

Charles took a list of names out of his pocket and gave it to her.

"I'd like to meet these people," he said. "Either directly or through their daughters. I want to become a member of the Jockey Club."

She looked at the list, then at Charles.

"The Jockey Club makes a very thorough investigation into every aspect of a prospective member's life. Especially if there are any dealings . . . financial circumstances, which—how shall we say it?—which were not entirely proper and are a matter of record—"

Charles had thought of that. He had been warned that parts of the English social system were still not completely corrupt. His dealings in Geneva were ten years old. He had married an heiress in Brazil. He knew of nothing written against him. So he gave the Lady his coldest look.

"I don't think there'll be any problems."

"I was making no such suggestion. I was merely pointing out that an investigation would take place, if your name is put before the committee—"

"Thank you, *madame*." Charles rose from his mock-Chippendale chair. "If all goes well, you can expect another payment in a month."

The Lady's eyes sparkled. Her mouth smiled almost girlishly.

"Thank you, Monsieur de Belmont."

"One thing." Charles stopped at the door. "One invitation a month in the best circles is good enough for me. I have done a lot of things in my life. But I have a low tolerance of boredom."

He saw the Season open with the debutantes all appearing in white, descending a staircase at Londonderry House at Queen Charlotte's Ball. They looked like a discarded *corps de ballet* on their way to an amateur performance of *Swan Lake*.

One of these young girls made him forget himself. She was Lady Claire, the Earl of Aubynne's daughter. Her father had a string of fifty racehorses at Newmarket and one famous sire, Petrone, the only horse ever to win both the English and French Derbies. Charles was interested in meeting the Earl and went to a house party at the family seat in Shropshire. When the girls left the men after dinner, to their port and cigars, Charles made himself liked by the Earl. He had researched the names of twenty of the Earl's bloodstock.

They talked about horse pedigrees for half an hour.

"You're a damned intelligent man, de Belmont," the Earl said.

Later Lady Claire took him for a walk in the gardens, her fingers clutching the arm of his red velvet smoking jacket.

She was beautiful in her way, slim where her friends were plump, hard from all the riding on her father's horses, avid for experience, with eyes that would not stay still, moving in green glances feverishly from side to side. When he kissed her, he found her tongue striking like a snake's head into him, her body pressing urgently against his, her nails clawing at the nape of his neck.

"For Christ's sake," she said, "don't stop. Don't stop, Charles. Not like those little puppies back there.

Grope and giggle—that's all they can do. Fuck me."

Only horses had kept her from the stableboys, and
even then she had had an affair with a trainer at sixteen. Now she was hot for Charles, making him come
into her as quickly and brutally as if she were one of
the black girls from the Carioca. The saxophones
were wailing silly fox-trots. The damp rising under
the garden bench where they were lying. Anyone
could arrive and find them copulating like cats in
heat. It made their drive into each other, their digging
hands and crawling flesh, into something fierce and
sweet. When they broke apart, she dropped her dress
back to her knees after wiping herself with her pant-
ies and throwing them over a nearby hedge.

They went back to the party by different paths, she
to the ladies room to repair the damage, he to the
champagne bar to think about the raunchy respecta-
bility of the English country girls.

He did not meet Claire again on her own. She said
she was madly in love with him, but he told her to
forget it. After all, she was only eighteen. He couldn't
risk a scandal if he wanted to be accepted by the
Jockey Club, where her father was a Steward. One
blackball was enough to exclude him, and he would
get it if their affair became known.

"Horseflesh," he told her, "I prefer horseflesh."

She was furious, but she forgave him privately. He
was the only man who had shown contempt for her
in all her short life.

His affair with Catherine came to a natural end.
They met a few times at his apartment in Eaton
Square in SW1. She was resentful of him now. She
said that he had ruined her relationship with her husband. How could she respect a man who owed her a
fortune over a gambling debt and would not pay? He

accused her of adultery, which she would not confirm or deny. The divorce, which they both said they wanted, would hurt his career and harm their children. So they went on living uneasily in the same house.

The few times that she and Charles made love together, it was as though they had been married for years. They went through the motions of being excited, but each knew the other was acting.

It was almost a relief when he saw a little man in a dark raincoat watching the windows of his apartment, standing by his Jowett Javelin parked in Eaton Square. Charles knew the type. He had worked with them.

"Your husband's got a private detective on your tail," he said. "We won't meet for a while."

Once their meetings were no longer expected, they let the affair die. After that, Catherine would think every day of her life of an Edinburgh hotel room and an ecstatic dying under a waterfall. Charles would also remember on the rare times he ever thought about the past.

At Ascot he had a pass to the Royal Enclosure; he was on speaking terms with thirty members of the Jockey Club, even the Duke of Norfolk lifted his gray top hat as Charles lifted his own.

He applied for his racing colors—orange and maroon with gold hoops and a diamond on the back—he was always lucky with diamonds. He was told that he could race under his colors provisionally. They could be confirmed next year after an investigation. On the surface, he was absolutely acceptable—and he was spending money on British thoroughbreds as a gentleman should.

Charles held parties in Eaton Square that were not like the other parties in London. He had felt the winds of change blowing in the world.

Clearly the days of the great land empires were finished. It was incredible that a small island in the North Sea had ruled a quarter of the earth for fifty years, winning two world wars. But it could never happen again. The only future empire for Britain and France lay under the oceans with their limitless untapped resources. Russia and America could afford to take over space with their *Sputniks* and von Braun rockets, now aimed at the moon instead of London.

So unknown sheikhs like the Harvard student Yamani came to his parties at Eaton Square. There was also a little-known underwater explorer, Jacques Cousteau, marine biologist from Cambridge trying to introduce fish-farming techniques, and Lebanese bankers from Beirut growing rich on investing Arab oil profits. His guests met the ex-debutantes who were only too happy to be invited on expensive evenings from their four-girl apartments and their dull jobs as secretaries at Sotheby's or Spinks, if they weren't shopgirls at Harrod's or Fortnum and Mason's. The wealthy men from the Persian Gulf and Beirut and Brazil loved the titled girls of London, freed by their families to sleep around if they wished, innocent in all things except the use of other people's money.

Charles sometimes felt he was running a *maison d'assignation*. He was a male madam putting together the alliances of the future. The rich young rulers of the new East were coming together with the impoverished aristocrats of England—so clever at finding fresh sources of income for their traditional tastes. Caviar never was cheap.

He began going to the 213 in Knightsbridge. He

had heard of it from a Brazilian friend as the most elegant brothel in the world. It was staffed entirely by society divorcées and young widows who had been used to the good life. Deprived of their husbands' income, having no trade except pleasing a man, lazy by nature, and used to earning fur coats on their backs, the women of the 213 chose to become the mistresses of rich men.

"After all, Charles," the most elegant of these women said to him one night, "we have men whom we excite, all expenses are paid, and we can play around before we settle down. We're not in a hurry to go to the altar again—all that boring social bit, you know." An enticing smile followed above a pair of bewitching and naked breasts. "Unless *you* were to ask me, Charles."

"You're perfect as you are. Why gamble on marriage?"

He started an affair with Lady Claire again because of her obsessive passion for him. He only had to touch her to set her on fire. "Christ," she said, "I'd strip for you in the middle of Piccadilly. I would too. Ask me." He did not ask her, but he believed her. If he put his fingers on her blouse, she would tear it off, the buttons popping in her haste.

"I know I shouldn't," she would say. "I should play hard to get. But if I didn't run after you, you'd bloody go away again. Fuck all that ladylike stuff."

"You are a lady—officially."

Normally he hated being pursued. He could not bear a woman crawling all over him. But with Claire he was secretly flattered. She was beautifully made, long-legged with tight buttocks and firm breasts and a profile that could have been cut out of a coin, so clear was its edge, so beautiful. Her body was good enough to have stripped at the Crazy Horse Saloon in Paris, her manners (when she remembered them) fine enough for Buckingham Palace (where she had often been). Also her pedigree was impeccable—two whole pages in Debrett. This impressed Charles.

There was still enough of the peasant in him to feel satisfied at the adoration of such an aristocrat, and enough of the forty-year-old man to care for the caresses of a passionate girl of eighteen. Knowing his weakness for her, he was careful to remain cool on the surface and discreet in public.

"You are a bastard, Charles. You never take me out anywhere. You only see me at parties. You never tell me what you really think of me."

"If I did, you'd leave me."

"Do you despise me that much?"

"No. I wouldn't like you ever to know how to call the shots on me."

II

His gray mare, The Interloper, was third favorite in the Ascot Gold Cup, bet down from fifty to twenty to one during the weeks before the race. Much of the backing came from Charles himself, who put twenty-five thousand pounds on the horse.

"I'll see you at Ascot, Claire," he phoned her. "You'll be there with your father?"

"If you're going, yes! Why won't you take me for the Gold Cup? Please."

As they walked around the Royal Enclosure, he knew that he should not have agreed to take her. She was wearing a hat; women at Ascot always wore hats—a huge white felt Borsalino, pulled down over her eyes, that made her look like a gay gangster. Her cream silk sack dress was cut right on her breasts and made the rest of her body seem to writhe beneath its bell shape. She was radiant with him and she made sure that she was seen, staying close to his side and holding his arm as she talked to him, handsome and serious under his gray top hat. Whenever she met one of her debutante friends, she would introduce Charles as "the man of my life." When she met one of her family friends, he would be "Charles de Belmont—The Interloper, you know."

They went to the paddock to see his horse paraded around before the Gold Cup. Rigg was up, an experienced older jockey who was one of the best. The coat of the gray mare was shiny and she was in perfect condition, the best she had ever been.

Then Claire tripped on a tuft of grass, accidentally or on purpose. She tumbled off her stiletto heels, embracing Charles to stop her fall. When he got her back on her feet again, he found himself looking at the Earl of Aubynne and a French Rothschild.

"Oh, Daddy," Claire said, "you know Mr. de Belmont. He's got a horse—"

"Which may win," the Earl said.

"Which will win," Charles said.

"If I were as sure as you," the French Rothschild said, "I'd trade my bank for bloodstock."

"Charles brought me here," Claire said, "to see The Interloper win."

The Earl of Aubynne stared at Charles. There was no expression on his face, just an appraisal of form. Charles knew, that moment, his past and his pedigree would be more thoroughly scrutinized than ever by the Jockey Club's investigators. To be the owner of a racehorse was one thing, to be the escort of Lady Claire was another.

The Earl's two hands seemed to invite Charles and the French Rothschild closer to one another. "You two should be acquainted, both coming from France, I mean."

"Actually not," the French Rothschild said. "We've

never met before, but I've heard the name. An associate of mine called Louis Durac—"

"Oh yes, I knew him during the war," Charles said. "I once did him a favor."

"And he still speaks well of you?" The Rothschild looked at Charles with mock amusement. "I never do people favors—that is why I still have a few friends. Why don't you race in France?"

"I'm just back from Brazil where I spent ten years. I've only had my horses for a year. When I've won the Gold Cup, I'll take a crack at Longchamps."

"Brazil," the Earl said, "that's an interesting place to make one's money in. I thought that was where the nuts came from." The French Rothschild and the Earl laughed heartily.

Charles lifted his binoculars to see the running of the Gold Cup. The jockeys were under orders and bringing up the horses to the gates. Charles could see Rigg moving the gray mare up fast as the field broke away. The trainer had told him not to take an early lead, but that was how it went in the first furlong, the gray striding four lengths ahead of Chateau Labelle and the favorite, War Game.

"We're in front too soon," Charles said.

Rigg was holding The Interloper close to the rails as War Game moved out to the center of the track, his jockey giving him the whip until he came up to a length behind The Interloper. Claire was shouting her excitement at Charles's side.

With a furlong to go, War Game was half a length ahead of The Interloper, who was neck-and-neck with Chateau Labelle. Charles did not think his horse had a chance now. Rigg used his whip. The gray lengthened her stride and slid along the rails, closing on War Game. As the two leaders passed the post, The Interloper was a short head in front.

"You caught him just at the post," the Rothschild said. "Congratulations."

Claire looked at Charles, the green of her eyes like two polished emeralds.

"Oh, Charles, she won! Did you have a big bet on her?"

"Yes," Charles said. That was not important. He wanted recognition in England, and he would be recognized now.

"I must lead the horse in," he said. "Please excuse me."

He went to meet Rigg, who had turned The Interloper around and was bringing her back toward the winner's enclosure. He saw the jockey smiling and patting the sweat that glistened on the horse's neck.

"That was a great race," he said.

"Nobody wanted to go to the front," Rigg said, "so I did and put them all to sleep. Bloody burglary, it was."

"Come and have some champagne when you've changed," Charles said.

He held the horse for just long enough to allow the photographers to take the shots they needed for the newspapers, then he walked back to Claire and the Earl of Aubynne. He knew that they had discussed him while he was away. The stare of the nobleman was even more pronounced. Claire must have told her father that she was attached to him.

"The Queen's here," the Earl said. "She'll present the Cup to you. It's quite an honor—you're not used to it, are you?—I imagine."

"Oh, I knew General de Gaulle pretty well," Charles said.

When he was presented to her, Charles found the Queen quite a small woman with a pleasant smile in an orange silk coat and a matching hat hung with clumps of cloth bells. There was nothing very remarkable about her except the way she talked.

"We are very pleased you won the Cup. We are told this is your first year racing. We congratulate you."

"We thank Your Royal Majesty," Charles said, taking the cup. "We—I mean, the horse and I—"

He looked at the Queen, waiting to see her take offense. But she saw a slight grin on his handsome face, as lean and hawklike as her husband's, and she began to laugh. As she laughed, the little group of ladies-in-waiting and dukes around her began to laugh as well. It was a well-bred echo of royal pleasure.

"Mr. de Belmont," the Queen said, "we are amused."

Two months after he had won the Gold Cup, Charles de Belmont's racing colors were withdrawn by the Jockey Club. The result of the investigation of his past was negative. The Stewards would give no explanation. There was no question of appeal.

At first, Charles suspected Claire's father.

"No father likes losing his daughter to a man who is nearly his own age."

"Daddy wouldn't behave like that. He'd never put anything personal before his duty to the Jockey Club. He thinks it's almost as holy as Westminster Abbey. There must be something in your past."

"Someone," Charles said, "gave false information about me."

"You hardly ever speak of anything before Brazil. Perhaps when you were in England during the war—

or in Geneva afterward, or when you were in art dealing—you had an enemy—"

"Wait a minute! I think I know."

The blackballing turned out to be the revenge of Catherine's husband, Charles Adam-Villiers. Through the Foreign Office, he had access to the files in M.I.5 on Charles's intelligence activities. His part in the escape of the Nazis to South America was strongly suspected and partially documented. He was considered a bad security risk by the British. There was also evidence supplied by French intelligence that his family background was untraceable. It was a poor dossier for a future member of the Jockey Club.

Catherine phoned Charles to tell him that her husband had boasted he had a lot to do with the action of the Jockey Club. "You should never have humiliated him in that bridge game," she said. "I know he was cheating, but many bridge players of that standard do. To them it's a kind of fine diplomacy, a way of outsmarting the opposition, not really dishonorable. If it's any consolation to you, my husband's new feeling of superiority over you has saved what's left of our marriage. He thinks I was led astray by a scoundrel who abandoned me. I could think of it that way, I suppose—although I try not to because I love you."

It was a lesson Charles still had to learn. However good the odds were, hatred and envy could always upset them. Men could make irrational choices to destroy a person they detested. They would even be self-destructive to eliminate an enemy. He would never push a rival that far again—unless he killed.

"What are you going to do now?" Claire asked.

"This isn't the only country in the world," Charles said. "The fight's just begun."

He flew over to Paris in his Lear Jet, and sent his

card to Louis Durac, now one of the leading merchant bankers in Paris. Durac immediately invited him to lunch at the Tour d'Argent. They sat at the best table by the curved windows overlooking the back of Notre Dame and the Ile St. Louis with its pretty apartment blocks making a tiny walled city in the middle of the Seine.

"You haven't aged at all, Charles," Durac said. "I wish I could say the same."

Durac had lost the young man inside the fat sack of an older man. He weighed nearly two hundred pounds now, and his English tailor had trouble hiding his stomach in his discreet pinstripe suit.

"Good living," Charles said. "That's a sign of good banking—eating with all those rich clients."

"Living at all," Durac said, "only because you were good to me once."

They were both thinking of the scene under the walnut tree in the forest at the end of the war, when Charles had been ordered to execute a traitor and had let him go. And three days later a traitor had given Charles to the Gestapo.

"How did you get off the tribunals after the war, Louis? They must have been after your head."

"I had a friend who was close to de Gaulle. He decided that the execution order had been a mistake. There was a man called Duroc, and somebody typed the name wrong. They didn't have much evidence against me, anyway."

His eyes would not look at Charles. They turned gratefully to the menu. It was a wonderful refuge at any time.

"The duck *à l'orange* is very special here. And the *tournedos*—I don't know where they get it, but the cattle must be fed on buttered hay, it's so tender. It slips down your throat—"

Charles never knew for certain whether Louis Durac had betrayed him to the Gestapo or not. He did not want to know now, for he wanted to cash in Durac's debt to him for his life. It was no good hating a man if he was obliged to you. You might prefer revenge to repayment. Charles was sure that he was the only witness who had heard the young Durac's confession about being a traitor. Now the merchant banker would have to give him what he wanted, to pay for his silence.

"I can't get my racing colors in England," he said. "For some silly reason they've refused me—I don't know exactly why."

"Those damn fools—" Durac nodded in sympathy, his two chins moving at the same speed and settling down above his tight white collar and pearl-gray tie.

"You're friendly with the Jockey Club people here, they tell me. I'm bringing my horses over to run here, and I've already ordered my silks at Hermès. Fix it and me—for old times' sake."

Durac looked at Charles's face, now relaxed in the restaurant. He sighed and smiled. Strange, the only man who could denounce him had asked for so little. It was surprising how a small amount of snobbery could discharge the greatest debts. And yet, he had to be sure that Charles was not asking for a first installment. Otherwise, he might have to use his contacts with the ex-mercenaries from Indochina and Algeria, who could deal with that sort of embarrassment.

"Of course your membership can be arranged, Charles. As you say, our people are more rational. A man who is prepared to spend money on horses and has good manners is always welcome. Anyway, the Head Commissioner owes me a favor—" He looked carefully at Charles. "And if there has been a little indiscretion in one's past—then that is of no consequence whatever. I am right, am I not?"

"I never remember anything about my friends," Charles said, "except that they are my friends—when they are ready to help me. Now let's get on to more important matters—the *tournedos* or the duck?"

Durac smiled.

"It was always a pleasure to deal with you, Charles," he said. "You're a man who understands when a man has to deal."

Charles flew back to London to arrange for his string of horses to be shipped to France—and to settle his accounts. If the Stewards of the Jockey Club thought themselves invulnerable and unaccountable, they would be taught that they were men too. Montaigne had said it first—even a king sits on his own ass. Charles knew where to strike, and he struck. He would force himself down their throats, while they choked and swallowed him whole.

He spent a night with Lady Claire, breaking her in like a filly. He made love to her for six straight hours, penetrating her through every hole in her body, making her serve him lying, kneeling, on all fours, squatting, hanging from the bed rails, her legs open or locked or bent back.

He let her sleep at dawn, then he took her again at midday.

When they had drunk champagne and orange juice before their brunch of scrambled eggs and smoked salmon, he told her he would marry her.

"You will, Charles? You're not asking me? You're telling me."

"Don't you want to?"

"Darling Charles, I'm exhausted. I feel as if I've just been raped by a Mongol horde mounted on elephants—and they let the beasts have me too."

"After brunch, again?"

"Charles, I couldn't."

"I never thought I'd live to hear you say that."

"I never thought I'd live to hear you say you'd marry me. The answer is—" she paused for no effect at all "—yes."

III

A quartet of lovers were singing in Italian, skipping heavily about the stage like baby jumbos. In the Royal Box at the Covent Garden Opera House, the Earl of Aubynne turned toward Charles.

"One day they'll fall through the stage," he said, "unless we reinforce it. Why are all singers overweight?"

Charles laughed, but not loud enough to disturb the orchestra playing *Così Fan Tutte*.

"Do you enjoy running an Opera House?"

The Earl of Aubynne smiled.

"We don't run it, we raise money for it. The fact is—I don't like music that much, I like the food."

The food was served at the intermission in the private dining room behind the Royal Box. It was the favorite picnic lunch of the Palace—cold ham and chicken, tomato-and-lettuce salad, bread and butter and Rhine wine, and chocolate cake.

"It's very simple," the Earl said. "Sit down and enjoy yourself."

He obviously enjoyed the food, although his wife did not. She could hardly get the chicken past her lips, which had congealed in an effort to be polite to Charles. She was not grinning and bearing his engagement to her daughter. She looked as if she were going under for the last time. Talk between them never reached the end of a sentence without dying of embarrassment. Even Claire was subdued, and the bad weather was not interesting enough to carry the conversation through the evening.

A bell sounded for the start of the second act. The Earl's wife walked to a part of the oak paneling, opened it, and vanished inside.

"Impressive," Charles said. "If a mob attacks the Royal Box, that must be the secret way out."

"No, it's the royal washroom," the Earl said. "People who wear crowns aren't meant to have natural functions. But if they do, it's hidden away."

When his wife appeared again like a ghost through the paneling, he sent her and his daughter back to the box for the second act of the opera.

"My ears are buzzing; I'll stay here with Charles and have a chat."

Charles admired the grace with which the Earl had engineered their confrontation. He had been a good host all evening. Charles might have been his favorite guest. But the moment the oak door to the Royal Box had closed and the two women were on the other side, the Earl's face tightened into anger, only just under control.

"Well," he said, "you'd better tell me why you are doing this to my daughter. If it's money you want, it's all locked up in a trust until she's twenty-five."

"I don't care about that," Charles said. "I have my own. I'm sure you know that."

"Then if you don't want her money, what do you want?"

"She's a beautiful girl, your daughter." Charles spoke precisely, flicking at the Earl's wounds. "Why should I want anything more? She adores me—passionately—"

"She is only eighteen. You are forty. Don't you think it's a little—um—unwise?"

"You mean obscene, don't you?"

"If you wish. Frankly I can't see your reason. Do you—love her?"

The Earl said the word *love* as if he were choking. He could not believe it.

"I love her in my way," Charles said.

"And what does that mean?"

"The way I choose to make my life. I don't like being held up."

The Earl of Aubynne sighed.

"That Jockey Club business—I was afraid it might be that."

"You know a lot about me," Charles said. "You were given information by an enemy of mine. You didn't bother to check it with me. It was a secret investigation without an appeal. Do you think that's fair?"

"We could not accept you in the Jockey Club once we found out how you made your money in Geneva."

"Does that mean I'll make my horses run crooked?"

"There is often a connection between the way a man made his money and the way his horses run."

"We can't all inherit it. And actually I don't have the money I made in Geneva." Charles's words were technically correct. He had been robbed by the Nazis. "More than that, if you ask Israeli intelligence you will find that I gave them the chief Nazi network in

Brazil. But, of course, you're not interested in the truth. You just want to keep outsiders like me—outside. Any excuse will do."

"So you're marrying my daughter for revenge," the Earl said. "I find that almost incredible for a man of your obvious talents. Also, as a father—what about her happiness?"

"I am marrying her because of her," Charles said. "Don't get me wrong." He flicked his words at the Earl again. "I want to settle down. I want sons to carry on the name of de Belmont. And you—don't you want grandsons? Think of it. Your blood and mine?"

The Earl winced. He stroked his cheek with his hand as if he had been slapped.

"How much do you want to go away? Claire tells me you're racing in France now. Please go there and leave her alone."

"I want one thing," Charles said. "I want to be a member of the Jockey Club."

"I can't do that," the Earl said. "The decision against you is final and is not reversible."

"Then I marry Claire as soon as possible and it's your family's duty to have a wedding and a reception. Of course you'll invite all your racing friends to see you give away your daughter to me."

Charles had taken the Earl too far. The other man was on his feet now, white and shaking.

"You bastard," he said. "I will refuse my consent."

Charles stood up.

"I don't think you will. Claire would elope with me tomorrow. We could marry in Las Vegas or Monterey. Eighteen is the legal age there. You'll read about it in the *Daily Express*. 'Earl's Daughter Flees with Wealthy Playboy!' "

"If I'd known the man you were," the Earl said, "I

would have blacklisted you out of every place in London."

"As it is," Charles said, "I shall be invited everywhere as the husband of Lady Claire. And when we have a son, you will want to see me because of that son. You have an estate—you need an heir. You don't have much of an option, my friend."

"I will never forgive you," the Earl said.

"Never is a long time. I used to think the mark of the true aristocrat was—to accept what happens gracefully. That's how you've survived all these years, isn't it?"

The wedding of Charles de Belmont and Lady Claire took place after an engagement of only two months. The ceremony was held in the family church. It was a family show with the villagers standing in the churchyard outside as Charles used to stand as a boy when the girls from the local chateau got married. Inside the church, the narrow pews were jammed with the Earl of Aubynne's guests in their frock coats or formal dresses and flowering hats brighter than the church's decorations.

Most of Claire's relatives were there and none of Charles's. Against two dukes and duchesses, four marquesses and countesses, thirteen ladies and fifty mere honorables, Charles could only show his best man, the dishonorable Louis Durac who had arranged his membership in the Jockey Club in Paris. The French banker found the whole occasion charming and ridiculous, but the bride was ravishing beyond words; her white silk dress and lace veil and orange-blossom bouquet made her seem like an angel of purity and light.

The reception was held in the big hall. The county gentry and the racing friends all came to pay their respects. As the members of the Jockey Club filed past in the greeting line with their wives and daughters to congratulate Claire and shake Charles's hand, they could see his mocking smile.

"We are spending our honeymoon in Paris," he said. "My horses will be racing there."

They looked back at him enjoying his triumph and were sure that he would never be one of them.

As the great hall filled and the loud talk rose to the stone vaulting of the ceiling, Charles looked at the laughing face of Claire alight with her own triumph over her unmarried girl friends. She had captured the most interesting and mysterious millionaire of the Season, who was sweeping her off to a life of unspeakable delights. Around her Charles could see the hundreds of people from her class and kin, the massed roots of the family tree grown into the earth there for generation after generation. He was only backed by a single collaborator and traitor. He came fatherless from a whore and the bleak stones of a village in Provence. He was utterly self-made, utterly alone.

When the wedding cake had been cut and Claire went off to put on her going-away dress, there was a speech by a titled uncle who praised her for her beauty and spirit and spoke of her parents' sadness at losing her "to a man whom we would all like to know much better."

Charles's reply was short and to the point.

"I thank the Earl and Countess of Aubynne for their gift of a glorious daughter."

Suddenly the noise of a helicopter was heard outside. The aircraft began dropping down in front of Clackborough Hall, while the sudden wind of its coming flattened the leaves of the banked rhododendrons.

"I wanted to catch the last plane to Paris tonight," Charles said to his father-in-law. "So I chartered a chopper to get us to Heathrow. I hope you don't mind."

They ran out of the front door, under the whirling blades. He jumped aboard and pulled Claire up through the hatch, and the helicopter lifted and spun away above the dark box of the Hall and the tidy stone walls of the park.

"Oh, Charles, you spoil me. Nobody I know *ever* left a wedding like that."

"That was the point, Claire."

In Paris he knew of a hotel so discreet that it had no name. In its cellars was one of the best restaurants in France; its telephone numbers were unlisted; its bedrooms each furnished differently, from the most famous brothels of the last fifty years. He took Claire to a glass bed made up of the bits of fifty mirrors. Above their bodies hung a reflecting chandelier. As they made love on the red satin sheets, writhing and twisting deep in each other through the September night, licking the champagne off each other's hair and nipples, proving Charles's contempt of her background and her own escape from it, he could see his hard brown limbs and her white quivering skin split into thirty broken images, sliced and magnified and sectioned like a sex guide, pieces of flesh chopped into all the angles of love—detached, anyone's bodies, any beautiful bodies at all.

The hell with where you came from. Heaven was the girl you came in.

IV

By the sixties, the wealthy could flaunt their fortunes again and get away with it. It wasn't very amusing making a lot of money without being able to throw it around.

Charles was too smart to buy a place in the gossip columns. He knew that the established families showed their breeding and their millions discreetly. So when he took Claire to Monte Carlo to the casino, he avoided the company of people like the Dockers with their big yacht in the harbor which was almost as new as their title. He did not gamble very much since he knew the odds were always in favor of the bank in roulette and *chemin de fer*. He only played when he wanted to impress some one he thought important. He would win or lose a hundred thousand dollars in an hour or two, joking afterward with the player he had set out to seduce. Money was no object. The point was to move up the social ladder.

Lady Claire was a great help in this game. Her title was in her own right and remained after marriage.

Her family knew the aged Sir Winston Churchill, who was spending more and more time on the Riviera and on the yacht of his new friend, Aristotle Onassis. Claire was also a distant relative of the Greek tycoon's wife Tina through her first husband, Lord Blandford. "Divorce," Claire would say, "has nothing to do with whose cousin is whose. Everybody's slept with everybody so much that we're all related. The thing is, we just *know* each other."

So Charles was invited on the *Christina* when it anchored in the bay, and Sir Winston was there sitting in the dry marble swimming pool in the stern. The old statesman would smoke the long cigars of his host Aristotle and drop ashes on the ancient mosaic of a boy jumping over a bull's back. One time Charles and Claire came on board to a barrage of Greek curses. The hydraulic gear that lifted the pool bottom up to become a dance floor had jammed. Aristotle and Sir Winston were stuck halfway between base and deck.

"A screwdriver," Sir Winston said majestically, "will fix it. It always does."

A screwdriver did fix it in five minutes. The mosaic rose to the deck. Sir Winston rolled forward in his wheelchair, his cigar stuck between his lips, leaving the Greek tycoon fuming behind him.

"Be a good girl," he said to Claire, "and get me a brandy. Ari's going to swear at engines and engineers all day. Never mess about with boats. They'll always end by messing about with you."

Charles could listen to the old statesman talking for hours. Sometimes with the brandy in him, Churchill would spell out the future of the world in the rolling sentences of the great warrior and prophet. He saw communism withering away. But first there was a half century of oil to come.

"We will not fight them on the beaches now," he said to Charles, "we will fight them in the deserts. Not on the sea, but under the sea. Not on the ground, but under the ground where the oil is to be found. The future lies there. Go there if you want it."

And Charles heard him.

At other times, the old man showed that he was more than eighty years old. He would doze off in front of everyone, his heavy round face sunk on his swelling body, his jutting features suddenly soft and senile. He looked like the ruin of the British Empire that he had once led to its last, lost victory. Now he was dying slowly on a foreign yacht, pitied for what he had once been.

No one disturbed the great man while he slept. They went away to the bar of the *Christina* and perched on the biggest pricks in the world—Onassis's little jokes. The barstools were covered with the fore-skins of whales. The women in the party put their asses on them with care.

"Do you expect me to shove this *inside* me?" Claire asked her host one day. Then she slipped off her stool and ran her hands up and down the rough skin of the gigantic whale's prick. "If I jerk it off," she said, "do we get a soda fountain?"

Claire was invited everywhere. She amused everyone, especially Churchill and Onassis. She had a sharp tongue and a dirty mouth, and a quick wit. If Charles had loved her, he would have been jealous of her, seeing that he would not always keep her. He knew that she was trying to provoke him into a reaction, but he never gave her the satisfaction. His coolness made her more daring than ever. She would have been scandalous if she had not been an earl's daughter. As it was, she was called outrageous—but good fun.

He wanted her pregnant and she soon was after a night in the Negresco in Nice under one of the yellow cupolas modeled after the lemon-shaped breasts of the famous courtesan Otero. He drove so deep into her when he came that she felt split in two by something bigger even than the barstools of the *Christina*.

"I'm never letting you go swimming again," she said at breakfast. "You'd get harpooned and they'd cut off your bit to be Ari's throne."

She complained a lot during her pregnancy, although in fact it made her more beautiful. Her breasts had swelled and there was a radiance about her. Charles was gallant with her and tried to distract her. Once when Onassis was away in Milan to hear *Tosca* at La Scala, Charles borrowed the bright yellow seaplane that was housed on the upper deck of the *Christina* and flew across to Sardinia with his wife to look over the Costa Smeralda. He had been told of its white beaches and unspoiled coast. It was ripe for development and the young Aga Khan was interested in it.

"There's millions to be made there," he said to Claire as the seaplane followed its shadow along the shoreline, the sun at their backs.

"Then grab it!"

"Ten years to develop! Maybe twenty! Whose got that kind of time?"

"It'll take that long for your child to grow."

"Then I'll spend my time with him."

"All the men I know with money always want more."

"I don't. I've got enough."

"What do you want?"

Charles looked down at the rocky island beneath him, set like a buckle on the blue belt of the sea. "I don't want more things. I want more—just more—"

Claire smiled and took his hand and held it against the swell of her belly, hoping that the baby would kick through her flesh at its father. But the weight inside her did not move.

"More what do you want?"

"More everything. More life. More feeling. More justice and more intensity. I suppose if you come down to it, more total risk."

Daoud provided that. He arranged to meet Charles so skillfully that Charles would have thought it luck except for the conversation. Daoud was very tall, dressed in white pants and a skin-tight jacket, so that he looked like a stork. He hovered over his victims with his head cocked sympathetically down as if waiting to pounce on something good to eat with the beak of his nose.

"Monsieur de Belmont," he said at a certain stage of the conversation, "they say you're a man who found a lot of money once and forgot how to spend it."

"Meaning I'm cheap?"

"No. You're bored. I might have something of interest for you."

"What interests others usually bores me."

"Guns," Daoud said. "Revolutions. Fortunes. They interest everyone."

"Algeria," Charles said. "That means assassinations. Colonels. Torture. That interests no one."

"I'm not talking about Algeria," Daoud said. "I learned what not to do there." He stared at Charles and held on his eyes until both of them smiled. "You've been tortured, too."

"How did you know?"

"Right at the back of the eye there is always a little pain. A blank area in the iris. Every time they make you suffer, they kill a bit of you. Did the Gestapo get you?"

"German boy scouts," Charles said. "So the French got you—and let you go alive?"

"So the Gestapo got you—and let you go alive?"

The two men looked at each other and laughed.

Daoud dealt in arms and subversion. He had learned his trade running guns to Algeria for the FLN guerrillas. When the French security forces had caught him, he became a double agent to save his neck. When his cover was blown and the Algerian assassination squads came after him, he fled to France. Now he dealt in petty revolutions in the Middle East and Africa. Nations were emerging, he said, at the point of a gun.

"Cash is the problem, Monsieur de Belmont."

"Is that where I come in? Seed money for subversion?"

"Think of the payoff," Daoud said. "You could take an Arab emirate in the Persian Gulf for half a million dollars in grenades and machine guns. Then you could collect a royalty off the oil wells forever. Revolutionaries are perfectly grateful as long as you're private and you don't want to interfere with them."

"And if the revolution goes wrong, what happens to my investment?"

"You back the next one. Double the interest."

"And if that one goes wrong?"

"Back the one after." Daoud laughed. "What is sure is that this is the age of revolutions, and you should get in on the ground floor. Every little African colony, every little Arab sheikhdom will all blow up and throw out the old men. If you help the change, which has to come with cash—without strings—"

"There's a big risk in it," Charles said.

"You'd like that."

"I'd like that. Certainly I would." Charles put on his serious face, lined with concern. "But, Daoud, you have left out the most important thing—"

"Yes?"

"Why should I do it? I am not a revolutionary."

Daoud laughed again.

"That's why I asked you. A revolutionary would make conditions. He would interfere, and that's bad for business. We will supply arms to anyone, anyone who wants a change."

"A change for the better?"

"It's always for the better?"

"Is it never for the worse?"

"How can any change be worse for all those millions of people starving out there in the deserts and jungles? For them, any change is a good change. It gives them hope."

"I'm all for change myself," Charles said. "I was born poor and now I'm rich."

"So you want change for everybody?"

"No!" Charles said. "I couldn't stand the competition. Anyway"—he stretched out the fingers of his right hand, then clenched them into a fist—"I hate the rich who didn't make it themselves. The old lords and sheikhs born to it. The fat bastards who didn't make it the hard way. I don't mind who knocks them off as long as they get knocked off."

"It's much easier knowing who you're against than who you're for."

"I'm for the poor having a better chance, as long as they're not taking it from me."

Daoud's laughter was long and loud.

"A man after my own heart." He put a scented hand on Charles's shoulder. "Can I count on you for—five million dollars?"

"That's a lot of money," Charles said.

"I promise you, there'll be a lot of fun and danger."

"OK, but never more than a half a million at a time," Charles said. "Never twice in the same country. Ten little revolutions in ten little places with certified mineral deposits over the next ten years. That'll keep the juices flowing."

"You want to be involved personally?"

"What else?" Charles grinned thinly. "You know, I feel young again. I've had too much decadent society lately. Wasting my time with rich freaks. I was just beginning to think the world was boring—or I was. And now, another double life—"

"You like living like that?"

"Yes," Charles said. "A double life means you live twice as long."

The Earl of Aubynne wanted Claire to return to England for the birth. The child should have a British passport, he said. Charles decided to let his father-in-law have his way. If the Earl loved the baby, then more pressure could be put on him later. And anyway, pregnant women were not very interested in sex. In her eighth month, he could only slip into

Claire from behind; his child would kick against him, trying to push him out.

"He's jealous," Claire would say, her heavy body lying against the hollow of his flat stomach. "He wants me all for himself."

"He's got good taste," Charles said, and he sent Claire back to England alone for the birth. It wasn't that he was being cruel or did not want to see her family. He had business, he said, which kept him in France.

There was business. Daoud had put his first half million dollars into the Mulele faction fighting Mobutu in the Congo. Most of the heavy Western money was on Mobutu—there was so much copper in the Congo that any investment was worth the risk. Mulele and his tribes had some Russian and Czech money behind them but no Western counterweight. They were an outside bet, but there was a lot to be had if they won.

"We'll start with long odds," Daoud said. "The minerals are there all right, though I don't have too much confidence in our men on the ground."

Mulele and his mob went down before Mobutu and his white mercenaries. Charles's investment was a dead loss. He asked for an analysis and was flown over to the Canary Islands. There a Cuban airplane put down for a refueling stop, and Charles was introduced to the Argentinian doctor whose bearded face was beginning to wave on all the youthful red banners and T-shirts of the world.

"Señor Guevara," Charles said in the Spanish he had learned to speak along with Portuguese in Brazil, "it's a pleasure to meet you—off the battlefield—"

Guevara smiled. There was something seductive in

the softness of his mouth, something hypnotic about his eyes. It was hard to resist the magic of this man.

"They tell me you financed our last arms shipment to the Congo—and you got it through. We needed it. Thank you, but—" He looked at his stained green fatigues, then at Charles's immaculate gray suit from Savile Row. "—why did you do it?"

"I was a guerrilla myself for four years in the Second World War," Charles said.

"You like profits," Guevara said. "I saw the piece of paper you made Mulele sign. Five percent of the copper royalties until you had your money back ten times over. Tough terms, *amigo*."

"I'm not yelling because I lost."

"Why not do it for the brotherhood of man?" Guevara's eyes held his and drew the strength out of them. "For the liberty of man under socialism? You are better than you want yourself to be. I know it."

Charles had to shake his head to break the spell of the man. Guevara should have been a preacher, not a guerrilla fighter.

"To hell with the motives," he said. "You got the money and the arms. I lost it. You may get more if you tell me what went wrong."

"More on the same bad terms?"

"You don't have to honor them."

"But we will. Revolutionaries have to honor agreements. Or they don't get more."

"Tell me what went wrong this time."

Guevara's face became sour and severe.

"We backed the wrong people," he said. "They were cannibals. They ate their enemies." His voice was sad and heavy with defeat. "I am a doctor. My job is to save lives as well as to win revolutions. I cannot fight with people like that. Even if they call themselves Communists, they can't eat the hearts of the capitalists."

Charles smiled and put his hand on Guevara's shoulder.

"Better luck next time, *commandante*," he said. "You're not ruthless enough."

"We won once in Cuba. Thirteen men—and we took the whole island."

"You had Castro. He's tougher than you are. He'd sit down to dinner with cannibals and ask for more."

"Will you get me arms again if I need them?"

"Yes," Charles said.

Guevara gave his generous smile that seemed to take in all the hope and faith that people had to give.

"It's fine to be able to lead," he said. "But to deliver the goods when you're asthmatic and putting on weight and nearing forty—" He sighed and stopped speaking.

"You'll go on," Charles said. "You can't stop anymore than I can. There's all of South America to liberate. And it's in a bad mess, I know—I spent ten years there."

"Yes, I'll go home again," Guevara said. He appraised Charles's lean strength and lightness on his feet. "If you'd like to come with me, *compañero*, come along for the ride."

"I might betray you."

"Not you," Guevara said. "You like a fight too much."

A son was born to Charles and Lady Claire de Belmont. Before the birth, the child had been inscribed for Eton. The waiting list for that famous school was so long that it was safest to bet on a boy and cancel the application if it were a girl. The Earl of Aubynne wanted the child to have the best of the English tradition he had been born to inherit. Charles could understand that.

Claire came back to him in Paris, where he had bought a nine-room apartment with a roof garden on Avenue Foch near the Bois de Boulogne. With her came an English nanny for her baby, a fearsome creature of fifty-five. When Charles complained, Claire said, "Someone's got to teach the kid right from wrong, and it isn't going to be you or me." When Charles fired the nanny after a week, Claire said, "Now he's going to be just as bad as both of us."

"Which means he'll get on in the world," Charles said.

"I'm not going to look after him myself. We've got to find someone else. Also I won't drive in Paris; it scares me out of my pants."

"OK," Charles said. "I choose the nurse, you choose the chauffeur."

So their perversity began, as if they had caught it like a disease. The pay they offered for the two jobs was so high, the apartment in the *seizième* was so beautiful, that there were hundreds of people waiting to work for them. Charles picked a German girl named Lena, who reminded him of an aristocrat he had once had in Geneva—thin in the thigh, and tight-assed, hard breasts with a pale blue stare, her full mouth held in control until the point of her tongue licked her soft lips, reaching for crumbs after a meal. She was greedy, Charles knew, and she loved discipline. He could manage her through her desires, and she could manage the little boy through his.

Claire's chauffeur was a pale copy of Rudolph Valentino, with black eyes that could widen in appeal, white cheeks and a mouth with a cruel pout. His brown uniform was as tight as a wet bathing suit around his ass, and he strutted and posed like a body builder even while he was changing a tire. He let his eyes linger on Claire's breasts until he caught Charles looking at him, and then he turned his eyes caressingly to Charles's body until his employer said to him, "Pepe, keep your eyes on the road—or I'll keep your pay."

The bedrooms of Pepe and Lena were in the maids rooms off the end of the apartment, but Claire brought Lena inside to sleep with the baby. One night after she and Charles had returned from Maxim's to celebrate another victory by The Interloper at Chantilly, they heard the whistle and smack of a whiplash from the baby's room. They ran along the corridor and Charles kicked the locked door open. The baby was sound asleep, but Pepe and Lena were standing facing each other, he with a whip, she with a cane. They both wore boots and their naked bodies were covered with bruises and welts. They turned to face their employers, Pepe smiled slowly as he looked Claire in the eye, his erection pointing at her. Lena covered herself with her hands and turned away.

Charles shut the door and took Claire into their bedroom.

"Well?" she asked.

"We can only dismiss them—or join them."

They joined them. First Claire let Pepe make love to her, starting as a mistress indulging her servant, straddling him lying supine beneath her plunging thighs—and ending on all fours below him while he took her with contempt, jerking his prick into her as casually as if he was putting a nozzle into the car's gas tank.

Charles took Lena with fierce coldness, beating her softly with his belt into the crawling submission she desired, then letting her lick him into a rearing anger so that he could rape her to the point of total collapse, her limbs slack and soft beneath him in her abject defeat.

The two couples made love in adjoining rooms while the baby slept. Sometimes Charles would have the two women at once, but he would never let the chauffeur touch him or Claire's mouth. His mother, the village whore, would not let a client kiss her.

No man could touch his body and survive. No man could kiss his wife on the lips and get away with it. Perversely, he liked to see Claire degraded, but he himself would never let the nanny or the chauffeur dominate him. They were his servants, not his dictators. He knew the dangers of sexual power—he had used it all his adult life as his most lethal weapon. He might play around in a foursome, but he always had to be the master of them all.

When he had enough, he would put on his silk Cardin bathrobe and say coldly, "Lena, go check on how the baby is! Pepe, report with the Mercedes at eight in the morning! I may not be down till nine, but I want to know you are ready."

Then Pepe and Lena would disengage themselves from Claire and stand foolishly upright, before going out of the room.

"But I wasn't finished," Claire would say.

"You've had enough," Charles would say, knowing that she never would.

Once the chauffeur came into Charles's dressing room in answer to the bell to find his master drying himself after a shower. He took this as an invitation. He threw out a hand to fondle Charles's buttocks and was unconscious in three seconds. Charles kicked him in the gut and chopped the back of his neck as he was going down. Pepe did not wake for two hours. After that, he never tried it again.

"Do you think we're being vicious?" Claire asked one day. "I'm worried. I love you madly, but—somehow, with more people, it adds something. Is everyone like that?"

"If you don't really like the way you're living," Charles said, "stop the whole thing."

"I always thought we had to get as much experience as we can?"

"Experience is a nice name for it. What you mean is, you're rich and you're bored and you're fucking around because you haven't anything else better to do than bringing up a baby."

Bringing up baby went surprisingly well. The fat little fellow grew up in two years into beautiful little Adam de Belmont, bouncing and loving and chattering with his few first words as happy as a sparrow.

Appeals came almost daily from England to bring him back to his home country, but Charles would not allow that.

"Let them sweat," he said. "When they accept my terms, he can visit his second home."

"You can't still want that Jockey Club thing," Claire said. "You're a king at Longchamps and in the Jockey Club here. Everyone knows you."

"They know enough not to ask me home, even though I'm married to you. It's supposed to be a secret, but word got around from that English Jockey club investigation. False evidence—but they believe it. I'll never be accepted now, except through my son."

"Surely I'm enough?" The arrogance of Lady Claire would have been offensive if it had not been so naïve.

"Darling, you're known to be quite a frivolous lady yourself—and far too kind to the servants."

"A frivolous lady who's all yours."

"When you're not all theirs."

"Only when you approve."

"Be sure to keep it that way."

Then Sir Winston Churchill died. His doctors and brandy could no longer keep him going. A great funeral at Westminster Abbey was announced. The family asked Charles and Claire to attend the ceremony because they remembered the old statesman's last happy days on the Onassis yacht.

So Charles took his wife and son back to England again, to sit in the Abbey and wonder which revolution against the Empire he would back with his money in the years to come.

V

The grand old man had been lying in state in the Hall of Westminster under the Union Jack with the four Horseguardsmen standing at the corners of his coffin, their shining plumed helmets and armored breastplates bowed over their sabers digging into the red carpet between their high glossy black boots. Long lines of British people passed by the coffin for many days and nights, carrying Charles along with them, to stare at the flag over the box of the dead man and to remember the war years when they had been one people together and there had been a purpose to it all.

Later Charles saw the coffin put on a gun carriage by a squad of sailors, then drawn at a slow march by the bluejackets rumbling through the streets to St. Paul's Cathedral, to lie under the high dome that bombs and the blitz could not bring down. There Charles hurried to sit in the back pews with Claire, behind the very best of them all—the Queen and Ben-Gurion, Dr. Erhard and the Russian Marshal

Korniev, and even General de Gaulle, who had come to pay homage to his old ally, his old enemy, his old rival in the great days gone by. The General nodded to Charles in a sort of recognition—they said he never forgot a face that had been useful to him. He towered over the rest of them, a stranded monument of the last world war which had given Charles the chance he would never let be taken from him.

The Earl of Aubynne was there as a steward, seeing that the old dukes got to their right places and had their balloons in their trousers to piss in if they could not last through the burial ceremony. He stared coldly at Charles, not knowing how this hated intruder had found his way into the holy of holies. And Charles enjoyed his father-in-law's annoyance and sang the dead statesman's favorite hymn with pleasure:

> *There's no discouragement*
> *Shall make him once relent*
> *His first avowed intent*
> *To be a pilgrim . . .*

The Earl met him the next day in the Turf Club. The sporting pictures and discreet ancient waiters and sagging leather armchairs seemed to have been there forever. But the Earl was insecure, twisting in his seat.

"Nice of you to come back, Charles. I suppose you couldn't resist such a grand occasion."

"Churchill mattered to me," Charles said. "I fought in the war. Risked my neck a few times. Did you?"

"I was a pen-pusher," the Earl said. "But they also serve who only push pens."

"Knifing and garoting were more my style."

"I imagine. You knew Sir Winston?"

"Yes, on the Riviera. I knew General de Gaulle, too. He gave me a medal. You can earn your invitations. They don't have to come automatically from the cradle to the grave."

"I can see that." The Earl was uneasy. "How's it going with Claire? I hear she's a bit *wild*—"

"She's your daughter—but we're very happy. And we've got little Adam. There's nothing like a child for keeping a family together."

"And apart from his family. But of course," the Earl added, "that wouldn't bother you too much. You don't have a family."

"It's an advantage sometimes."

"Most people have families and most people want to be close to their grandson." The Earl was making a real effort to inject warmth into his voice. His upper lip was nearly split from the effort of unstiffening it. "Look, Charles, I would like to get to know you better. If there has been a past misunderstanding—"

"There's been no misunderstanding. You put private investigators onto me. You were told lies by a sexual rival of mine which you chose to believe. You wanted me thrown out of the Jockey Club and you got what you wanted. You say that can't be changed. How can I misunderstand?"

"The procedure was normal for vetoing a new applicant to the Jockey Club—"

"Abnormal, I bet you. You didn't use a fine-tooth comb on my life, you used an enema."

"That's all over," the Earl said soothingly. "Water under the bridge. Now if you would agree to send the child to us for the holidays at Clackborough, while you and Claire go off and enjoy yourselves—"

"You mean you're inviting the three of us to meet your friends?"

The Earl sighed and rallied.

"That would be delightful, though I'm sure you'd be bored. A man of your international reputation—"

"I'm notorious all over the world!" Charles threw a long leg over the arm of his chair to show his sense of relaxation. "I just want to know one thing. Can you get the Jockey Club to reconsider or not?"

The Earl shook his shoulders. There was real sadness on his face.

"You're very determined, Charles. Isn't there something else you want? Anything."

"I never lose in the end."

"You must. The Jockey Club has never reconsidered. Never."

"In my experience," Charles said, "never is negotiable."

"Not in this case."

Charles rose to his feet, blocking the light from the Earl, who sat in his shadow.

"I'd like Adam to get on in life as I did. I don't think French is the language of the future—Winston told me it might be Arabic for the next fifty years. So I think I'll pull up stakes in Paris and go to Beirut. The climate's fine, there's a lot of action, and—it's a long way from home."

The Earl rose to his feet as well. Faced with disaster, he had regained his coolness.

"If that's the way you want it," he said, "there's nothing I can do. As long as Claire follows you. As long as you stay with her—which may not be forever."

"And with her reputation," Charles said smiling. "I agree with you about staying with her always. Forever is certainly negotiable."

And he left the Earl of Aubynne in the Turf Club.

They did not get to Beirut immediately. They went to Portofino and Capri and Taormina. But however much the little islands and the rocks and the bay could be shuffled around, the sea was always the sea, and even the sunset was just another sunset day after day after day.

Charles took up water-skiing and aqualung diving to give himself exercise, but there was no thrill in the sports for a man who only liked forcing his body to its limits, if it were a question of surviving or killing or making a fortune.

"I can't tell one resort from another," Charles said. "Vacations are hell."

"You must rest," Claire said. She had smeared the white circles on her breasts with brown grease to make them the same color as the careful suntan on her body. Now she began to put rouge on her nipples, exciting their tips with her fingernails.

"Fuck resting," Charles said, and took his young wife violently, trying to spend his sense of uselessness in the warmth of her body. He forgot during the next hour of strain and pleasure, but the waste of his days came back to nag at his nerves again.

He saw Gaia, the Contessa Frescaviolli, with whom he had had an affair in Geneva, in her boutique in Taormina. She had come back to Italy and founded a "Maison de Mode" which developed into a big chain, including cosmetics and perfumes. Claire had dragged him inside to choose silk blouses and pants to add to the thirty pairs already hanging in her hotel closet.

"A girl never has enough clothes," she said.

The many years since their last meeting had made Gaia very beautiful in Charles's eyes. Time had refined her, hollowing out her cheeks and shaping her body into a slim hourglass of fashion. Her lips were so outlined that she looked more like an Egyptian mummy than ever, a Queen Nefertiti of modern chic. She smiled mockingly as she watched Charles following Claire on the prowl through the racks of bright silks, but her hand trembled when he took it.

"You look well, Gaia," he said. "Do you know my wife Claire?"

Gaia considered Claire, younger and blonder and more vital, the obvious object of blatant desire.

"Claire, I'd like you to meet an old friend of mine, Gaia Frescaviolli."

"I've heard of you," Claire said, "and not from Charles—he's so *discreet*. You've got your own brand of cosmetics and a fashion line. Frescaviolli—they're very smart."

"In these days," Gaia said, "we have to put our titles to work."

"Not if you marry," Charles said. "Didn't you ever marry, Gaia?"

Claire had turned away, pulling out a handful of blouses and fingering them, turned on by the splendor of the brand name. Gaia held Charles's eyes.

"I never met the man I wanted to marry," she said. "Or if I did—he went away, didn't he?"

Charles sent Claire back to Paris. He said he had business in Italy. Claire knew it was the Countess, but said nothing. A helicopter took Gaia and Charles from Taormina to Selinunte. There they wandered over the acres of fallen classical columns and sprawling blocks of stone. Vengeance had come from Syracuse and the whole ancient city had been destroyed, its people sold as slaves. Gaia and Charles visited the quarry where the building blocks for a new Greek temple had been left for two thousand years, half-cut out of the rock face.

"It's like us," Charles said. "Like our relationship. Suspended in time. I'll build you a temple of love like you've never seen," he promised.

There was only one little hotel in the fishing village between the ruined city and the Libyan sea, over which the hot wind blew from Africa. The best room was almost bare of furniture, and the two lovers did not even have a double bed. They pushed their twin beds together and made love on his side or hers. Once they fell through the divide between the beds, crashing onto the stone floor in a gale of laughter.

She wanted him fiercely and resented him all the way.

"Damn you," she said, "I hate you. I have never slept with a man I disapproved of more than you. You left me—and you kept your power over me. I despise myself for being with you and wanting you."

Yet she did want him and fought him only to increase the force of her climax. She would push him away so that he had to pin her wrists against the mattress and crush himself into her narrow cleft no bigger then a girl's. Her twisting pelvis would try to throw his prick out of her, but soon the sideways jerking would become a pushing up and down, until the explosions of their orgasms would break her into a shuddering surrender.

Yet as her passion ebbed, she would turn to her cigarettes and complain, "Oh damn you, damn you, damn you—Charles de Belmont. You're cruel, you're a swine, you come from nowhere, you succeed! It's intolerable. You marry a hot English Lady, you have millions. There's no justice in you, Charles. No mercy—just having to have your own way."

And he would stop her mouth with a kiss, crushing out her cigarette in the palm of his hand. And he would have her again.

While they were eating the grilled fresh sardines and the tomato salad which were the gourmet treats of the village, Gaia tried to find out who Charles was. "Why do you go for aristocratic women?" she asked. "Why Claire and me? Do you like proving yourself against our assumptions?"

"I've had savages too," Charles said. "Prostitutes and Indian girls. I just like sex, that's all."

"Finally your drive is futile," Gaia said. "You can't win me or Claire. We'll leave you in the long run. You're too intense; your style's too desperate. Terrific for an affair, but—"

"But what?"

"You frighten us. You obliterate us. We want that—but only briefly. I've got a career, Charles—"

"Selling perfume and blouses. That's a trade, being a shopkeeper."

"For a woman these days, it's a career. I'm rebuilding our family's *palazzo* with the money I earn—I haven't any brothers to help. You'd be surprised to know how much comes in from my *trade*. But let's not change the subject. I know you hate talking about yourself, but that's what everyone else likes to do."

"Everyone likes to talk about me?"

"About themselves—and you, when they know you."

"I don't. I never do."

"You don't do what others do. You never did. You think it makes you fascinating—mysterious—intriguing."

"No. I don't like explaining, that's all."

"All right, Charles, but—where do you go from here? You haven't found your woman—not me, not your hot English Lady either. You need someone as tough as you, a real match for you. I could be, but—you're not going to give me a chance and I think I know why."

"Give me a reason," Charles said, "and I'll hear a lie."

"Something very important, which most people who come from nowhere and make a fortune don't know. They ruin the rest of their lives trying to buy and force their way into a society which will never accept them. Old blood will kiss the new rich, take their money, sleep with them—but they won't accept them. We always remember how they made their way. And you—you just violate us, watch us degrade ourselves for you, and then abandon us."

"I'd like to join you and share my energy—"

"On your terms."

"On my terms."

On the third and last day of their stolen time together, a local boatman took them to a secret grotto where Tiberius and Caligula and other Roman Emperors were said to have held some of their orgies. Weird salt pillars writhed their white limbs from base rock to high roof, stalactites and stalagmites made columns of twisted bodies leaping from the still sea inlet or falling from the overhang of the cave. There was a cold little beach hidden halfway up the grotto. There the boatman left them with a mattress and camelskin rugs, two bottles of the best white Corvo, and a kilo of cold Adriatic *scampi* flown in from Rome. They ate and drank and stripped shivering in the chill of the air, then they worked themselves into warmth with the flame of their desire.

Lying with Gaia under the strong scent of the camel-skins, Charles could look out of the long ridged grotto toward the glare of the sea entrance. It was like being in the womb of his mother again, looking out to the light of birth.

"Gaia," he said, "I could almost love you—"

"If you didn't know better."

"If I didn't know better."

"I'd always patronize you, Charles, because I'd remember your background. So you'd violate me to keep me quiet for a while. That's not good for a long affair."

"All the same—"

Her body that day was like the earth, warm and yielding and taking him into her, not the dry, barren fields of summer but the soft land wanting to be broken and turned.

"Charles, my Charles, go away quickly—or I'll never be able to leave you."

When they heard the boatman coming back from the glare of the afternoon, standing at his two oars like the black ferryman of death himself come to take them away from all life and delight, they dressed quickly, shocked into sudden apartness by the chill of the grotto. So completely one, so soon alone.

Charles said on the voyage home, "I will never forget you; I will always love you."

"I too."

"Then we must remember—to never meet again."

Daoud involved Charles in two dangerous games at the same time. The first was in Zanzibar. There a small group of Arab merchants had ruled the black majority since the time of the slave trade. Something had to give soon, and there was a payoff.

"Spices," Daoud said. "Cloves in particular. I know it sounds old-fashioned, but spices once made Europe rich. You'd be surprised how profitable they still are. And anyway, how nice if the interest on your investment can smell so sweet."

The second situation was a split one and a sophisticated one. Daoud had not been in Algerian and Arab politics for nothing, where no one ever knew if the friend of today were not the enemy of tomorrow.

"Split your half million between two rebel Arab movements, the Kurds in Iraq and Iran, and the Yemenis in Aden."

"But they haven't got any minerals," Charles said. "Aden is just a desert. And there's nothing in those mountains where the Kurds are. Who'll pay me off and how—if they win, which isn't very likely?"

Daoud smiled from his thin height like a bird of prey opening its beak.

"When the Kurds are doing well—and the Marxist Yemenis on the Saudi Arabian border—then you withdraw your support, for a price, for a great price from the Shah and the King of Arabia. It would be worth a lot if we can time it just right."

"Money for betraying friends," Charles said. "That's not quite my game."

"Who's talking of friends? We are talking of profits. You will never even see the Kurds or the Yemenis. You will provide arms regularly—and the big vital shipment won't get through when they're ready for victory. Leave it all to me. Arms are strictly neutral."

"What about the Palestinians?" Charles asked dryly. "If I backed them and left them in the lurch, the Israelis would pay me off."

"The Israelis are too dangerous," Daoud said. "They might eliminate you first. They know everything that goes on in the Middle East practically before it happens."

"I once did them a favor in Brazil. They owe me something."

"Then keep it that way, Charles. And keep alive. You may need them."

"You tell me that as an Arab and a Muslim?"

"An Arab who drinks whiskey daily," Daoud said, "and is religious enough only to eat pork between meals. We nearly took all Europe once—I wish we had. French cooking would have destroyed the ridiculous prohibitions of Islam. In the old days, we always got along very well with the Jews—and I'm old-fashioned. Perhaps we will again."

"When everyone's killed everyone else with our weapons," Charles said.

"How can they, my friend, when our weapons are invisible at the vital moment?"

Charles offered Daoud another whiskey.

"I'm moving my family to Beirut," he told Daoud. "I'd like to see just how and where my money is going."

"You'd be very exposed there to retaliation."

"I said I wanted to be involved. I'm getting bored."

"Your skin," Daoud said, "not mine. If the Kurds betray you or the Yemenis, you'll have visitors. It's a great city for assassins."

"And sheikhs, and oil money, and gambling."

VI

They lived in a palace that used to belong to the Sursock family near the great Casino of Lebanon that flaunted its wealth on the tip of the horn of the bay curving north from the old city. The walls of the palace were hung with silk prayer rugs, and blood-red and cobalt-blue Persian carpets covered the marble floors. Small octagonal pools were set in the center of the high rooms with edges raised to ankle level. Once Claire landed among the water lilies floating in a pool and sprained her leg. "Goddam water hazards," she complained. "This isn't a house, it's an indoor golf course." But Adam loved the pools that seemed built for a small boy.

Charles made many connections with the bankers of Beirut. He was not surprised to find that old families like the Chehabs had as many financial interests in Tel Aviv as in their home city, and that Christian Lebanon was very much the middleman between Israel and the Arab nations, preparing for their perpetual wars. Much of the arms trade of the

Middle East and Africa was financed out of the twisting streets of the old Phoenician city—and half the hashish trade of the world. Up near the evil ruins of Baalbek, where the dark stones were still stained with ancient blood from the sacrifices to Aphrodite, the opium poppies blazed over hundreds of acres.

"We live as we have always lived," one of Charles's bankers told him. "We supply human greed and human need—gold, drugs, and young flesh. Really, nothing has changed here for thousands of years and nothing will ever change."

Charles met the black revolutionaries from Zanzibar and personally gave them the first installment of their money. He arranged for a shipment of Czech submachine guns and Luger pistols to be sent out to Zanzibar floating in grease in sealed oil drums. Soon after its arrival in the docks there, the revolution broke out. Rumors of massacre shocked the whole Arab world. The black slaves had risen and were cutting their old masters to pieces, violating their women and the rules of Islam.

Charles took a plane to Dar es Salaam and chartered the only helicopter there to fly him across the straits to Zanzibar. The new regime had sealed off the island, but they had no air force which could shoot him down. The helicopter flew in low over the steaming city on its hot lagoon. On the dockside, there were small red pyramids that splashed around their edges. At Charles's command, the helicopter hovered above them. He could see the piles of human heads, little hills of hands hacked off, tiny mountains of the parts of men and women. He flew back to Beirut sickened and ready to quit. Daoud flew across from the Riviera to calm him down.

"Never again," he said to Daoud. "I won't finance such massacres. It's revolting, inhuman, barbaric."

"Revolutions are revolting," Daoud said. "Good revolutionaries get rid of all the opposition in one swift surgery. The dead are soon forgotten. Slow killing of reactionaries is bad for publicity, while a quick massacre is usually all over and buried before the press gets there."

"I can't tolerate that."

"You are softening, my friend. Is it your child and your marriage? I thought you were hard."

There was a knock at the door of Daoud's hotel suite. A boy entered carrying a *nargileh*. He knelt in front of Daoud to suck at the mouthpiece of the *nargileh*, making the hot water inside the glass bowl bubble and the heated coal flare on the brown lump of hashish.

When the boy had gone, Daoud offered the mouthpiece to Charles.

"Smoke," he said. "Forget your scruples in easy dreams. If you leave the world alone, the poor will die slowly. If you try to change it, the rich and the poor will die quicker—and suffer less. Choose."

Charles said, "I want out of our deal."

"Too late, my friend. I have already committed you to the Kurds and the Yemenis. And you know too much. I might have to—proceed against you myself. Or let it be known in certain places exactly what you have done."

"Are you threatening me?"

"Just pointing out the realities of the situation before the smoke gets in my mind. Charles, wait till the profits come in. The first spice shipments will arrive in Egypt in two months. Revolutions don't matter—

the blacks are Muslims, too. The game goes on. Wait and forget. Stay with me—you must, you know."

The shipment did come in and Charles made his investment back five times. He did not forget the horror of the heaped corpses he had seen from the air. He waited to find a way out of the arms dealing after his connection with the Kurds and the Yemenis would be over. One evening as he was going back to the Sursock palace, his trained eye saw a shadow in a doorway that had never been seen there before. Another morning, he saw a scratch on the hubcap of his Mercedes. He had Pepe drive it to the nearest garage; all the wheel nuts had been loosened. So he began to carry a pistol, and he hired two Phalangist bodyguards from the local Christian militia to protect Claire and Adam. He could look after himself, he reckoned.

He was not surprised one evening when one of his new bodyguards brought him a visiting card—*LEVY, EPSTEIN, SOLOMON et Cie*. He recognized the sallow man with rimless glasses who was shown into the room.

"Good to see you again, Solomon," he said. "It's been a long road since Rio."

"Yes," Solomon agreed. "They tell me you are now in the export trade as well."

As they talked, Charles could see they had a common interest. On the old principle of backing the enemy of one's enemy, the Israelis were sending supplies to the Kurds and to the Marxist Yemenis as well. The first lot of rebels kept Iraq occupied; the second started a second front on the southern borders of royalist Saudi Arabia. Solomon had heard that Charles was financing the same people and had been sent by Israeli intelligence to interview his man.

"I can't believe you're doing it for love of Israel," Solomon said. "You're not a Zionist; you don't buy our national bonds or fund-raise for us. You're putting your money into private wars—and yet you can't hope to get anything back out of them."

Charles could see that Solomon's information was only good as far as it went. He did not know of the return on the cloves from Zanzibar.

"Perhaps I'm bored. I'm much more interested in markers. You owe me a favor for giving you those Nazis in Brazil."

"Yes," Solomon said, "we do."

Charles walked over to the barred window of his study in the palace and lifted the edge of the curtain, keeping his body back against the wall. He peered out across the street and saw a man in a caftan selling rugs to the empty night air.

"There are people following me, trying to kill me. Are they yours?"

"No," Solomon said, "you're helping us, whether you mean to or not."

"Find out who those killers are. And who they're working for. Then get your people after them to scare them off."

"Then our debt is paid?"

"Then your debt is paid."

Solomon rose to leave.

"You're a strange man, de Belmont. You don't think what you're doing in Kurdistan and the Yemen makes us obliged to you?"

"I'm not doing it for you. I'm doing it for myself. The Nazis in Brazil—I did it for you."

"And yourself."

"Both." Charles smiled. "Help me now. You'll be

helping yourselves too. That's the only way which really works."

Two mornings later, the assassins struck at Charles. As Pepe was driving him up the coast road to a meeting in the Phoenicia Hotel, a donkey cart loaded with melons swerved and blocked the road. As the Mercedes pulled up, two gunmen ran out of a shop and opened fire on the car with submachine guns. Bullets ripped through the interior, giving Pepe a flesh wound in the neck and peppering Charles's cheek with broken glass. The Mercedes plunged into the curb and the two gunmen ran up for the kill. Charles had his Luger out and was crouching behind the front seat, but he knew he had no chance in the cross fire.

Behind him a Volkswagen drew up and two men in black mackintoshes erupted from its doors. They held long-barreled automatics in their hands and they began to fire at the attackers. One of the Arab gunmen fell with two bullets in his back. The other gunman put a last burst into the gas tank of the Mercedes so that the car spouted and roared into flame. As he turned to deal with his new enemies, their bullets cut him down.

Charles found his clothes on fire as he dragged the bleeding Pepe out of the driver's seat through a pool of blazing gasoline. The two Israeli agents ran up to him and knocked him over, rolling him around on the dirt until the flames on his clothes were put out. Then they picked him up, and he found himself charred and hurting and smiling.

"Thanks," he said, "we're quits now."

The two agents did not stay, but ran back to their Volkswagen, backed up, and drove away before the

wailing sirens of the police could reach the scene.
Charles had one bad day in the hospital while his
burns were treated, and two more bad days in the
police station. But the Lebanese security forces could
get nothing out of him, even when they threatened to
deport him. It was not a serious threat. What small
country would throw out a man who had brought
two million dollars in cash into their banks?

The next approach of the Arabs to Charles was
more polite. It came in the form of an invitation.
Charles read:

> *The Emir of Qa'a'rat would be pleased if*
> *Monsieur Charles de Belmont would join him in*
> *a hunt and a reception in his honor. Visas and*
> *transport have already been arranged.*
> *R.S.V.P.*

"I'd be delighted to come," Charles said to the
young eunuch. "Traditionally you never murder your
guests."

"Not until after dinner, *m'sieu*," the eunuch lisped
in French.

"That's good enough for me."

The antelopes flew across the desert, their horns
laid back on their neck in fear. Behind them the
Land Rovers roared, churning up the sand. Bullets
from the Mannlichers whirred and sprang off the
rocks. A lucky shot hit one of the white antelopes in
its hindquarters and it fell kicking, then rose to
scramble forward on three legs. A bull mastiff leaped
off the seat beside the Emir and pulled the wounded
animal away. He was followed by a Bedouin with a
whip who lashed the hound off his prey, then bent
and slit the antelope's throat with a curved knife.

Then he threw the bleeding corpse into the back of the vehicle and jumped aboard with the hound. On they went across the dunes, sliding and skidding after the other Land Rovers pursuing the game.

"Will there be any more?" Charles shouted to the Emir. "Antelopes, I mean."

"Allah always sends more." The Emir blasted off three more shots from his rifle, hoping that fate again would send one home.

"What about conserving them?"

"Allah conserves us all. Look!"

Two desert foxes broke away through the rocks, their light tails flying. The Land Rover stalled in a patch of sand. Charles shot once, twice. Each shot dropped one of the foxes dead in his tracks. Nobody could shoot as well as that, and yet he had.

"Allah is in your sights," the Emir said, and for once Charles could not disagree with him.

At the feast under the date palms of the oasis, three whole lambs were served, spitted and roasted to a crisp. The guests squatted on Bokhara carpets laid out on the sand with Charles on the right of the Emir. Almost mockingly, the Emir scooped out one of the eyes from the skull and presented it to Charles. From his smile, Charles could see that his host expected him to fail this traditional test of desert hospitality. But Charles took the eye and swallowed it whole and belched profoundly. His manners were perfect.

"Another one?" the Emir said.

"I could not keep such a delicacy from you."

The Emir sighed and took the other eye. He considered it before putting it in his mouth and swallowing.

"Most Europeans can't," he said. "Where did you learn the trick?"

"On the prairies of America," Charles lied with a straight face. "Every time we killed a buffalo, we would swallow its balls raw in a glass of blood. You've heard of the drink?"

"What?"

Charles's face was innocent.

"Prairie oysters."

The Emir began to laugh until he choked.

"You are a humorist, my friend. I spent several years at the Sorbonne. Paris, you know, is where all good Arabs hope to go before they die. We used to drink prairie oysters after our hangovers. Now at last I know what's in them."

The two men had become friends by the end of the feast. The Emir explained to Charles what he had never understood, how the British with so few men had held the oil of the Persian Gulf so long.

"It was not Lawrence of Arabia, it was British intelligence. They were the best—I am sure you know that."

The Emir looked hard at Charles, who nodded in silence. It was good that the Emir thought he had real power behind him.

"The British always knew where our enemies were, and they would help us kill them. They always paid for their information in gold sovereigns—no paper trash. They honored all us Emirs and sheikhs, flying their whole air force past to show respect—and to remind us of their power. They understood that a few people must always rule over the many, as we do. They loved our desert as if it were their sea. And they never touched our women. That's where the French failed—"

"The British preferred your boys?"

The Emir laughed again.

In a small tent made entirely of carpets from Istaphan, the Emir finally had a serious interview with Charles.

"You are hurting Arabia, my friend, by supplying arms to the Marxists in the Yemen. You are hurting our friends in Iraq by helping the Kurds. Why? Are you like that mad guerrilla Orde Wingate—a Zionist without being born to it?"

"No," Charles said, "I just like to gamble."

"You are more serious than that," the Emir said. "The Kurds are doing too well. They'll soon have an independent state and then Iraq won't be able to aid us against Israel. The Royalists are doing badly in the Yemen, which means that the red plague might spread even to Arabia. Your arms and money have been very useful to our enemies."

"Would you say the arms had become necessary?"

"You could say that."

"And if they were expected—" Charles said, "if they were counted on—if they did not arrive on time or at all—and if you knew they wouldn't—"

The Emir considered Charles. Then a slow, rich smile, spread across his face.

"Who trained you, my cunning friend? Or were you always that way?"

"I've survived in places worse even than deserts," Charles said. "Now will you get your assassins off my back?"

"Of course," the Emir said. "I think we will need you."

Claire was withdrawing from him into a private world of nightmare and fantasy. Pepe was bringing her hashish every day and feeding her with it to assert his control. She insisted on hiring more servants for the palace, pretty little boys smartly dressed in red fezzes and embroidered vests and baggy pants and red boots with turned-up toes. The rooms were full of whispering and the sound of running feet. Wherever Charles went, he felt spied upon except when he visited Lena in the nanny's room.

She, too, felt isolated in Beirut. She asked Charles to get her a horse so that she could ride over the nearby hills toward the Dog River. He bought her a white Arab stallion from the best stud in Lebanon. The sight of her lean beauty in her white riding outfit on the strong flanks of the superb horse with its arching neck and tossing mane quickened Charles's blood.

Sometimes when she came back from her rides, he would rip down her riding breeches and take her standing, from behind, while she bent forward and gripped a chairback, her legs straddled wide to receive him. It was a hard quick way, but it fulfilled some fantasy of horses and mastery and completion.

He hardly slept with Claire anymore. When he tried to make love to her, she was drugged and drowsy. He found small bitemarks on her breasts—from the mouths of the Arab boys, he presumed. She was slack beneath his hands and stupid when she answered him in her slurred voice.

"You must begin to make sense," he told her one day. "You're twenty-one now."

"Don't bully me," she said wearily. "I don't need you. I don't need anyone. Except Abdullah. He's sweet and he gets the pipe just right. It's not everyone who can get the pipe just right—"

Charles grew close to his son because Claire was

drifting away from her little boy. Adam was happy in the house full of servants ready to caress him and play with him. He always had attention. With the casualness of the very young, who hardly notice their parents' indifference, he ran around the Sursock palace playing with boats in the lily pools and sliding up and down the marble floors on the silk prayer mats. He loved his daddy and his daddy loved him—when he had the time for it.

Sometimes when he looked at the face of the little boy asleep in his lap, Charles could see himself so clearly that he felt the old pain inside him of being abandoned, a child alone, the whore's son who nobody wanted to know. Would Adam do better? His mother was a whore, too, in her way, even if she were an earl's daughter. Adam's father was a wanderer, a man who could not feel at home even in his own place. Yes, he did love his son, but only when the child was there in his arms, so soft, so trusting, so utterly his. But when he went away, his heart would harden toward the little boy.

If I could get along without any help from anyone, Charles would say to himself, *so can he. He has a fortune from his mother and a fine family. He doesn't need me. I never had a father, and already he has more than I ever had. Perhaps all we can do is pass on to our children what life has made us be.*

One night Charles said he would be away with Daoud, but a terrorist explosion had closed the airport, so he had to return home unexpectedly. Claire's bedroom was a blaze of lights. She was lying naked and half-conscious on a silk Persian rug with three young Arab boys trying to have her at the same time. Pepe was standing over them filming the action with a sixteen-millimeter Eclair. He had set up the black-mail, but on the wrong night.

For the first time in his life, Charles went berserk with rage. He did know what he was doing as he moved like a killing machine across the room. When he came to his senses, he found himself surrounded by the dead and the wounded. He had broken Pepe's neck. All three Arab boys had broken arms or legs and were badly bruised. Claire was untouched, but she was crouching against the wall and whispering, "No, no, no."

The Phalangist bodyguards and a hundred thousand dollars for arms for their Christian cause solved the problem. Pepe's head was blown to pieces with a grenade and his body dumped in the Dog River—it looked like one of the endless Christian-Muslim executions that were driving the Lebanese government toward civil war. The three Arab boys were treated for their wounds in the palace, then they were given some money to emigrate to East Africa. Claire went back to England with Adam to see her father.

"I want a divorce," she said. "You're a murderer."

"I want a divorce, too," he said. "You're a whore."

He had two prints made of the blue movie Pepe had been shooting of his wife. He ran it through one night and vomited. There was nothing Pepe had not done to degrade the drugged Claire. If Charles himself hated the aristocracy and wished to violate them, Pepe must have hated them more and must have wanted to put them all in the same sewer with him.

Charles shuddered and saw where his loathing of them might lead him. There was a path back from degradation, he hoped, to a sort of love, the intense holding together he had with Isabel Portalena before she died and deceived him. He would not follow his chauffeur down into the inferno of vicious desire. He had never been anyone's slave. He would not be ruled by his own perversity.

At the same time that Charles's marriage collapsed, the government of Lebanon fell, and General Eisenhower sent in the Sixth Fleet and the Marines to wave the flag and to show he meant business.

VII

The Americans marching through the streets playing "The Star Spangled Banner" took Charles back to the simple days of the war again. Just before the liberation of France, the old peasant women had stitched little Stars and Stripes out of the colored rags and bits of blouses to hang in their windows when Patton's tanks came roaring past. It had never been the same in Europe again. Last year's savior was this year's object of envy. But in Beirut, the warring factions, both Christian and Muslim, put down their arms before these helmeted intruders from beyond the sea—and from outer space, as far as could be seen, with their huge aircraft carriers bristling with Phantoms and their arsenals of weapons waiting to explode into flame.

Two days behind the Marines came Annette Kilroy. In the World War, little drawings had been found everywhere, behind the enemy lines. A face peeped over a pair of hands and a wall—under it was always written, KILROY WAS HERE. Now it was the name of the most popular interview show on American television. The mass audience could count on Annette Kilroy being there only a day or two behind the news, if she was not making the news herself.

Charles met her at the Phoenicia, blazing a trail to the bar, her red-gold hair flying behind her shoulders that were squared off by the padded jacket of her tailored green pants suit which managed to suggest simultaneously a French jungle uniform from Indochina and a dress collection from the Faubourg St. Honoré. Annette Kilroy liked having the best of all possible worlds at once, even when they were in conflict. There was nothing she could not straighten out and record on tape.

She pounced on Charles as he sat at the bar watching this new phenomenon erupt.

"I'm Annette Kilroy and you're Charles de Belmont, a mystery financier who has something to do with the arms trade. You're certainly aware of what's cooking here, and—" Charles could not swear to it, but he was almost sure that she gave him an outrageous wink. "—you're by far the most attractive man in the bar right now."

"Have a drink," Charles said. "Pick my brains, I am all yours."

"Lucky for me." Annette Kilroy climbed up on the barstool next to his. "Scotch on the rocks."

She was a native Texan, born in a little town called Rising Star. Her degree in journalism from Southern Methodist University was almost as important to her family as her being head cheerleader for the basketball team. In New York she lost her Texas twang, which she recovered when she was upset or excited, and that was often. She was a total liberal and presented her views objectively. She was a great favorite of television audiences and the networks paid her a big salary. Shortish, but well-made, she had thin legs with a round small bottom. Her waist was tiny and her breasts seemed firm under the flap pockets of her army-style jacket.

"The luck is all mine, Miss Kilroy."

Her green eyes were wicked as she smiled at him while he ordered their drinks from the barman.

"You're married, I presume," she said. "Everyone always is."

"I was till last week. Let's drink to liberty."

"I was married till they renewed my contract. Then I had to choose—husband and daughter, or getting the news to the world and the world to the news. Since then I haven't been able to stop."

The two glasses were put on the bar. He touched the edge of his drink to hers.

"To another gypsy," he said. "I'm a bad husband and a bad father, but I've made my way in most parts of the world."

She pumped him expertly in the bar about the situation in Lebanon, and she went on pumping him in the French restaurant where he took her to dine. It was run by one of the last of the local Gaullists who had never gone home again after the fighting in 1944. He would always give Charles a special Armagnac and talk about the great General and the good old days when the Free French and the British forces had actually fought each other to control their old colonies in the Middle East. He knew the politics of Lebanon aboveboard and underground, and he did all Annette Kilroy's homework for her while the three of them drank themselves into a sleepy happiness.

"I was never briefed so easily in my life," Annette

said. "Maybe I can rest tomorrow morning and have time to realize what country I'm in."

"That's a very good idea. May I take you back to the Phoenicia?"

"You may take me anywhere," Annette said and laughed in his face.

He took her to the Phoenicia and he took her in the Phoenicia. She had one of the best suites overlooking the gray American warships in the bay. She proved expert and enthusiastic in bed. She was at the best age of a woman of her style, in her middle thirties, with the body of an athlete and the mouth of a sinner with her lips and scarlet fingernails plucking all over him. Her long red hair brushed his belly as she hung over him, her nipples softly swinging against his thighs.

"You're a beautiful man," she said.

He found that she had awakened some of his lost gentleness. He ran his hands in long strokes over her freckled breasts until they rose against his palms. Then he stroked further down her body to where the muscles of her belly writhed under his touch. Then softly, softly, into the red fur that hid her sex. He tormented her too, refusing to penetrate her until she begged him. Then he put her small buttocks into his lap and her two breasts into the cup of each of his hands, while he moved into her slowly and deeply until she pushed one of his hands down and held it against her clitoris and rubbed herself into ecstasy.

It was only the beginning of a long night of lovemaking, but by early morning, Annette Kilroy was crying quits. She had to sleep; she had a job to do, even if he was the most fantastic lover in the Western world and the Eastern world and anywhere else you could mention.

"I want you on tape too," she said. "Tomorrow."

"Like this?"

He looked down on their two naked bodies streaked with their juices glittering in the moonlight.

"I want you dressed and talking on tape just as if you'd never met me."

"We'll start right now and pretend we're making love for the first time."

"Oh, Charles—"

Annette Kilroy recorded her program next day and left that evening for New York. Yes, she would meet Charles again if she ever recovered from their last meeting. She could not say where or when, but she would meet him every time she needed a rest cure by complete exhaustion.

Charles received a letter from the attorneys of the Earl of Aubynne, formally demanding his divorce from Claire and full custody of the child. Charles sent a print of Pepe's blue movie by special messenger back to the Earl. He stated that he would be in Deauville in two weeks' time to play polo. He was playing for a Brazilian friend of his, who was competing mainly with hired Argentinian riders and ponies. He could spare the Earl a brief interview then, he wrote—in between chukkas.

The Earl did not arrive at the polo ground until the finals. Charles's team, Eldorado Park, was playing the Blue Devils, a scratch team from England which had had a brilliant winning streak because of one player and his pony, Eduardo Garcia Jones on Hacienda. Jones had a nine-goal handicap and he seemed to grow out of his roan pony like a centaur. The mare could stop on a dime and accelerate like a twister. She would plunge in and crash her rivals aside and come out with the ball time after time. No one could catch Eduardo Garcia Jones before the posts, and the Blue Devils would score again. The rest of his team were competent British gentlemen players—and sometimes the Duke of Edinburgh joined them.

Eldorado Park had no stars. It was an all-around team of "assassins," the hired Argentine riders who were the roughest players of them all, a Brazilian playboy captain, and Charles de Belmont, who had quick catlike reflexes. The *gauchos* had trained their ponies by the brutal methods of the *pampas*, the rawhide loop around the tongue and the quirt on the cheek, the gallop into walls and barbed wire, the breaking by fear and force that made the Argentinian polo ponies the best there were.

In the first two chukkas of the final, no one could hold Eduardo Jones. Even with his handicap, Eldorado Park went down two goals. When the Earl of Aubynne arrived for the third chukka, his first sight was his son-in-law charging down the field, hacking a long ball at the Blue Devils' posts, which Eduardo Jones intercepted and whacked back contemptuously into a scrimmage of horses and riders. There was no getting past him and Hacienda. He blocked the way to the goal and scored when he chose.

Perhaps it was seeing the Earl on the sidelines that gave Charles his mean streak. He was not a good loser, especially when one of his enemies was watching. As the ball came loose and one of the "assassins" hit it over to him, he saw Eduardo Jones coming at him like a thundercloud, his stick held high in the air. Charles seemed to hesitate on his pony, waiting for the other man to hit. As Jones struck, Charles slashed at the ball deliberately high, breaking Jones's stick just above the head. He swung again and scored clean and true between the posts.

"Sorry, Eduardo."

"Fucking Frenchman!" Eduardo said.

A minute later, one of the *gauchos* was riding hell bent for leather at the Blue Devils' goal. Eduardo Jones was closing the gap while Charles was boring in from the side. As Jones bent down from Hacienda's saddle to sweep the ball out of danger, Charles bumped his pony into him and sent him crashing to the ground. Jones lay there, stunned, and when he was picked up, one of his shoulders had dropped six inches below the other. His collarbone had snapped.

"Sorry," Charles said.

Eduardo Jones spit at his face and missed. Charles smiled.

"The truth is, Eduardo, I meant it."

If his captain had not taken him off, the referee might have disqualified him. As it was, Charles removed his helmet and went to stand beside the Earl and watch his team win the Cup without him by six goals to four. Without Eduardo Jones, the Blue Devils were not good enough. Gentlemen trying to compete with players, amateurs faced with *gaucho* professionals.

The looks of the spectators around Charles were even more sour than the Earl's, who was standing among the group of English players and their friends. Their hatred of Charles's tactics was vocal. "Damn bad show" was the best thing they said about him, "frog bugger" next best. But Charles just grinned and took the Earl by the arm and led him away to a quiet spot under the trees that looked toward the distant Channel and the invisible English coast.

"I suppose," the Earl said, "I should congratulate you on winning again."

"Yes, why not? I'm sorry you had to see me at my ruthless best."

"Was it meant to be a warning?"

"You could call it that."

The negotiations between the two men stretched out all afternoon. Charles was hungry and insisted on an early snack of *langoustines* and Sancerre. He knew he held the Earl in the hollow of his hand. Yet somehow he found that he could not squeeze him ruthlessly. He did not feel charity or forgiveness or even pity for the older man who had no cards to play. It was just that there was no pleasure in rubbing the face of a defeated man in the dirt. Better to help him up, then cripple him with a sort of respect, if not a kind of gratitude.

"With that film of Claire," Charles said, "I could get a divorce in any court in the land—and ruin your family's reputation. I would certainly get custody of the child. You know that."

"It was a horrible thing," the Earl said. "I could not have believed—Claire tells me you killed the maker of the film. That's why she had to leave you."

"There are no witnesses I have not taken care of," Charles said. "And nobody would take Claire's word against mine once they have seen the film."

"Still, you did kill him."

"You would have done the same."

The pale face of the Earl was bony with suffering. He nodded.

"I would have done the same."

"I have one other print. I will destroy it and the negative. You can destroy the print I sent to you. That will take care of it."

"What do you want for doing that?"

Charles ignored the Earl. He was coming down to business too soon, even if they had been talking for hours.

"As for my son, your grandchild—"

"I won't oppose you having full custody. His mother's not fit to look after him. I can only beg you to let us see him sometimes."

"Take him," Charles said. "I know he'll be raised better if he stays with you and your wife."

The Earl looked at Charles as a dead man might look at the doctor who had revived him.

"You will give Adam to us?"

"Yes," Charles said.

"I never expected—"

"Can't you understand?" Charles made his voice sound harsh and impatient. "I'm only doing it because I'm selfish. Without him I'm free to be as ruthless as I like. I love him in my way, but he makes me too soft. What sort of life can I give him anyway? Wandering from hotel to hotel, trying to find a mother in his nannies or my mistresses? You'll give him what a child needs—security, a single place to live in the country, a tradition—"

"All the things you hate in us."

"Yes, all the things I hate in you—but I know Adam will need. I certainly can't give him that."

The Earl stretched out his hand to Charles across the table.

"I do not believe you are as ruthless or as selfish as you make yourself out to be."

Charles looked at the Earl's hand. He took it briefly.

"I am ruthless and selfish," he said. "Or I was made to be."

"I owe you an apology I thought I would never make. If I could undo that Jockey Club blackball, I would. I will tell them that we received false information. But I am afraid that they would rather save their face than change their minds."

"I believe you," Charles said.

"I know it hurt you, taking away your racing colors. It was meant to hurt you. It was a despicable victory."

"No more apologies," Charles said.

The Earl of Aubynne nodded.

"I understand. The terms of the divorce—is there anything you want?"

"Yes," Charles said. "I'll settle a million dollars on Adam, which he can control at the age of twenty-one. The interest can take care of any expenses. I don't need the money. But I want one thing—Claire's estate in Scotland. Call it a souvenir."

"But that's family property!"

"That's why I want it," Charles said. He looked at the Earl, testing him, hoping he would pass the test.

"It's been in the family four hundred years, Charles. Ten thousand acres in Sutherland. Just for fishing and shooting now. Why would you want it?"

Charles said, "You asked me what I wanted. Can I have it?"

"Yes," the Earl said. "I think you are most reasonable. And even generous—it's not worth a million dollars."

Again he put out his hand. This time Charles held it and shook it until the Earl took it away. Then he smiled.

"I only want the use of the estate for my lifetime," he said. "Then it can go to Adam and back to your family. I'm sure you'd like it that way."

"That's more than generous."

Charles got to his feet. The interview was over. "Now let's go to the Eldorado Park party—we're really unspeakable when we win."

The *gauchos* were dressed in their full costumes, wide flapping leather trousers and silver spurred boots and leather belts glittering like the starry night with gaudy scarves at their necks. They were turning huge spits to roast twenty slaughtered lambs over live coals. In the background, a pale Andalusian Gypsy girl with camellias in her dark hair was strutting and singing flamenco, stamping her heels like volleys from a firing squad. Whiskey and gin were flowing out of gold taps; champagne corks were popping more often than the firecrackers and rockets that exploded in the sky.

"You may be bad sports," the Earl of Aubynne said to Charles, "but you do give damn good parties."

"You haven't seen the worst of it."

Down the marble steps leading from the hotel to the party gardens, five *señoritas* swayed, stamping their heels on the stairs. They were thin and cruel-faced, their fierce eyes blazing above high cheekbones and mouths painted like wounds in gashes of crimson and orange. In their tight long skirts flaring with flounces, they seemed like five wild beasts trapped in nets. Their fans, larger than palm leaves, fluttered from their bony fingers over their flat chests. But as the guitars struck up the Spanish dances, they swung into graceful whirling and stepping, their shawls swinging behind them in arcs of triumph.

Now the Queen of the Night rode her white pony down the steps, its hooves picking delicately at each stair while its rider sat sideways on its back, her long red skirt spread out like a banner, her auburn wig sparkling with a crown of diamonds. The pony almost seemed to dance to the music, treading in time to the clicking of the castanets and the tapping of the heels of the dancers.

"*Olé*," the *señoritas* shouted in harsh voices, and the Queen of the Night raised her golden scepter to confirm her reign.

"Isn't that your Brazilian friend on his polo pony?" the Earl asked Charles. "And aren't those *señoritas* the rest of your team?"

"Yes!" Charles said. "They love to dress up like women."

The guitars quickened their rhythm. A frenzy of music stirred the air as the false *señoritas* kicked their feet high and pulled their skirts up to their knees, showing their slim legs in skin-tight thigh boots above high heels.

The guitars were savage now. The Queen of the Night leaned forward and hit her pony's cheeks with her fan, rat-tat-tat, rat-tat, tat, controlling her mount with knee and touch and rap. The pony seemed to quickstep above the bottles placed on the floor, high-stepping and balking and turning and floating like the winged horse of the gods.

The false *señoritas* were squatting now to the screech of the guitars, kicking and jumping like cossacks. The pony reared among the bottles. Its back hooves splintered the glass as it twisted and slipped and came down on another Piper Heidsieck with its front hooves. Bleeding at the fetlocks, it reared again, throwing the Queen of the Night, who tumbled across a river of yellow bubbles and broken glass, laughing wildly in drunken delight.

The guests ran forward, the English to lead off the pony and bind napkins around its wounds, the *gauchos* to pick up their Brazilian captain and wash his cuts with gin and pour more champagne down his throat.

"We look after what we love most," Charles said to the Earl of Aubynne. "I should have looked after Claire better, but—"

"You did not love her enough. I'm sorry."

Charles had to return to Beirut to clear up his affairs. He gave up his lease on the Sursock palace at the end of the month, and called Daoud to meet him for a final conference and evaluation. The Americans were pulling out of Lebanon again, leaving it in its inexorable drift toward civil war. The Marxists were winning in the Yemen, giving the Royalists a hard time in their last strongholds in the mountains toward Arabia. The Kurds were pushing back the Iraqis and threatening the Shah with a declaration of independence. Both groups needed one last large shipment of antitank weapons and machine guns to win decisive victories. They were begging Daoud to get them the munitions quickly—their other suppliers were hanging fire, wanting them to keep fighting. If they won, they would no longer be bargaining counters in the diplomatic game.

"I've already sent them the bills of lading," Daoud said to Charles. "They think the shipments are already on the way, one on boats coming around the horn of Africa, the other coming through Turkey on trucks and donkeys. They expect it will arrive in a month at the latest."

"Will they get it?"

Daoud laughed from his thin height and thinner lips.

"Do you think I would waste your capital, my

friend? The bills of lading speak of shipments of coconuts; who would send coconuts to Yemen? The trucks and the donkeys are carrying pottery and dried figs officially—exactly what the Kurds need."

"For once the bills of lading are correct?"

"Exactly, my friend. The Yemenis and the Kurds will get exactly what we specify, for once."

It was Charles's turn to laugh. The joke really was a good one.

"You mean, Daoud, we are really being honest merchants at last? The Yemenis will have to pelt the Royalists with coconuts, while the Kurds jam the Iraqi tank tracks with figs—" He paused. "Of course our friends the Iraqis and the Saudis don't know we did not send the arms."

"Of course they do not know."

"So we sell out now and take their offers?"

"Yes, but—" Daoud bent and put his fluted hand on Charles's thigh. "You know how wily we Arabs are, my friend. If they know we did not send the arms, they will not pay us. They will wait for us to be killed by Yemeni agents. Then they will never have to pay. We have to hurry, and none of my people likes to be hurried."

"Do you think it's possible," Charles said, "if I set up a special sort of occasion, if I excited them—or confused them—"

"You think you can do that? Delay is a way of life for us Arabs. Our excitement lies in considering things for years."

"I think I can arrange something. Get my friend the Emir of Qa'a'rat here in two weeks' time! I have something for him."

"What?"

"A horse, a girl, and two dogs—what more can a man want here?"

"A horse, a boy, and two dogs," Daoud said, laughing.

Charles worked with Lena and her white Arab stallion for the next two weeks, putting them through their routine daily. He sent to England for a pair of dogs, which had already been trained for what they were meant to do. He set the stage in the inner courtyard of the Sursock palace by the marble fountain under the palm trees and the oleanders with the pointed Moorish arches on the covered walks serving as the backdrop of it all.

Persian carpets and camelhair cushions had been set on the ground for the Emir of Qa'a'rat and the six other sheikhs he had brought for the occasion, all of them representing interests in Arabia and Iraq and Iran.

"We do not have to have total agreement," the Emir explained, "because that could never happen before Allah called us from this earth. But we have to have a general feeling that we are right to proceed—which may take time."

"There's no hurry," Charles said. "Our last two arms shipments were the biggest and your enemies are doing well. We can arrange to stop the shipments in the next few days—but as Allah wills."

"And as we decide."

To the recorded music of flutes and dulcimers and zithers and hand drums crying of some erotic pain in some lost Arabian oasis, Lena rode out bareback on her white Arab stallion. Holding him on a right rein, she wheeled him around and around a small pomegranate tree set in a tub of blue tiles and crowned with a cage of quails protesting at their prison. At each slow turn on the horse, she began to strip—first her riding jacket and then her white silk blouse, leaving her hard breasts pointing the way to the horse's head.

Now she bent forward and rubbed her front along the stallion's neck and mane, exciting him and exciting her, so that the horse jerked and pricked up his ears and fretted while she shook her long blond hair loose from her riding cap which she tossed to the sheikhs. They were all leaning forward on their cushions, intent on this *houri* of delight on a stallion of their dreams.

Now the music changed to Wagner and the thunder of Siegfried, as Lena lay on the back of the circling stallion and undid the zips on the back and legs of her white riding breeches, playing with the cloth until she threw it away like a white gull in the air, then sprawling on the horse's back with her pale skin on his white one, naked and spread-eagled with an arm and leg falling down each side of his ribs, her hair like a saddle blanket on him and her breasts cocked high like his ears.

Now she rose and bent toward his hindquarters and caught the tip of his long tail and began to play with it like a tassle between her legs. Then she turned around to straddle him, feeling down and kicking at his lower belly. His great black prick began sliding out of its sheath. The Emir and the sheikhs were standing now and crooning, their eyes glazed and glistening like peeled grapes as Lena slid off his back. For she was only wearing her high black boots which seemed to meet in the little blonde patch of her sex, backed by the quivering legs and mighty black prick of the stallion.

She raised one arm in a gesture that looked like a Nazi salute, but Lena was only stretching for the cage of quails on top of the pomegranate tree and opening it.

Two English pointers ran out behind her and froze like statues to see the birds, each turning and quivering and raising a leg and pointing at the game. As the birds flew away and the stallion whinnied, the Wagner orchestra crashed to its finale. The show was over, the deal was begun.

The Emir and the six sheikhs were mad for the girl and the horse and the dogs. They were offering Charles oil wells for them—never a girl like that in any harem, never a stallion, never a hound that could point its leg to show the sitting game. Charles only said, "Those are your *gifts,* my friends, when we have done our business."

He had already arranged to pay Lena a hundred thousand dollars for her to spend one year with the Emir in his harem. "It'll be enough to buy me a Porsche now and a dress shop later," she said.

The business was done that night. The Emir and the six sheikhs put up a bank draft for seven million dollars to get Charles out of the arms trade in the Middle East and Africa, and to stop the two final arms shipments to the Yemenis and the Kurds.

"The days of the private dealer in war are over," the Emir said. "You're right to get out. It must be the time for the big boys."

"I agree," Charles said.

"As for your gifts," the Emir said, "how can we refuse them? Unfortunately, there are only four of them and seven of us. To find out who gets which of them, we may have to buy your arms and go to war!"

"Surely you have seniority, Emir," Charles bent to

whisper in the Emir's ear. "She prefers you; she told me so."

"I do not like to share, you know."

"She goes to one person alone on a one year's contract, unless you can persuade her to change her mind. I am not a white slaver."

"And I am a man of honor," the Emir said, "and too much desire." He sighed. "You are very clever, Monsieur de Belmont. You will get what you want. She will go with me."

"Thank you for obliging me."

"It will be a shame not doing business with you anymore—and quite a relief, my friend. They tell me you are leaving us."

Charles put his hand affectionately on the Emir's shoulder. He liked the man and his style.

"I have learned a great deal in the Levant," he said. "See Beirut—and what more can one learn of the human race?"

Part Four

ODDS AND EVENS
America, 1967–1977

I

Charles had heard they were hunting Guevara like a wild animal trapped in the Bolivian jungles, so he flew out to La Paz to see what he could do. He was no longer in the arms game, but he had told the Argentinian that he could count on his help if he went out again as a guerrilla. Now the aging doctor was trying to conquer a whole continent with thirty men. The odds were hopelessly against him—Charles liked him for that.

The Bolivian police took a long time with his passport at the airport. They did not want foreigners coming into La Paz while they were trying to get rid of Guevara. Every stranger was a suspect—and so were most of the Bolivian people. He knew that a car followed his cab through the shantytowns with their mud walls and tin roofs and squatting Indian women wearing brown derbies on their braided hair. He was followed as he walked from the hotel along the potholed streets where even the sewer covers had been stolen for their metal. He had a contact in La

Paz, alleged to be in touch with Guevara, but when he reached the address he had been given, Charles could see soldiers milling about, so he did not stay.

Next day, the newspapers announced the killing of Guevara at Higueras. They printed a photograph of his body, stripped and surrounded by a pack of grinning fools. Charles cursed himself for arriving too late. He went to visit another contact he had in Bolivia, Sancho de la Puente Ramirez, one of the ministers in charge of the nation's development whom he had met in Beirut buying oil.

The minister was free to see Charles suspiciously fast. He was a small man, sweating in his blue suit, although it was cool in La Paz at that time of day.

"Why are you here, *señor?*" he asked.

"Everyone wants to know that," Charles said. "You all seem obsessed. You think that everyone here has something to do with Guevara."

"You are right." The little man's eyes became points behind the lenses of his horn-rims. "How about you?"

"He always interested me," Charles said. "But now I hear he's dead. Is it true?"

The minister said, "Guevara will never die."

He took Charles by the arm and led him over to a water fountain and started the mechanism.

"We can talk now—I never know when they have bugged my office or not."

"It's a good old American custom," Charles said.

"The average life of a minister in this government is six months. Then you're arrested, tortured. You disappear—if you don't ask for asylum first. You've only got two places to go. America, which won't have you because they're supporting the generals here. Or Cuba—but you have to have something to give them."

"Do you have anything to give them?"

"Yes, I think I do now—the relics of the martyr."

"In that case," Charles said, "there's a deal to be made. I want to see Guevara's body and pay my last respects. I admired the man. And—you want his remains as a passport to Cuba before the generals come and get him."

"They have ordered the body burned. They are scared of his becoming a hero, a saint. They don't want any trace of Guevara left on earth."

"Can you get a military plane to fly us to Higueras today?"

"I will try. With a little cash I think it's possible."

Charles had come to La Paz with a hundred thousand dollars for Guevara, in case it would be of any use to him. He paid two thousand on the minister's instructions and in three hours, they were on an airplane headed toward the jungles in the south. They arrived in time. The body of the guerrilla leader had not been burned yet.

When the town's chief of police and the local military commander saw the minister's credentials, they took him and his guest straight to the body, which was lying on a table in the school. It was naked from the waist up to show that there were no bullet marks. In fact, he had been assassinated by an automatic fired in his belly and his legs, which were covered up. His face looked hollow and starved, the true face of a martyr. The authorities were stupid to record it.

But the local men in power had to have photographers. It was their town's only great occasion in its whole history. They posed with Charles and the minister beside the hero's body for the sake of

posterity. They presumed time would praise them as
Guevara's killers.

It was the first compromising photograph of himself that Charles had ever allowed to be taken in his
life. But he did not care. He had spent all his years
avoiding commitments, and he had found few men to
admire for their courage in defying the odds—General
de Gaulle and Winston Churchill when they would
not surrender to a Nazi victory, and Che Guevara trying like Bolívar to unite the whole of South America
into one land. Success and failure did not matter—the
dream was all. It was time for Charles to stand up
and be counted by the murdered hero. So he waited
between the minister and the grinning officials for the
flashbulbs to do their dirty work like a firing squad
over the corpse.

For another thirty thousand dollars, which Charles
paid, the minister got his relics. Soldiers were
watching the next day while Che's body was burned
to ashes on a secret pyre. But he was decently wrapped
in a tarpaulin now, except for his face. Nobody could
notice that his arms were missing. Charles's money
procured the two relics wrapped in plastic in a kit
bag ready for the flight back to La Paz.

"Do you really know what you are doing?" Charles
asked the minister. "You are making a saint."

"I am getting a passport out of Bolivia when the
time comes," the minister said. "Will you go to
Havana with his arms when I have had them embalmed—and tell them that I'll be there soon?"

"To be a Bolivian in the government," the minister
continued, "is to be in danger. The moment there is
a coup, we wait to have our heads chopped off by the
next coup. I did not want to be a minister, but the
military needs civilian front men with good names.

They made me a minister at the point of a gun. And I believe—"

"What Che believed?"

"In living."

"His body," Charles said, "will save your skin."

A week later he flew with the embalmed arms of Che Guevara to Mexico City. There he went to the Cuban Embassy and told his story. He was given a visa and put on the next airplane to Cuba. On his arrival, he was taken immediately to see Fidel Castro. The Cuban leader interrogated him for three hours, wept twice, and accepted the arms of his dead comrade.

"We will not make him a saint," he said.

"The South American people will," Charles said.

"His cathedral shall be the continuing revolution!"

A government car took Charles back to the Havana Libre Hotel, which had once been the Hilton. Charles found a friend waiting for him in the lobby. It was Annette Kilroy, dressed in red and green like a cockatoo, and alive with curiosity and desire.

"You mystery man," she said, "what are *you* doing here?"

He did not tell her. It was too difficult to explain his few loyalties to brave men, those who would take the risk and die for it. He had no time for politics.

"Traveling around," he said, "looking for you. What are you doing here?"

"Interviewing Fidel about Che's death."

"I thought Americans weren't popular locally since the Bay of Pigs."

"Oh, he'll see me!" Annette's green eyes were alight, wicked, and glancing. "He always sees beautiful women reporters with an international reputation. He sees them *alone*—for hours! He thinks it does a lot of good for his macho image. You know how these Latins are—"

"How about your image?"

"Oh, Kilroy is here, as always—isn't she?"

A government car took them both to the only grand nightclub left open in Havana since the revolution. There they watched the bright *señoritas* dance sambas and rhumbas with swaying breasts and bodies that had not been touched by the change. It was the pheasant on the menu which Charles found difficult to understand. He asked the waiter about it.

"*Compañero,* does everyone eat the same in Cuba?"

"Yes, *compañero.*"

"Then why are we eating pheasant here?"

"Everyone is eating pheasant this week. It is the ration."

"Are there enough pheasants to go around? In France, pheasant is only for the rich."

"Fidel ordered a drive against pheasants. We all eat it this week."

"And next week, do you have a drive against lobsters?"

"If Fidel asks us."

"And if there aren't enough of them to go around—isn't there ever any special treatment?"

"If Fidel says it is for everyone, it is for everyone."

Charles waited for the waiter to go and get their pheasant.

"That solves the problem of equal distribution," he whispered to Annette. "What Fidel says is true—and no one can check it out."

It was difficult and stimulating making love in the Havana Libre. They were sure that their rooms were bugged. The sense of a hidden listener or an intruder waiting silently behind the wall put them off and turned them on at the same time.

"Big Brother is watching you," Charles said as he took Annette into his bedroom, identical to her own.

As they undressed with quick fingers and began caressing each other in the hot Havana night that steamed through the motionless air conditioner, Annette flinched from the hidden bug or camera eye toward Charles, crouching against him as if he were her first date.

"I don't like it," she whispered, "being watched by someone!"

"Perhaps we should give them something to see."

For a moment he felt the unseen eyes or ears holding him back as well, but his usual boldness overcame his fear, and he lay on his back and guided Annette's hand to his groin and set her to work.

"Hell," he said, "they'd better see what they're competing with. Latins always think they're the best lovers. What they lack is evidence."

"You're arrogant, Charles."

"At least I'm not indifferent."

As he felt the power surging into his loins, he turned toward Annette, stroking her sex and widening her legs as she softly fought against him, then let him enter her slowly, forcing himself deep into her protesting body, moving above her as strong and steady as the stud bulls Castro was known to love. She came with him in a long-drawn-out wail.

"I didn't mean to shout, Charles."

"I didn't mind. I liked it."

"People could *hear* me."

"They're listening to us anyway. What does it matter?"

"You're so strong and so certain about things."

"Aren't you?"

"When I'm with you, I kind of feel—I've been everywhere alone too long."

The sense of conspiracy around them drove them closer and closer. The government guides did actually take them to a cattle-breeding station, where imported Canadian bulls were being crossed with Indian heifers to produce the humped *zebu* cattle that could do well in semitropical countries. When the guide showed Annette the mounting block on which the bull was meant to rear so that the scientists could steal his sperm for artificial insemination, she began to giggle and gave Charles her camera. She jumped on the block, her legs spread wide in her green pants, and Charles took a picture of her.

"It is not allowed," the guide said in a shocked voice. It was as though she had jumped on an altar.

"That's why she did it," Charles said.

The bull cult on the island went even farther. On the evening before Annette was due to film her interview with Castro, the guide took them to the latest painting exhibition in Havana. The gallery was split up into stalls. In one stall hung a large canvas—bright and opulent with streaks of red and whirls of purple, yellow banners and orange clouds, full of confidence in the future. In the next stall stood a large bull, chewing on some hay. Then a painting again, then another bull.

"Which is the work of art?" Annette asked.

"Don't ask me, ask Fidel."

Annette would never tell him of what Fidel did or said off the record. She hinted at great follies and sexual glories, and she did not come to his room when she returned late to the Havana Libre, but Charles was sure that she was trying to make him jealous. From all accounts, the Cuban leader preferred haranguing lady journalists.

On the edited television interview, Fidel did answer the question about the bulls.

"We need them. They will make Cuba great again. The bull is strong, economic. From one ejaculation, we can have three hundred calves!"

"Yes, but don't you like bulls because you are basically a *Spaniard?*" Annette dared to ask. "Because of your *machismo?*"

Fidel answered coldly.

"All I do is for the revolution. Personal reasons have nothing to do with it. Next question."

By the time they left Cuba together, Annette had fallen in love with Charles. He was attracted to a woman who was clearly his equal. She had to return to New York to put together her Castro show, but he agreed to meet her in a week's time in Cozumel, the Mexican island resort off Yucatán. If they spent two more weeks together, they might learn how much together they should be.

"Strong personalities," Charles said. "The two of us? I don't know—"

"Nor do I, but it's exciting—"

"I'm hoping for that."

"If you're looking for Kilroy, Kilroy will be there." Annette's cheerfulness suddenly became hesitant. "Would you mind if my daughter showed up for the last few days? I want you to meet her—just so you know what you may be getting into—"

"Aren't you afraid of young competition? If she is half as beautiful as her mother—"

"I love Jacqueline, but if you like her—if you want to go with her—you'd better sew a crazy quilt on your

jeans and put a daffodil behind your ear. With that
crowd, father figures are out."

Cozumel was a wonderland. Its long beaches were
bleached white by the sun. Flights of pink flamingoes
patrolled its azure seas, so clear that the huge conch
shells were visible fifty feet below the surface. The
windless days made no waves except those from the
stern of the fishing boat Charles had chartered for the
two weeks. The brown Mayan owner would take him
and Annette out to sea along the shoreline of palm
trees, while they lounged under the deck awnings,
drinking tequila punch out of coconut shells. He
would stop the boat over a reef and they would dive
for their lunch, swimming down with goggles and
spears to bring up little octopi and conches and tropical fish with pouting mouths and luminous streaks
of yellow and blue along their backs. Then the boat
would be driven onto the shelving beach and they
would wade ashore and the brown Mayan would cook
a fish stew with pineapple and cayenne pepper,
sweeter than any *bouillabaisse* from the Mediterranean.

Charles and Annette would lose themselves further
down the beach in an inlet among the palm trees.
There they would drop their swimsuits and make
love on the edge of the nibbling waters, the curious
tongues of the sea plucking at their bodies as they
twined their legs and arms around each other, her
whole belly melting in her want of him, the muscles
of her groin and back contracting and quivering. The
crash of the breakers of her desire drowning her so
that she moaned and let her ease wash away as she
felt again the soft salt teeth of the splashing sea.

He found her so young and free that she might
have been a girl again, bounding with slim legs along

the white heat of the sands as light as an antelope, barbecued by the sun into a firm bronze of flesh. Yet she could talk as a woman of the world about the far places where she had been. Her views of the great people she had interviewed were wicked without being malicious, witty without being catty, shrewd without being unfair.

She was also able to stand up to Charles. He had always destroyed his women by his reserve, his silence, and the force of his sex. But when he said nothing to her for hours, staring out to sea with lost eyes bluer than the Caribbean, she would either caress him softly or lose herself in her own reveries. Or she would break his mood by telling him stories about her trips abroad that would make him scream with laughter.

As for the strength of his lovemaking, she took it into her and absorbed it and flowed around it.

"That's the secret," she said, "with an irresistible force. You have to be a movable object and let it flow through you—and resist it only after the force is gone."

So she would manage him quietly after sex was over, trading with him so that he had some of the things he wanted if he gave her the same.

Shortly before her daughter came out to Cozumel, they had their first blazing row. She had bought turtle-oil cream, the marvelous cosmetic of the island and asked him to spread it all over her body as a moisturizer, but when she was slippery and aroused under his hands, he took her brutally and against her will. She was shouting at him to stop.

He raped her bloodily on the stained sheets, and she swore that she had never hated a man so much.

He was a pig, a brute, a bastard, and a son of a bitch and a whore.

He slapped her hard in the face for the first time in her life. She burst into tears and they made up, huddling together promising never, never, never to do that again.

It was only the first of their quarrels in their spectacular coming together. Neither of them was used to serious opposition, or even needing another person in their lives. Both had made their way by their own ambition, and they fought against the obligations of a love relationship. Yet that was becoming necessary to both of them—and equally intolerable.

Jacqueline arrived at Cozumel two days later. She had hitched from California, she said. Sure, it was easy to get a lift in Mexico, if it didn't bug you giving a bit.

"A bit of what?" her mother asked.

"Oh, Mother," Jacqueline said. "Hey, is it true, there's a new sort of magic mushroom out here that takes you to the other side of Venus?"

"Yes," Annette said, "and a new kind of Mexican clap that eats penicillin for breakfast."

Jacqueline was overweight in an appealing sort of way. She bulged slightly through the holes in her torn jeans and faded T-shirt, so dirty that Charles could hardly read its message, CLEAN OUR AIR. Her wild blond hair was as shaggy as the fringe of her Tibetan coat. Her beauty lay in her large green eyes, even larger than her mother's, and the lazy charm of her voice coming from her squashy mouth, which had never known any form of control.

For a day she was rude to Charles and even tried to patronize him. He was silent, remembering the defensive arrogance of his own youth. Then at dinner she gave him his cue.

"I mean," she said, "I mean, like, what would *you* know about the kids—I mean, about being spaced out and flower power and how it's got to be and Che Guevara, who was simply the beautifullest man, and you killed him—"

"He was a friend of mine," Charles said. "I helped him. He asked me to fight with him. What do *you* know?"

It was a cheap victory, name-dropping like that. But the victories of the young were cheap, too, as they excluded everyone who was older, who didn't speak their hip slang, who didn't worship at the shrine of the new gurus like Leary and Kerouac and Dylan and the Beatles.

"I've been a wanderer," Charles said to Jacqueline, "like your mother has. But there was a point to it. It wasn't just hitting the road because it was there. You never find God or money by stumbling onto them. You work for them. You have to have a plan."

"Shit," Jacqueline said, "that's what you all say. I mean, like, it's in your head or it isn't. And it *isn't* for you, it can't be. You don't understand."

"Eat your fish," Annette said. "It's good for you."

"Oh, Mother!" Ostentatiously Jacqueline took a hand-rolled cigarette out of her embroidered bag and lit it. The smell of marijuana drifted across the restaurant table. Charles took the cigarette from her mouth and crushed it in his hand and put the stub in his pocket.

"Get yourself arrested if you like," he said. "Not your mother and me."

"I'm splitting," Jacqueline said. "Tomorrow. You're

too much. I'm heading back to Arizona. Dropping out with the Indians. Turning on."

"It may surprise you to know," Charles said, "that I dropped out with Indians in the Amazon for a long time. Less civilized Indians than the Navajos."

"And—?"

The contempt in Jacqueline's voice hung in the air.

"And savages are savages. There wasn't any sort of vice or murder I didn't have to commit. I even ate people—"

Jacqueline began to laugh.

"All right!"

"It isn't, you little idiot—it's plain horrible. Ever since then I've tried to live as far from the jungle as possible. What you have to learn is this—being civilized may be boring. It is expensive. It does limit your desires. But if you ever give way to what's really in you, that tiger in your belly—that rat in your brain—you'll hate yourself for what you do. It isn't flower power that runs us, it's brute power. I know it. I've had it. I've used it. And I hate it."

Jacqueline slowly clapped her hands together and got up from the table.

"Quite a gig," she said. "When does the big band come on? You've got yourself an actor, Mother."

"He means what he says." Annette's voice was urgent. "Sit down and listen. He's learned it the hard way."

But Jacqueline walked without a word to the door of the restaurant and was gone into the night air. She took the first boat out of Cozumel in the morning and vanished for several months.

"She only writes to me for money," Annette said.

"She says she doesn't worry about me—she can always turn on the TV and see I'm fine."

"Do you send it to her when she writes?"

"That's what a mother's for these days, so she gets the money . . . and love—but she doesn't want that."

"Love is money," Charles said, "in an odd sort of way. It's a link between people, and it does help—even if it just lets them be free of us."

"I try not to worry about what will become of her. But I do."

"Don't, Annette. I never understand how any of us ever survive being seventeen. We all do such dangerous, crazy things. We should be dead, or depraved for life. But something looks after us—perhaps our innocence or our arrogance. We survive to become everything we despised—pillars of the community, stinking rich, even—parents—"

"But I'm failing with her."

"Did your mother fail with you?"

"Yes, but I thought—I wanted to be her friend—I gave her everything she wanted—"

"Dr. Spock has more to answer for than Hitler in certain ways," Charles said. "I'd hang him next to Freud. There should be a peace criminal trial for people like that. Permissive education—and claiming you're warped because of what your mother did to you when you were too young to remember—that shit has made two generations sloppy, unhappy, and cowardly."

"You're quite a reactionary, darling, but—it's a good conversation piece. Would you say it to some shrinks on my show?"

"I'd say it anywhere to anyone because I mean it.

I'm a man who does things, and I don't want to know the reason for it."

"You're also a man who never mentions his mother. Who was she?"

"Have another Tequila Sunrise, Annette. I'll come back with you to New York to burn the bones of Doctors Freud and Spock."

So Annette filmed him for her show. He was announced as a mystery man and a millionaire. His lean charm made him an instant success, although he attacked the sacred cows of American psychiatry like a cattle butcher. KILROY IS HERE had never received so many telephone calls or fan mail about any of its guests—even the angry mail wanted Charles reeducated, not deported or executed. He was not the man you loved to hate—he was the man you hated to love.

II

The cities of Europe and America were exploding in 1968. The children and the students were fighting in the streets of New York and Chicago, Paris and London, Hamburg and Warsaw. Che Guevara's face rippled on their breasts or flew on their banners. His death seemed to be their war cry at the old rulers—Get out, get out, get out! Get out of Vietnam, get out of Poland, get out of Ireland, get out of the White House, get out of the Elysée Palace, get out of atom bombs, just go!

"Let's go to Scotland," Charles said to Annette, "and find a little peace. I've got a place there I've never seen. And a son I'd like to see again."

His divorce from Claire had become final, and the deeds of her Scotch property had been made over to him for his lifetime. He had settled on Adam the million dollars he had promised. His son was coming up with his nanny to meet his father. It amused Charles to confront the all-American, Texas-born An-

nette with the old style, which he once had wanted
and now had adopted him.

They were met at the Glasgow airport by an ancient Daimler driven by a one-armed Highlander
called McPherson. He used the hook on his other
wrist to steer while he changed gears.

"We were expectin' ye, sirr," he said, "for a wee
while. But now ye've come, we'll not be expectin' ye
to go."

"I must," Charles said, "but not for a wee while."

There was a castle on the estate, which had been
restored and modernized in the thirties. It had no
windows in the thick granite walls of its first two
floors, only slits and winding stone staircases. But the
upper two floors were marvelous, a great paved hall
opening into a huge kitchen and dining room, with
circular bedrooms in each of the four little towers
that rose on the corners of the castle, overlooking the
lake where the Scots mist haunted the waters at dawn
and dusk.

"It's very ancestral here," Annette said. "Yours?"

"No, not mine," Charles said, "but I have a feeling
I'll be called on to play an ancestral role very soon!"

He was, almost at once. The head keeper was at
the front door early next morning to take him to
the rifle racks in the gun room.

"Your stags are starvin'," he said. "Ye'll have to
cull them, sirr. When will we be stalkin'?"

"Now," Charles said. "I'll put on my boots."

"Give me five minutes to make up," Annette said,
"and I'll come."

"If you want to crawl on your belly up a rocky
stream for a few hundred yards, that'll be great. Otherwise, I can't recommend it, darling."

"Then I'll try to make the castle look more like

home," Annette looked up at the stone ceiling arching high above them. "I don't think drapes will help." Her eyes fell to the thick granite blocks under her feet. "If an Englishman's home is his castle, no limey ever saw this one!"

Charles knew the two keepers would put him to the test, but he also knew that they did not reckon on his fighting training and his jungle survival. When they sighted the first twelve-pointer six hundred yards away, they wanted Charles to crawl half a mile around a scree to get in an easy shot upwind. He ignored them, crawling forward so flat against the ground on the belly of his jacket that he looked like a turtle, then aiming at five hundred yards with the stag already scenting him and breaking for safety, so that he had to drop it running with a clean shot through its neck and head that brought it down in a tangle of hooves and horns.

"You're lucky, sir, with that one. Next time ye'll be heedin' me."

"My job's to kill stags," Charles said. "I won't let you down, but I'll do it my own way."

When he had killed his third stag of the morning, they put him to the test of blood at lunch. They spread out the cold grouse and the egg-and-watercress sandwiches and the oatmeal biscuits and the flasks of coffee and cherry brandy on a tartan rug. Then they skinned and cut up the dead stag nearby, spreading the joints around Charles as he ate, so that the heather smoked with bloody meat. Charles ate on, ignoring them.

"Will you join me?" he asked. "It's delicious."

The head keeper came up to him, a red hunting knife in his hand, with his other arm hugging the whole stag's head to his body so that its horns seemed to grow out of his cap. Blood dripped from its severed neck a foot away from Charles's biscuits and turned the heather from purple to crimson.

"You'll have to have this one mounted, won't you?" the keeper said, turning the glassy dead eyes of the animal to stare at the sitting Charles. "Sixteen points. He's a fine braw beast."

"Don't bother," Charles said. "I've shot bigger." He stuck an egg sandwich on the point of the man's reeking knife. "Eat, my friend. Keep your strength up. We have work to do this afternoon."

He was as ruthless a killer as he had been in his army days. He kept them stalking until it was almost too dark to aim, but even in the gloaming, he killed his ninth stag with a shot through the eye from three hundred yards. The keepers had never seen stalking or shooting like that, neither the uncanny silence of his movements nor the lethal accuracy of his rifle. They were used to fat Englishmen who could hit a bull's eye at fifty paces, but who could not get through the heather better than baby elephants and were too winded to aim straight when they did.

"Ye're a bonnie stalker," the head keeper said. "I do not remember a day like this in all my thirty year here. But the Earl, he was sayin' to me—"

"What Earl?"

"The Earl of Kirtlemuir. His land is next to this."

"I know him," Charles said. "At least, I know his land. I was here in the army. And I know his daughter too."

"Do ye ken her?" The head keeper's smile was slight, but too knowing. "She's home, they say. Shootin' with her father and teachin' her two wee lads. Her husband, he's away over the sea, I hear."

Charles appeared to ignore the news.

"Shall we start at seven in the morning tomorrow?" he asked. "If you need any more stags culled."

"We'll be needin' two days to bring these in," the keeper said. "We'll not be troublin' ye, sirr, for the now. But there's the birds, of course. No fishin', it's not the season, as ye'll be knowin'."

"I know."

When Charles told Annette of his stalking that evening, she was appalled.

"It's slaughter, Charles. It's a damn blood ritual. Putting you in a circle of bleeding meat! Didn't Jack the Ripper do that? Cut up his broads and drape them around the room?"

"Yes, it's a blood ritual, but it has to be done. If there are too many stags, they can't live on what there is to eat on those fields. They get stunted and diseased. They fight each other to death. Killing them selectively is right."

"All hunters say that. Killing to be kind! It's just putting a ribbon on murder."

"They expect me back every year here."

"It's horrible," Annette said. "For Pete's sake, Charlie"—her Texas heritage surfaced—"are there any ghosts in this castle?"

"Only a headless green maiden," Charles said, slipping off his loafer and stretching out his foot stealthily under the table. "You don't see her, you *feel* her suddenly—"

Annette screamed and jumped up, knocking over her chair as his foot touched her thigh. Charles fell back in his seat, laughing.

"You bastard!"

"Darling, this is Scotland! Have a Glenfiddich! Drown your fears in the best malt scotch."

"I'll never believe you again!"

"Will you marry me?"

"Liar!"

"Then I'll ask you like the Scotch—will you not marry me?"

"Of course I will, you dirty deceiver. You cheat! You'd sell snake oil to your dying grandmother!"

"I'm glad you've discovered the real nature of the man you're going to marry." Charles's voice sank deeper than the grave. "Did I ever tell you of the unspeakable presence in the west tower?"

"That's *you!*"

"Dead right, darling." He advanced on her with the triangular black Glenfiddich bottle and drank standing from the bottle, guzzling down the whiskey like soda pop. "It's a Scotch birthday—drink!"

"You'll kill yourself!"

He coughed and handed her the bottle. As she began to wipe the neck on the sleeve of her dress, he interrupted her.

"Leave it! Lips that have touched my liquor ever shall touch mine!"

Annette laughed.

"You're a drunken Celt who claims to be French. I'll drink to you—and swear never to wipe your kiss off a bottleneck again!"

So they drank and decided to get married in three weeks. It took that time to be qualified for residence there.

Adam was a joy in the castle, running around like a puppy in all directions and going to sleep like a puppy very suddenly with his arms and legs in the air. He was at the enchanting age of small boys with enormous blue eyes and blond hair and enough love to hug anything from a Shetland Pony to the head keeper's boot. He rushed into embraces like a pigeon to its home, giving wet kisses on demand without being bribed by a sweet. Annette and the castle staff all adored him, and Charles looked as smug as any pleased father.

"You don't deserve such a dear little boy," Annette said. "You're such a hard case yourself."

"I'm waiting for love to soften me."

"Oh, that! If you had any more, you'd drown in vanity."

She did lavish her body on him in the tower bedroom with the four ribs of the pointed ceiling making an arched vault above them, a dark converging cavern like the replica of her own desire that tried to engulf his lean limbs within her body and her legs, straining to cram his strength so deep inside her that he would be crushed whole into her womb, Charles as a child again in the very depths of her, her lover, her beloved, her son within her.

"I have the most incredible fantasies when you take me," she told him. "I don't dare tell them to you. They're too *female*. They're so personal!"

His true nature eluded her as always. Although he did show more affection, suddenly catching her breasts through her silk blouse from behind with both of his hands before sitting down for breakfast, or licking her ears till she shivered with pleasure at her dressing table, she never felt that she had put her hooks into him. She could not penetrate his reserve. He said he needed her, he seemed to show it, but—she did not believe him.

"Charles, please, Charles!" she would cry in the night. "Let me in."

Charles felt that he would never be accepted by his Scotch neighbors. Shooting was the test of a man's opinion of the locals. So he set up a shoot of wild caliber in these parts, shooting and drinking and the grouse. He brought in black-and-white German hounds, the fastest there were. He mobilized all the keepers and their families and their friends. The land-owners were asked to appear from fifty miles around in the Highlands. The Earl of Kirtlemuir and his daughter Catherine were also invited to stay on for dinner.

By eleven o'clock, the station wagons had arrived and the long line of shots was assembled. Catherine Adam-Villiers was polite when she met Charles again and her tall, stooped father in his baggy tweeds was curious. But nothing much was said and Charles put them to left and right of him in the line. The keepers and their helpers were driving the birds up the slope in a great semicircle across the moor. The hounds were loosed and darted away, flushing grouse from their secret hiding places.

These were not the fat, hand-raised birds of the south. They were not flipped out of cages into the massacre of the hired guns. They were the wild breed, crafty and swift, and they veered as they flew, dropping and sliding and rising unpredictably. The guns blazed out their barrages, missing the skittering birds four times out of five on the left and right of the line.

In the center where Charles stood between the Earl of Kirtlemuir and his daughter, the grouse were falling steadily onto the heather, their feathers drift-ing down after their bodies in a soft hail. Catherine was bringing them down with every second shot, and the Earl rarely missed, but Charles was the true killer, his instant reflexes gauging the exact swerve and rise of each bird, sending the message back to his trigger finger. He would fire once, twice, and two birds would plummet out of the sky. The loader behind him would have the second of his pair of Purdys in his hand almost before he could give back the first. His skill was exact and deadly. The best gun of them all.

"Damn fine show," the Earl said when the drive was over. "When I was up in the House last time, Aubynne told me I'd find you—redoubtable. That was his word. He was right."

There was tension under their talk at dinner. It showed in the sharpness of Annette's answers to Catherine, in the flush in Catherine's cheeks, in the precise questions the Earl put to Charles. Catherine had kept her looks well with her high color and flawless complexion, but the red of her hair looked rough and wild against Annette's groomed blood-orange, silken spread, and her clothes were badly cut on her fading body, while Annette's gown flowed clean from her low bodice to her feet.

By the end of the sherry broth and the claret and the venison pie and the mushrooms on toast and the sherbet with Chateau Yquem, silences had begun to settle around the table. The two women were looking at each other waiting to talk it out, and the men were glancing at each other waiting to do the same. Charles blessed the old British customs and rose to his feet after the decanter of port had been served.

"Perhaps you would like to show Catherine where she can arrange herself, Annette. We'll join you later."

Annette would normally have fought the point of the ladies leaving the men over their port—women's liberation against feudal ways—but she wanted to be alone with Catherine. She had seen the other woman looking at Charles with the hurt, hot eyes of the rejected lover. She had to know.

"Take as long as you like," she said. "Let's get moving, Catherine, and we'll let our hair down."

When the women had left the dining room, the Earl brought his chair to the side of Charles. He took another glass of port and waited for Charles to fill his own.

"Aubynne said I was redoubtable," Charles said. "Why?"

"He could hardly avoid it—you are." The Earl paused. "Since Catherine left her husband—did you know?"

"No, I didn't. I'm sorry."

"Since then, she's talked to me about you quite a bit. She's very fond of you."

"We met during the war here. Then again in South America."

"When she heard you'd split with Aubynne's girl Claire, she was very hopeful. And when she was told you had the estate and were coming here, she was more than hopeful. You can imagine her disappointment—"

"I'm marrying Annette."

"Forgive me for saying it," the Earl said, "she doesn't seem quite the type. She's rather formidable, wouldn't you say?"

"That's what I like," Charles said. "She's the first woman I ever loved who could stand up to me."

"You *like* that?"

"It's new. And believe me, there's not much new left to interest a man who's lived a life like mine."

The Earl smiled, a drowsy smile that did not hide the shrewdness in his eyes.

"I'm sorry about that. I really am. Catherine told me you'd make a good father to her two boys."

"I'm not even a good father to my own son. I'm a wanderer, and very selfish."

"You'd come back. You asked for the estate here, Aubynne told me. You want to settle in your way."

"For the hunting season? That's not enough. Catherine's a fine woman, and she needs a full-time husband. I'm not her sort. Annette is far more like me."

"A pity," the Earl said, "I'd like you for a son-in-law. You'd shake things up a bit. We need it."

"You'd like me in the family?" Charles had to laugh. "I'd never thought the day would come when a man like you would *invite* me, Charles de Belmont, to be his son-in-law."

"Aubynne told me he had got you wrong. He told me he'd done you a dirty trick, and that you were a good man in a tight spot. I believe him." The Earl filled up his glass of port again. "It's a pity about my daughter, but—I'd still rather be with you than against you, Charles, if I may call you that."

"So would I," Charles said, also filling up his glass of port. "I don't mean to sound arrogant, but knowing myself, I'd much rather work from inside my own skin than have to deal with me on the outside."

In the drawing room, Annette was into the Grand Marnier while Catherine was lowering the Drambuie. A box of chocolates stood pillaged between them, crumpled brown papers littering the carpet.

"But you're not *right* for him! I know Charles."

"You've no goddamn right to say I'm not right! Do you think *you're* right for him?" Annette laughed. "I can see you don't know him too well."

"He's desperate and lonely. I knew him when he was a commando here, before he disappeared in France. He was a trained killer, brutal, dangerous—"

"And he turned you on."

"I couldn't do anything with him. I was far too young. But later I felt I understood him. If I hadn't had two children when we were in Brasília, and a diplomat husband— I would have run away with him—"

"Did he ask you?"

"He would have. He didn't think it was possible."

"He's asked me to marry him. And I will."

"Not if you're wrong for him."

"Who the hell are you, Honorable Miss, to tell me I'm wrong? I'm Annette Kilroy. I tell the whole fucking world they're wrong. I don't have to take this shit from anyone."

Her cheeks blazing, Catherine managed a smile.

"Hearing you talk like that," she said, "I know exactly why you're wrong."

Annette would have slapped her, but that would have meant throwing the game away.

"Look, you Scotch deep freeze, just because he had you doesn't give you any claims on him. He's through with you British broads and your titles. He told me so."

"I suppose you're a *challenge* to him?"

"Call it what you like. I'll marry the son of a bitch, even if I have to divorce him the next morning."

"It'll be a great mistake," Catherine said in her most prissy voice. "I simply can't see the two of you together."

"I'll see to it you don't. We'll be in the Arctic Circle to get away from you. And come to think of it," Annette added, "I won't divorce him the next morning. I wouldn't give you the pleasure—you'd still be waiting!"

In their bedroom later that night, Annette shouted at Charles for half an hour.

"She was drooling over you. She'd marry you tomorrow! Go ahead, why don't you? I bet you've fucked the whole of Who's Who and What's What and a piece of Shit's Shit! Big deal! I suppose there's not a whore with a title tattooed on her ass you haven't had. The whole fucking House of Lords is full of bastard Belmonts! Well, Kilroy's better than that. Kilroy's pretty exclusive. And y'all can shove it up your ass!"

"I'll shove it up yours. Don't insult *me!*"

It was a savage skirmish. She ripped the silk quilt to pieces; she broke the washbasin into twenty pieces of porcelain; she tore a pillow into a storm of feathers. He took her brutally and when it was over, she was so broken that she could only sob helplessly, repeating, "Bastard, bastard, bastard—"

He picked her up in his arms and took her to another bedroom and cradled her all night, whispering to her and soothing her and promising her that all would be well, better than well; they would have a closeness that he had never had with a woman except in his dreams. He did not talk of his closeness with Isabel Portalena—that had been brief and she was dead.

"I've never held anything against you that you did before I met you. I've never even asked—I don't want to know. It doesn't matter. You can't hold anything against me either. Surely, I was a real bastard for most of my life, but now, I can see—maybe a little dependence, a holding onto a special woman like you—"

"Oh, Charles, if I could believe what you say—"

She believed enough to hear him take the marriage oath in the registrar's office at Inverness where they drove for their quiet wedding. The Earl of Kirtlemuir was one of their two witnesses. Catherine had returned to London.

III

The young had made it impossible for the American President to go into the great cities of the nation, and they had forced him not to run again for fear of meeting their rage at the Democratic Convention in Chicago. Their anger seethed in the streets and brought out the riot squads across the world, policemen with black boots and truncheons, plastic shields and tear gas, that cracked the skulls of the dissidents and sent them sobbing and bloody back to their classrooms. Sometimes the National Guard or the tanks had to go in, but the results were always the same. They took a beating for trying to take over before their time had come.

Annette's daughter Jacqueline went underground that summer. Just before she disappeared, she came to New York to ask her mother for a thousand dollars. Charles was in the Hotel Pierre with his new wife, and he was shocked at the change in Jacqueline. Where there had been a plump, rude adolescent, now there was a wraith as thin as a Giacometti. Anorexia had stripped the fat off her so that her breasts were flat under her red T-shirt, her pelvis pushed out two blades of bone through the cloth of her jeans, and her legs seemed to run straight up to the crosspiece of her crotch.

Annette burst into tears to see her daughter.

"You're starving yourself to death. *Please* eat!"

"Don't tell me what to do, Mother, just give me the money. I have to have it."

"You're a junkie, Jacqueline," Charles said. "You're living on drugs and forgetting to eat. That money's just for your habit."

"Don't preach, man. Don't you know drugs are for the people, and we're the people?" Jacqueline laughed. "I'm on to something bigger than that. Just give me the money."

Annette gave her the thousand dollars, and Jacqueline promised to return the next day to spend a week with them in the Hamptons, resting up. She never appeared at all. There were bomb explosions in a U.S. Army recruiting office. Two people were shot and badly wounded. Photographs of the group of terrorists began to appear on the Most Wanted Lists in every American post office. One of them was Jacqueline Kilroy.

"I can't believe it," her mother said, after the tenth visit of the FBI agents. "It can't be true. But they did pick up someone just like her in that last holdup. The informers say she's one of them. What did I do wrong?"

"You didn't do anything, Annette. It's not your fault; it's the times we live in. Revolution's fashionable these days, and I know about that. I'll tell you what worries me—you've got a bunch of amateurs playing urban guerrillas. They'll hurt themselves and they'll hurt the wrong people. I know. I was a professional."

A homemade bomb exploded in a Seattle slum house, killing four of her group. Jacqueline escaped with the three survivors. Annette went on television appealing to her daughter to come home. Her loyalty to her daughter and her public grief made her more popular than ever. Kilroy stood by her own. Kilroy was always there when you needed her.

"Charles, if you love me, find her! You've told me you were an agent once, a guerrilla. You knew people like Che Guevara. You could find her if you tried."

"When the FBI can't?"

"You've got the professional skill. Please—for me—"

"OK. I'll try."

Charles set off into the radical underground of 1968. He started among the top circles of the people he despised—the rich revolutionaries who funded the movements and did not want to get their hands soiled in the process. They said they were Maoists and lived like Manchu Emperors. If they lived on rice for a meal or two, it was wild rice with Peking duck washed down with Tokay or double Scotches. Their military jackets buttoned up to the neck were made of Thai rough silk, and they helped the Red cause by buying T'ang pottery made in Hong Kong.

"We are not hypocrites at all," explained Mrs. Duplessis "Tigerlily" Smith to Charles in her Gold Coast penthouse on Lake Shore Drive during her Chicago fund-raising evening for dropping two bombloads of a hundred thousand red roses on Hanoi as a gesture of solidarity. "While capitalism lasts, we feel we should go in for the ultimate in conspicuous waste to bring it down sooner. When a society is as rotten as ours is, it is our duty to make it more rotten so that it will wither away faster. But, of course, when the revolution comes—"

"You and your friends will work happily waist-deep in mud and flies in the Illinois paddy fields?"

"Oh, there aren't any flies in China now, Mr. de Belmont. Mao asked everyone to kill ten flies a day until there weren't any left."

"So when he comes here," Charles said, "we'll throw away our fly sprays and use our fingers?"

He mingled with these people, who were using the revolution to add a kick and a reverse status to their lives, but he did not hear any news of Jacqueline. So he dropped down toward the Chicago campus, shucking off his suits for old army fatigues, letting his beard grow and speaking with a strong French accent. He bought two old submachine guns in the black ghetto and rendered them useless by taking out their firing pins. He then wandered about the campus coffeehouses, letting out that he was a deserter from French Indochina and was giving ideological courses in weapon training.

"The red flower is a warm gun," he would say, "but first you must know how to strip it."

When the militants picked him up, he took them to a room he had hired back of a launderette. There he stripped the submachine guns and explained their parts and assembled them again.

"The course," he would say, "is called The Power and the Art of Machine-Gun Maintenance."

He told them that he would not teach them how to use the weapons until they knew them thoroughly.

"Never use a gun unless you know it won't jam on you."

He recognized an FBI stool pigeon one day. He was the bearded one who talked too much and wanted to get the hell on with using the weapons. Charles set up the date of the FBI pounce on them by fixing a time and a place in the Illinois woods for firing practice on the following Saturday. The day before, he took off with LeRoy Lincoln Watkins, the only one of his pupils who did claim to have links to Jacqueline's friends. They caught the Greyhound bus to San Francisco to shake off any tails.

"We were penetrated," Charles said to Watkins. "I know it in my bones."

The black student agreed.

"Yeah, they were close to us, man. Like—I could feel *ants* on my skin every time that beard moved."

The next two weeks were spent hanging around People's Park in Berkeley. Charles was filthy now and slept in his bedroll in the open air, and the students respected him. He knew about street-fighting and jungle war, about Molotov cocktails and *plastique*, about killing with thumbs and piano wire. The fact that he would not talk about his age or background gave him even more prestige. He was generally thought to be a professional revolutionary like the young Ho Chi Minh, sent to "help" raise American consciousness by the comrades in Europe.

On the news, Charles heard that Senator Robert Kennedy was coming to California in his bid to win the state for his shot at the presidency. Annette Kilroy was also coming out to interview him, and Charles wanted to spend the night with her and brief her. So he took the long walk over the Bay Bridge into the city and wandered into the elegant old lobby of the Mark Hopkins Hotel on Nob Hill.

"Miss Kilroy will not want to see *you*," the receptionist said, looking with horror at the bearded figure in stained fatigues.

"Tell her it's her husband Charles. And if she doesn't have a bath ready by the time I get up to her, she'll die of lockjaw or poison gas."

As Charles entered the elevator, two old ladies nearly broke a leg as they tried to rush out. When Annette met him at the door of her room, first she laughed and then she cried and then she insisted on scrubbing his back and soaping him all over like a virtuous Japanese wife.

"You shouldn't be doing all this," she said.

"I'm enjoying it," he said. "It's great to be young again."

He made love to her twice quickly until she was in continual orgasm, the first spasm triggering the next and the next and the next in a rush and a tumble and a foam of desire, no sooner in the lull than the race to the crest to come, the spray and shatter and slack, the rapids settling slowly down to the slow stream of knowing that her man wanted her and she wanted him more than ever.

"Tomorrow, darling, you're coming to dinner with me and the Senator in Los Angeles, where I'll be recording him. We're staying close."

"I'll be seen by the Berkeley kids. It'll blow my cover. It's dangerous."

"But you like the risk? You like being with me?"

"Both," Charles said, and he took the risk against his judgment of the odds.

So he was walking near Kennedy in the shortcut through the kitchen of the Ambassador Hotel when Sirhan Sirhan shot the Democratic leader down. He saw Kennedy fall and he saw the secret servicemen jumping the young assassin. He also saw a movement by the far doorway of the kitchens, and he was off in pursuit before Annette could stop him, a killer again in the hunt of killers.

As he reached the street, he saw a figure slip past. He ran across and around the corner. A black-haired young man was getting into a four-door Chrysler. Charles reached him as the rear door was closing and the car was gunning away from the curb. He wrenched the door open and threw himself across the rear seat, slashing with the edges of his hands at the faces above him. The car accelerated down the hill. Charles found two revolvers pointed at him, one in his ribs and one in his face. Three Mexicans or South Americans were looking at him.

"Quiet, *amigo*. Or you die."

He was blindfolded and tied by the people in the car, which drove for at least two more hours until it pulled up. He was frog-marched a little way along a gravel path, then thrown onto the concrete floor of a garage and left in the darkness. Some hours later, he was pulled to his feet and walked over more concrete and down some steps. He was then seated on a chair, which had been bolted to the floor. Handcuffs were put on each wrist and attached to the chairlegs so that he could not move. He could not see his interrogators through the blindfold.

"This is a revolutionary tribunal," a voice said. "We meet for the trial of a fascist mercenary spy."

"What's the news?" Charles asked. "Did you kill Kennedy?"

There was a silence. Then the voice started again.

"Kennedy has been executed. It is now your turn after positive identification. You have been observed spying on radical activists in the Berkeley area. You have been identified as the husband of the reactionary media person, Annette Kilroy. Your name is Charles de Belmont. Do you deny that?"

"I do not."

"Your motive for these reactionary activities?"

"I'm looking for Annette's daughter, Jacqueline Kilroy, who has gone underground. Do you know where she is?"

"That is not the purpose of this tribunal. Do you expect us to believe that this was your only motive? You were also informing to the FBI."

"I have told you the truth," Charles said to his unknown judges. "I have nothing to add to that. You will aid yourselves by freeing me—and telling me where to find Jacqueline."

He felt a burning sensation on his wrist. Someone had stubbed out a cigarette on his skin. He smiled.

"The Gestapo tortured me in the Second World War," he said. "Some Nazis tried to beat me to death in Brazil. Don't play your kid's games on me. You're wasting your time."

"Execute him!"

The new voice was a woman's. For a moment, the blindfolded Charles hoped that it was Jacqueline's voice, but it was too harsh.

"Not yet," another voice said.

"I ask the tribunal for an immediate vote," the woman said.

There was a silence, presumably for the raising of hands.

"The vote is for execution," the woman spoke. "Let us do it now."

"One thing," Charles said. "I would check first with your friends. Ask the Cubans about me. Ask Fidel. He might tell you that you are making a bad mistake."

There was another silence.

"You are deliberately delaying us," the woman said. "We will execute you now."

"I strongly recommend asking the Cubans," Charles said. "Or you will be executing yourselves later."

There was another silence, then a discussion began in Spanish and English. Who knew anything positive about Charles de Belmont? Why was he near Kennedy at all? As Annette Kilroy's husband? What if the Cubans had put him there, and not the FBI? No one believed that Sirhan Sirhan was the only killer. There must have been others—or others set up to kill. What if the tribunal did execute a leading Cuban agent?

"We will check," a voice said finally. "But if you are lying, we will shoot you in the stomach and leave you to die very slowly."

The handcuffs were taken off Charles's wrists. Still blindfolded, he was led back to the garage for a long wait. Twelve hours later, he was released into the custody of a fresh-faced boy, who removed the blindfold and drove him to a deserted place near the cliffs on the Pacific Ocean. There the boy cut the ropes on his wrists and waited while Charles rubbed the circulation back into his hands. He did not apologize, but he was plainly scared as he balanced uneasily on his sneakers.

"The Cubans told us," the boy said, "that if you died, we would die. It came from the top. Jeez, what did you *do* for them?"

"I helped them make a saint of a man you now worship." At last the pain in Charles's hands was settling down to a puffy hurt. "Professionals like the Cubans always do things for other professionals. Now they owe me nothing. Maybe I owe them."

He moved very fast to slap the boy on both cheeks,

bringing tears into his eyes. As the boy went for his gun, Charles kicked it out of his fingers so that it fell onto the grass. It was easy.

"Fucking amateurs," he said. "When will you ever learn?"

He put his forearm across the boy's neck and the point of his knee in the small of his back.

"Where's Jacqueline? I'm getting bored."

"I don't know. I swear it."

Charles dug his knee in deeper so that two of the boy's vertebrae clicked and cracked. It was not serious, but it sounded dangerous.

"Oh, Jesus, don't! Don't! She's grassed! *We're* looking for her too!"

"What?"

Charles released the boy so that he jackknifed onto the grass, feeling at his back to see if it was broken.

"Tell me more, or I'll break your spine for real."

"She's on junk. Unreliable. After the bomb blew up, she was picked up, we think. The FBI went on supplying her with coke—and they fed her back in to pick up the rest. Yesterday the other three were all grabbed. So she split. She's scared."

"Where did she go?"

"Either the FBI has got her stashed away as a witness, or she's split into Haight Ashbury. Like I told you, she's got a habit, and all junkies end up in Haight."

"Thanks, kid."

Charles put down a hand and pulled the boy back up off the grass. He hit him with the flat of his hand in the middle of his back, forcing him to straighten up.

"Stand up. I didn't hurt you. I was playing."

He bent down and picked up the revolver, breaking it open and taking out the bullets before handing it back to the boy.

"Go easy with this till you know how to use it."

"What are you going to do?"

"Well, I'm not giving lessons anymore to punk kid guerrillas. I'm going to find Jacqueline. I said I would."

The boy was visibly scared. Even the empty gun in his hand did not seem to give him confidence.

"And the Kennedy murder? They'll talk to you. You—you could tell them about us. We weren't really connected. What will you tell them?"

Charles shook his head. When would they ever learn?

"I won't say anything. Nothing at all. It's not my war. I'm not the law. I do what I say, no more, no less."

IV

The ice cream was special in Magnolia Thunder-pussy's café in Haight Ashbury. It was made into obscene sculptures, food for the loins. "The Montana Banana" was a peeled, unsplit banana which reared from two balls of vanilla ice cream for the Caucasian customers, two chocolate balls for the others. It was complemented by "The Pineapple Pussy"—half a scooped-out pineapple filled with strawberry lips of whipped cream on either side of a cleft of pistachio fudge, all decorated with little hairs of shredded coconut.

"I'll have a plain mocha," Charles said.

He had carefully chosen a table in the corner of the psychedelic café, the walls painted with soaring clouds of purple and orange and red. He had to wait and he did not want to be conspicuous. He was wearing a plain cotton shirt and chinos. He also wanted to stay out of trouble. They wouldn't bother him, the sad children slumped over the tables, seeking comfort in the sickly goo they used to have at home. Trouble could come from the Hell's Angels, who also had a yen for Magnolia's specials. The Harley-Davidsons were stacked along the street outside the café window, and the Angels were stamping in and out in their battered boots and filthy studded leather, jackets with Nazi insignia, the mindless storm troopers of a new fascism, waiting for trouble to pass the time of day.

Charles knew the principle of waiting, which was a technique like any other. There was no need to look. If you sat long enough in the right place, a guide would come and take you to what you were looking for. And after ninety minutes or so, a tall thin shape with sunken cheeks and the loose limbs of the Appalachian Mountains drifted across to lean over Charles.

"You wanna score?"

Charles finished his last scoop of ice cream.

"What have you got?"

"Speed. Acid. Bennies. Uppers, downers. Most kinds of shit."

Charles put a hand in his chinos and brought out five hundred-dollar bills. A dull gleam appeared in the hollow eyes of the Appalachian kid.

"Pussy, too?" Charles asked. "I like to get high on young pussy. OK?"

"Sure. For that kind of bread you got Lolita."

"No professionals. New kids on the junk, so they have to put out what I want—"

"Fourteen. Twelve, sweet 'n twelve! You like that? Huh?"

Charles rose, crumpling the bills back into his pocket.

"Minors? Are you crazy? You think I want to break the *law*, man?"

The Appalachian kid laughed so high that it was like a train whistle.

"Shee-it! You don't wanna break the law? Shee-it! You're crazy too!" He put his long fingers on Charles's shirt-sleeve to bring him back to the table. "What *do* you want?"

"I want them thin. I like them sweet and thin. I don't want them to have anything on their bones. And eighteen. There's no law about what you can do to a girl of eighteen. It's the age of *consent!*"

"That's weird. Sure I know some chicks—"

"Fresh too! Just arrived! I want to break her in. None of that used-up pussy. And like a telegraph pole."

"I got the chick for you."

Charles let himself be led through the streets of Haight Ashbury. Below the high-gabled houses built after the earthquake and the fire, with their gingerbread woodwork and white fronts, the sidewalks were littered with trash. Some of it was alive. Winos were lying like bags of dirt in doorways, the booze dribbling from their lips. Junkies sat like beaten boxers, their heads between their knees, looking for a way, any way to get up. Begging girls with torn jeans trailing tasseled velvet tablecloths around their bent shoulders pushed forward and held out a chewed hand.

"Gimme a quarter!"

The jungle was never like this.

The Appalachian kid took Charles up an outside wooden staircase which led to a green door. He knocked three times, then twice, then three times again. Bolts were drawn and Charles was admitted by an old brown man into fetid darkness. The stench of bodies and vomit and sour wine and cats' piss was bitter in the stale air. The shades were all drawn, but streaks of daylight cut around the edges to show up the bodies in the stripped living room. Eight young people lay sprawled on the floorboards or on dirty cushions. They were naked or half-clothed. One of them, a girl too young to have grown more than vague swellings at her breasts, was moaning and sobbing. There were four more girls and three boys, all unconscious in the stink of the room.

"Any turn you on?"

They had all been used too often, and they had abused themselves. There were lice crawling on their bodies, and their arms were pocked with scabs and needle marks. One girl, her face down on her thin arms, was as emaciated as Jacqueline. Charles turned her over to find a Belsen-faced child who had lost her two front teeth.

"Nothing for me here, but—" he held out a hundred-dollar bill to the Appalachian kid—"that's on account. Let's keep moving."

"You lookin' for someone particular?"

"No, I'm just particular about who I'm looking for."

So they walked all day through the tragedy of the times. Bare rooms—wasted children, chattering with the agony of withdrawal—girls with beatific visions staring into space while cockroaches crawled on their unwashed feet—boys with dull eyes and dishrack ribs waiting for the fix that must come if they ever had the strength to scrape themselves off the floor to hustle their bread—the Beatles singing from the record players of a Yellow Submarine or Lucy in the Sky with Diamonds while Mick Jagger and the Stones hammered out songs of street-fighting men and the revolution all the young thought they were making, except they were losing it and opting out for the flowering deserts of the inner mind. And around this total destruction of young flesh and the hope of a generation, the wolves lounged in huge hats and silk pants, pushing the little pills and packets of white dust—to hook, to hold, to spoil, to crush, to finish.

"Do you like the scene, man. Isn't that something?"

"Yes," Charles said.

In the evening they came to the place where Jacqueline was. A squat studio stood on the heights with a sheer drop of a hundred feet down to the roofs below. A tall black gay was at the street door. He wore two silver stars embroidered on the tight buttocks of his purple satin pants, and two more golden stars on his crimson leather vest.

"We wanna score," the Appalachian kid said and showed the hundred-dollar bill.

The gay unlocked the door and let them into the studio. The colored wool bedspreads on the floor and the Madras cotton cloths on the walls could not hide the squalor of the large room on the cliff, where Cuban posters shouting VENCEREMOS were pinned up side by side with pop posters suggesting DROP DEAD. Near them, a paunchy white man in a sailor suit had dropped his pants and was shoving inside the ass of a black boy on all fours, weeping with his face on his arms. Over by the couch in the corner, a thin girl lay naked beside another heavy man. He had spread open her two buttocks and was trying to widen her asshole with his finger and thumb.

"Give, baby, give—" he was saying, "if you wanna receive!"

She turned a terrified face toward Charles at the door, and he could see the haunted hunted look of Annette's daughter.

"Jacqueline!"

Her eyes glittered in a terror of recognition. She hunched up her thin body and clasped her legs in a fetal position, blocking out all sight with her knee-caps driven into the sockets of her eyes.

Charles began to kill. That is all he wanted to do. He moved like a panther across the room and tried to jerk the heavy man to his feet by his hair. A blond toupee came off in his hand. Charles kicked him in the throat. As he lay vomiting and gasping, he took him by both ankles, bent backwards against the weight, and began to whirl his whole body off the floor, his head hitting the boards. The turning body knocked over the Appalachian kid, moving in to help. When the momentum was great enough, Charles let go of the man's ankles so that he skidded across the floor, his skull crushing against the edge of the stone mantelpiece.

The Appalachian kid was getting up once more as Charles jumped at him with both heels driving forward, slashing his face and slamming it back onto the ground. He landed on his feet, already lunging at the paunchy man who had got up with a knife in his right hand. As he sliced, Charles caught his wrist and pulled, then a fist in his back and a kick on his ass sent him plunging toward the low window at the back of the studio. He could not stop, but hit the glass and the frame and took them out with him over the drop, falling and screaming a hundred feet down to smash onto the ridge of the roof below.

The Appalachian kid had not risen from his knees. He looked at the broken window, then he looked at the crushed skull of the bleeding body lying by the mantelpiece.

"I'm prayin' to you, mister. I'm on my knees! Jesus, sweet Jesus, don't!"

Charles walked forward and kicked him in the face with the toe of his shoe, splitting his nose into blood and bone and shreds of flesh.

"Get out," he said. "And get out of pushing drugs! Or you'll meet me again."

He turned to the naked black boy who was shivering on the floor.

"Get your pants on and move! Or the cops'll get you."

Panic sent the Appalachian kid and the boy scuttling out of the studio, taking with them the doorkeeper in the purple pants. Charles ripped a colored quilt off the couch and wrapped it around the shaking Jacqueline, still crouched in a ball. He lifted her with ease—she must have weighed no more than seventy pounds. He walked with her in his arms to the door and the street. In the distance, he could see the three running figures who had got away.

He struggled along with Jacqueline for two blocks, then he found a cruising cab.

"Take me to a hospital," he said. "This girl is sick."

She could only be given sedatives at the hospital, while she screamed night and day for her drugs and lapsed into delirium. Annette flew in from New York and sat by her bed with Charles. They consulted specialists and visited drug-withdrawal centers, but they were frightened by what they saw. Jacqueline was so thin and frail that a cold-turkey treatment might send her screaming into madness.

"I never dared tell you," Annette said, "how her father died. He committed suicide."

"Why?"

"I don't know, or I don't want to know. It wasn't business worries. I think—he was a closet gay. There was a boy who was putting the screws on him. He did it without warning."

"Did you feel you'd failed?"

"How the hell should I? I felt sort of lousy because I'd chosen my career and not him and Jacqueline—and maybe it was just too much for him to be Annette Kilroy's husband—" She put on a sarcastic voice. "And what do y'all do, Mr. Kilroy? Wash the dishes?" She paused and spoke normally again. "But all the same, he was a skunk to kill himself like that. He cut his wrists in the bath, and that poor kid found him. She was fourteen; she had just started menstruating. She was under analysis for two years after that until she quit."

"So you can hardly blame her for anything?"

"How can I? I just know—she can go over the edge, just like that—"

Charles stared at Annette's green eyes. He saw concern in them, but also the ambition which had always been there.

"Can you quit the show and look after her?"

"I can't, Charles. I've got a contract like a leg-iron. After that last Kennedy show before he was killed—it was number one on all the ratings—they'd sue me. I'd be wiped out. I've got to go on."

"Do you want me to look after her?"

"Charles, why should you?"

"Because I've never done anything like that. Because I hate what the kids are doing to themselves. I'd like to see if I can bring one back, the hard way, the natural way. Do you want me to try?"

Annette stared at Charles. She could not understand him. "Hot damn, are you trying to be the saint of the year?"

"No, I'm doing it for me. It's a challenge, and if I win—how many times do you think I've ever played the *beau rôle* anyway?"

"I'd always be grateful, but—when will I see you?"

"Very little for three months. You've got to be in New York, doing your shows. I'll take her up into the Rockies and keep her there—look after her night and day. We'll sweat it out alone. I'll put thirty pounds on her and bring her back, all sinew and roses. I'll try to."

"I'll be jealous!"

"Of that crazy scarecrow? I love you, Annette—but you've got a contract and I don't. So I've got to do something if you still want to have a daughter. But I warn you, I may fail—and that's something I hate to do."

He took her up to a cabin in the high pines by Lake Tahoe. There the wind in the trees rustled like a softwater river, and the squirrels sat on their hind-quarters with their tails high to eat the pine kernels, and hawks hunted the mountain meadows, and even an eagle stood still in the heavens above the high sier-ras.

The first four weeks were hell on earth. Sometimes Jacqueline sobbed and ranted and beat at his face and chest with her hands. Once she gouged strips of flesh from his cheek with her fingernails. Usually she slouched apathetically on her bed until the bad odor from her made him change her nightdress and sponge her all over, wondering that there was still some life left in such a sad sack of gray skin.

He was her nurse and keeper, guard and guide. Once

she escaped toward the local town, but he caught up with her as she was trying to hitch along the highway, and he threw her into his station wagon, kicking and swearing. But she did not try to escape again, spending her time chewing at her thumbs and staring out at the trees. Slowly she stopped throwing up and her appetite returned, starting with cereals and ending with the huge T-bone steaks he brought home from the market.

She liked knocking herself out with the gallon jars of red California wine, Cabernet Sauvignon and Pinot Noir. He encouraged her to drink herself into a stupor because she would sleep at least six hours afterward. And she would wake the better for it, rested and able to walk through the forest.

He himself stripped all civilization off his body. Every dawn he would run ten miles through the woods, slipping in and out of the tree trunks as if they were an obstacle course. Then he would return to give her breakfast, the scrambled eggs and link sausages that reminded her of her childhood. After the meal, she would come outside with him, even jogging a mile or two until her weakness made her stop.

One day they found a baby bobcat. The mother had been trapped and died of loss of blood after gnawing off one of her two legs caught in the steel jaws. The baby cat was still mewing and pulling at its mother's cold teats when Charles and Jacqueline found it and ran it down and took it back to the cabin. They fed it on milk until its teeth ripped open the rubber nozzle of the feeding bottle, then they switched to hamburger and stewed beef and spareribs. It played like a kitten although it was bigger than a tomcat after two months. It scratched all the curtains down from the windows and made the tablecloths

look like streamers. But it grew tame and sat for
hours on Jacqueline's lap, while she combed its
tufted ears and rubbed the sensual bump on the top
of its skull.

So the weeks passed raising the bobcat, chopping
wood for the log fire, cooking three large meals a day,
running and jogging through the pines, then later
swimming in the snow-chilled waters of the lake that
cut the flesh cold down to the bone marrow, but
made the blood race wild and tingling afterward in a
sprint along the shore. The high air was brandy in
the mouth, making the breath bubble and laugh as it
came out of their lungs, the bouquet of the pine
needles sweet in their nostrils.

Charles wondered why he had ever left the hills
and the jungles. Each time he ran in the forest, he
was an animal again, hard of thigh and lean of arm
and quick of eye. But he was also being born a man
again in his care of another, his heart soft in him for
the new girl slowly budding out of the corpse of the
old, her skin browning, her flesh firming, her feet stepping light and quick with the spring and the dance
of the young bursting free again.

One night after twelve weeks together in their
cabin, she had gone to her bed in her room, but he
could not sleep. The moon was haloed by clouds and
bright in his eyes, the crickets and the bullfrogs were
making an orchestra in his ears, and he was restless.
Cures never seemed to end. Virtue had to be its own
reward, because it certainly went on too long—

Then his muscles tensed, he found himself
crouching, ready to spring. A shape had come into his
bedroom—Jacqueline in her night-robe. She opened it
to him, showing her lean flanks and small breasts,
which the food was beginning to fill out again. Her

mouth was loose and full and glistening in the moonlight. She did not speak, but she came over to him and put her body against his while her fingers felt between his legs.

"Don't speak," she said.

He felt his stomach stir and his prick harden as he grasped her buttocks with his hands and pulled her against him, ready to take her. Then his fingers let go of their two handfuls of young flesh and he walked away to the window.

"No," he said.

"I told you not to speak."

"No."

"You don't want me?"

"Of course I want you. You're beautiful now. Close your robe!"

He spoke harshly, and she buttoned up her robe. She sat in the rocking chair looking out at the moon, her flowing hair powdered with a nimbus of pale gold.

"You rescued me, Charles. You've looked after me for months. Nobody's ever done that for me. Won't you let me give you something I want to give?"

"Not that. What about your mother?"

"I knew you'd bring her up. I've been thinking about it. I've been thinking for weeks, ever since I knew I wanted you. Then I said to myself—like, Annette will never know. Even if she did know, she wouldn't be bugged by it, because—look, it's just *now!* We both want it; I'll split later, I just want you now! How else can I show what I feel for you?"

Charles walked over to stand behind Jacqueline in her rocking chair. Very softly, he began stroking her forehead with the tips of his fingers. She pressed the back of her head against her chair and sighed.

"Oh, that's good—good—"

"Look, Jacqueline darling—" Charles's voice was tender as it had never been tender. "I want you too. I feel for you too, or I wouldn't have done all this. You're beautiful and I'd love to sleep with you. And it isn't even Annette who really stops me—"

"Don't tell me you're being good?"

"No, I've never been good. I'm not sleeping with you for your sake."

"Oh, Charles, don't give me that shit!"

"I mean it. Look—like it or not, when I married Annette, I sort of became a father to you."

"I've got George Kilroy, the great suicide! He loved me so much he killed himself in front of me! You're not my father—you're a man who happens to be married to my mother. That's what you are. It's not incest."

"You're very beautiful and bright. Now you're well again, you can get any man you want. But there'll have to be one man in your life you can't get, who can be a father figure to you. And that's me." Charles laughed. "I wish it wasn't. I'd rather fuck you, if you really want to know. But that's how it is."

"Mummy always said you were a beautiful man," Jacqueline said. "But she never said you were a soft man."

"I'm the original hard case. You know that."

Jacqueline stretched in her chair and yawned.

"No, you're not. You're a pussycat with butter fingers. Mmmm—I'm nearly asleep."

Charles picked her up in his arms and took her to her bed and laid her on it and kissed her softly and left her sleeping under the moon.

When Jacqueline reached her target and tipped the scale at a hundred pounds, when she became as radiant and fit as a young animal let off the leash, Charles wired Annette that they were both coming back to New York. That last night together, he asked her for a celebration dinner in Reno. They could have a wild time, he said.

She refused. She wanted to spend her last night with him in a little cave they had discovered by the lake. She shopped for their meal, thick country ham and cold asparagus, Napa grapes and four bottles of Kenwood Pinot Noir seven years old. As the light began to settle on the glittering lake, they swam naked along the rippling blade of the setting sun on the waters. They rubbed each other's body down and dressed and lay together under the rug in the cave to get warm. Then they ate the food and drank wine until the moon rose into the dark heavens.

All night they lay side by side, holding each other, but they did not make love that last time of their greatest temptation. The warmth between them was the seal of their comradeship. No coupling of the flesh could make them closer than they already were.

So the full moon shone down on their faces as they lay. And the bobcat came and spread itself on Charles's chest, its fur hot on his cool skin, its jaws open on his neck. He could feel his windpipe quivering between the teeth of the beast, dreaming of the chase and the kill. But it slept on quietly like his loved comrade at his side on her pillow of golden hair. At any time, it could have closed its fangs and ended his life.

Yet he did not care. He felt that if he died that

V

It was hopeless for the three of them to live in the same apartment in the Hotel Pierre. There was an electric jealousy that crackled between mother and daughter. Jacqueline had only to look at Charles for her mother to snap at her.

Charles could not take the atmosphere, so he decided to go and ski in the Colorado mountains, where an October snowfall had started the season early. He hired a split-level chalet near Aspen with a large picture window overlooking the white peaks. He told both Annette and Jacqueline where he had gone.

He went up on the ski lifts in the morning, trying to recapture his feelings of peace and seclusion at the time when he had been a young man on his long trips over the Swiss mountains. But he found the ski slopes crowded with smart people—and the people they attracted. Everywhere the ski suits blazed in scarlet and gold, while the gossip about the visitors drowned the rattle of the cocktail shakers in the bars. Even the slopes were like a traffic jam on the Los Angeles freeways, the people plunging down at sixty miles an hour along the ruts in the snow.

When Jacqueline came to see him, Charles found the reason for being in Aspen. They locked the door against the outside world for three days and nights. She had set up an alibi for her mother—a visit to Miami to stay with a girl friend, who would tell anyone who asked for Jacqueline that she was out sailing and could not be reached.

"I have to have you, Charles, or I'll go mad."

So they made love in the time that was left to them. Her thin body coiled among his limbs like a beautiful serpent's, drawing out of him all his strength and his passion. She was like a virgin now, the muscles of her thighs and belly writhing against him so that he had to come again and again inside her while she shuddered and shook and sobbed beneath him, "My love—Charles—my dearest love!"

There was something animal between the two of them as if they were both creatures of the wild that had survived the soft erosion of captivity, the deceitful debility of disease. They had come out on the far side as beings close to nature and their own nature. They needed to mate, procreate.

"Darling, I want to conceive. I want to have your child."

"That would wreck everything."

"Wreck? Or make? It's all the same. As long as it's yours—inside me—"

"Jacqueline—you make me lose all control, all sense in my life! But I don't care. Let it fall where it does!"

She would scratch him lightly with her fingernails, playing with his naked skin like a kitten, exciting him into more lovemaking. There was no repetition in their sexual frenzy, but a seeking of justification for their betrayal of Annette. They fiercely sought in each other's bodies the proof of their love, as if the intensity of the flesh would demonstrate how close their two spirits had come together in one flame of feeling.

"Charles, we can't go on like this."

"We'll try! You must move out to a hotel. Wait until your trial is over and see what happens. We'll keep this marvel of ours a deep secret. And when the trial's over and you're free, we'll go away together."

"And Annette?"

"If we follow our hearts, we must break hers."

Jacqueline agreed to be a witness for the government at the trial of the surviving members of her group. She had no choice, if she wanted to stay out of jail.

During the trial she broke down in court, sobbing until it was adjourned. Sometimes she could not meet the cold stares of the accused, who looked at her as a traitor. Sometimes she was defiant, declaring that she had been misled, but now she had learned. There was a simple way of living, she said, which had nothing to do with the destruction of society.

The security operation to keep her alive was enormous. The television cameras waiting outside the courthouse could hardly catch her because of the bulky agents surrounding her. Her mail was filled with threats to her life. She became the target of radical groups, a symbol of bourgeois treachery. However, to most Americans, she represented something else— the good girl gone wrong and now coming out straight again. Charles saw her daily suffering and courage. She had become what he had often been—

one of the hunted—and she was trying to live with that.

"I suppose I'll never be safe unless I drop out and become someone else and never see anyone I really dig again."

"If you want to be safe," Charles said, "that's what you should do. Taking another name means you can start again—I know it."

He looked at Jacqueline, appraising her. The trial had made her into a woman, capable of a choice and a hard choice.

"Who wants to be safe," Jacqueline asked, "if it means being sorry?"

"I hoped you'd say that."

Annette hated the obvious complicity between her husband and her daughter. She had been immensely grateful when Charles had brought her back radiant from her months in the mountains, but she had been jealous ever since. He swore that nothing had happened between them, and she had to believe him. There was a bond between stepfather and daughter, and she was supposed to feel good about it. It was too damn close for comfort.

"I don't like it," Annette said. "You've risked your life so much already; you shouldn't put it up for grabs again. Perhaps you shouldn't stick around with us where they know how to find you. I can't keep out of the public eye, but you can. Though we'd hate not to see you for a time—"

"Would you, Mother?"

Jacqueline looked coolly at Annette over the coffee percolator, while Charles looked carefully between the two women. He was pretending that he was not aware of the motives behind their words.

"Of course I'd hate not to see you," Annette said.

"You're my girl and I love you. But it would be selfish if it meant risking your life. I'm thinking of your safety."

"And your own?"

"I'll look after everyone," Charles volunteered.

"I'm sure you can," Annette said. "I'm sure you'd just *love* it!"

"I don't want to be in the way," Jacqueline said. She rose from the breakfast table. "I know Charles is married to you, Mother. If he wasn't, well—"

"Well what?"

"Well, he'd be up for grabs like my life, wouldn't he? But my life's mine. And I'm not going to spend it living in a hole in the ground because I don't dare get in the wind."

"Good girl," Charles said. "There's nothing wrong with risk—it makes you live more."

"Or less," Jacqueline said.

"Or less."

"You can't just expose yourself," Annette said. "You'll get killed."

"I'm not going to run away, Mother. Let them come and get me."

Three of the accused were sentenced to fifty years for their part in the bombings and bank robberies, while Jacqueline was given a suspended sentence because of her testimony and cooperation with the government. She was offered the chance to disappear into a false life, but she said that she had been underground too long already. If she were an informer, she would live with it.

"Judas may have been a fink," the press reported her as saying, "but he didn't have plastic surgery to change his face."

She only survived for three weeks after the trial.

She seemed almost to be flaunting her notoriety, inviting her execution. She walked every day from her hotel at the same time along the same route to have lunch with Charles and sometimes Annette. She did not even check to see whether she was being followed. She held her head high, looking past the stares of the curious. Television had made her face familiar to millions. She refused to appear on talk shows, even her mother's. For once Kilroy was not there. And she also refused to write her true story for the best-seller list. She would not even talk to a ghost who would spare her the trouble of writing it.

"I've had enough of spooks," she said.

The killer found her easily. She was going from Fifth Avenue into the lobby of the Pierre Hotel when the young man pulled the pistol out of his mackintosh and slapped her on the back. As she turned, he put the gun muzzle into her stomach and fired twice. She slipped down to the sidewalk, her hands on her belly, crouched over with the blood seeping between her fingers.

She turned up her face, in appeal, to the windows of the hotel. So Charles found himself looking down on Annette's dying daughter and his love, watching the young killer sprint across Fifth Avenue toward Central Park. It was the same person who had released him after his trial by the revolutionary tribunal, the fresh-faced boy who was studying to be an urban guerrilla and now had become one. Charles had even given him back his gun, perhaps the same one that had killed his Jacqueline.

It took him ninety seconds to run down the emergency stairs and reach her. People stood around, doing nothing. He knelt and took her head in his arms. She looked up at him and tried to say something, but the words would not come out of her mouth for the pain. She could not even tell him she thought she was bearing his child.

"I love you," he said.

She tried to smile. Then death covered her eyes with a white blank film. She stiffened and her neck seemed to break.

Charles rose, putting her head gently on the sidewalk, her blood on him. His mouth opened, then his face set in a killing anger.

He turned away and began to run between the cars after the killer. Horns blew at him as he dodged in front of the radiator grills and behind the exhausts. He leaped over a dog racing across his path on the far sidewalk, and he hurdled a child on a tricycle as its mother screamed. He could not see the killer, but he expected him to be going right, toward the reservoir, then across the park to the west.

He ran along the brown curves of the dry grass, leaving the joggers in their bright track suits gasping at his heels. And as he came over a hill, he could see the fresh-faced boy slowing to a walk ahead near a little artificial lake. The killer thought he was safe. It was a fatal mistake.

He loped up behind the young man in the mackintosh, making no sound on the hard dry earth. He was only ten yards away when the boy turned and began pulling out his gun. The killer hardly had time to aim and fire as Charles left the ground in a long flying tackle, his shoulder hitting the boy's knees and knocking him backwards. The gun flew free. Charles rolled and shifted and squatted on the boy's chest, knees across his arms, right hand raised ready to kill him with a swipe to the windpipe.

The boy looked up at him, sick with fear.

"You little bastard!" Charles said.

"Please—"

Charles chopped him on the windpipe, enough to make him choke, not enough to kill. Then he dragged the retching boy into a clump of bushes at the edge of the water that hid them from most of the park. He held the boy's head by his hair and pushed it under the water, making him drown for a minute. Then he brought him up again, coughing water out of his lungs.

"It didn't have to be you," Charles said. "I gave you a chance."

He pushed the boy's head under the surface again and held it down for two minutes. His body thrashed about on the bank, then kicked into stillness. Charles pulled his head out of the water again and pumped his ribs to get the water from his lungs. He could revive this dead idiot, but he could not revive the dead girl he had loved.

The boy choked and vomited back to life again. He gulped in air greedily, then he sobbed at his tormentor above him.

"Kill me! Just kill me—"

"You want to die? That's easy."

"Please."

There was no point in torturing the killer. He had nothing to reveal. Even revenge was finally pointless, without a purpose. It would not bring Jacqueline back to life.

The cold water on his hands and face began to bring Charles back to his senses. He had meant to kill the boy and leave him as the presumed victim of a mugging in Central Park. But people had seen him kill Jacqueline and he would be identified. And more people had seen Charles run after him. There were too many respectable witnesses this time to let him be his own law.

"I'm turning you in," he said, "only because I don't want to stand trial for killing you."

He chopped at his neck again, making him unconscious. Then he bent and picked up the body and put it over his shoulders. He carried the dripping weight until he found a police car cruising the park roads. It pulled up beside him.

"Any room for a murderer?" he asked.

There was and for the witness to the murder. The two police officers frankly admired the job Charles had done in working over the boy.

But Charles could not listen to their praise. He found himself weeping out of control. Jacqueline was lost, and all innocence with her.

"I'm sorry," he said to them. "It's not like me."

And it was not.

Annette was inconsolable. She blamed Charles for Jacqueline's death.

"You live on risk. Your blood's ice water and you need danger like other people need a Scotch. But you encouraged her to risk it. Look what happened! She shouldn't have listened to you."

"She wanted to do what she did," Charles said. "She knew the risk. She was part of them once in the underground, too."

"But you didn't have to agree with her! You had a great influence on her. She would have listened to you!"

"I did what I thought was right. And so did she. She gambled, she lost."

"For Pete's sake, Charles, life's not a goddam game of poker! You don't gamble with it."

"Yes, you do. Daily. Every time you cross the street or drive a car. The thing is—do it boldly! Smash, or go softly! Not many live like that. Jacqueline did and I admire her for it."

"She'd be alive *if*—"

On the next performance of KILROY IS HERE, Annette broke down on the live part of the show. She suddenly began to tremble and weep. Her makeup ran down her face in long streaks, making her look like an old woman for the first time. Her audience knew of the death of her only daughter, and the millions were thrilled to see real grief. It was superb television. The network agreed with Annette to suspend the show for thirteen weeks and sign a new contract after she had time to recover.

They went traveling. Annette had wanted to go to the smart places of the international set, but Charles insisted on putting her in shape again. He took her to Nova Scotia to a fishing village called St. John's. Besides, there was something he wanted to check out there, an absurd story of sunken treasure and tidal suck and drowned men. He had heard it from two reliable sources at different times. It was worth taking an aqualung and the rest of his diving gear.

His first priority was to restore Annette to health. He stayed with her in a widow's cottage from which the fisherman husband had sailed out with the fishing boats on the day of the black storm five years before. Half the men of the village had died that night, and the boats which had come back out of the raging waters were little better than wrecks. Since then, the men who lived shared their catch among all the households in the village and even some of their money from the canning factory. The children had to be kept until they grew and took their fathers' place.

Then there were the summer visitors like Charles and Annette de Belmont. The landlady, Mrs. MacPhee, did not recognize Mrs. de Belmont.

"It's fish every day," she said. "I hope you won't get fed up with it."

"We'll get fed up," Charles said, "and we'll love it."

They did. They liked the fish stew boiled with milk and the baby squid which Charles insisted on frying himself. They walked at least ten miles every day along the sea grasses above the granite cliffs, and some nights they would go out with the fishing boats. It was ghostly, the lamps gleaming off the stern of the rocking boats, the lump of fat dropping deep into the black sea off the end of the leaded rope, the waiting under the cold starry heaven, then the winding-up of the rope until the fat bait came up with squid after squid wrapped around it and each other, with their greedy tentacles, a huge writhing and trailing ball of undulating skin and bulbous eyes.

"There's horror in that deep," Charles said.

Yet as the days and nights passed, and as Annette became whole again, he was anxious to begin his search for the sunken treasure. But first he waited for Annette to seek him in the night, crossing over to his twin bed across the weathered boards of the attic under the stone roof of the white cottage. She would slip into the narrow space at his side, and he would hear her voice gentle as it used to be.

"Hold me; I'm cold."

Then he would hold her until her shivering stopped and he would warm her until the icicles of her toes thawed into life, and he would feel her breasts until the nipples stood against his palm, and he would rub her belly and thighs with the tip of his prick until she began to part her legs and guide him against the lips of her cleft, and within her, pressing him deeper and deeper into her body, crouching down and pushing onto him until she was spitted and roasting over the coals of her desire.

"Dammit," she said, "you're a hard man. That's why we love you. Forgive me—you're not to blame at all. You saved Jacqueline; you didn't want her killed at all. She asked for it."

"You know, she said I was a soft man."

"You are, somewhere deep inside you, but—it's not for me. I wish it was. It's for younger people, vulnerable people—and you don't see me like that."

"Everybody's like that somewhere."

"I can't show it to you. You can't show it to me. We're in sort of a love war with each other."

"That's why I'm nursing you back to health again—so we can have a good fight! Like the good old days."

Annette laughed.

"You're a dear, lovely fuck and a great fighter—and it's been a hell of a good life for me ever since you came into it."

Mrs. MacPhee confirmed the stories of the sunken treasure near the rocks off the headland. Some said it was a bullion ship blown off course from the Spanish Main that had gone down there. Others said that Captain Kidd himself had buried his gold there so that nobody could ever bring it up again; he alone knew the trick of getting it out. What was certain was that a hundred years ago gold ingots had been found in shallow water there, and ever since men had tried to dive for it and they had died. The fishermen from St. John's would have nothing to do with the treasure. They said they heard the souls of the drowned dead haunting the place, and if it was just the barking and singing of the seals on the rocks, well, everyone knew that drowned men always came back again as seals to wail.

Once Annette was well again, Charles took her and the diving equipment out to the headland. He looked down at the killing ground below. Some of the problem was clear. Two currents clashed so that the sea seemed to boil and froth and suck around the rocks, which were sharp and pitted like ancient teeth.

An hour later, Charles was equipped with his aqualung and wet suit and flippers and mask. Annette begged him not to dive, but he insisted. There was nothing in the world that he would not explore once. The ocean was bitterly cold as he went slowly into the water, the current so fierce that it nearly swept his legs from under him. Then he was swimming, the current taking him toward the frothing cauldron off the rocks. He tried to kick away, but he could do little. He had to race with the flow, looking ahead for the granite edges before they cut him apart.

As the current reached the rocks, it met the second current in a whirlpool. Charles was whipped around and around as in a giant cement mixer, battered by the roaring blows of the spray, bruised by the slap of a granite boulder as he was dashed past it. As he spun in the whirlpool, he was dragged down by the swallow and the suck of the sea. He was sure he would never come up again, never at all. The force of the water seemed to break his bones with its chop and thrust. He could see nothing through his mask, only the white fury of the ocean. His ribs ached from the slugging of the twisting waters. He would die soon, stupidly, powerless in the deep.

Yet as he was dragged down, he was suddenly squeezed out, shooting sideways like an orange seed. He found himself swimming in still, clear, dark water. Around him was a circle of rock like a well, with only a narrow fissure leading to the race of waters outside. An overhanging cliff hid the top of the well from above, and its sheer sides made it impossible to climb down into it. Below him on the sea floor, Charles could see vague shapes among the weeds—the straight lines and square edges must mean man-made objects down there.

He swam deeper, noticing that the well opened toward its base. Its walls were no longer smooth now, but held cracks and small caves. Nearer now on the sea floor, he could see broken boxes of chests, and close by, small oblong shapes which could be ingots. The treasure was there, not difficult to reach, if he could find a way out.

Then Nature or Captain Kidd played their trick. Through a fissure in the rock wall, the current swept in cold force. It caught the diving Charles and hurled him toward a cleft in the far rock face. From it, tentacles hung and waved, looking for their prey. They wrapped themselves around the man and drew him in, helpless in the suckers of the deep.

Charles had one arm free. He could see the dull and bulging eye of the squid and he struck at it with hooked fingers, tearing it open. Blacker fluid stained the dark waters. The sea beast lurched and loosed its hold on the rocks. The current caught it and its victim, forcing them through another fissure below the beast's lair. Charles was protected by the tentacles of the squid, but its body was shredded and lacerated by the granite sides of the crack as the current thrust it through the grating edges as in a gigantic mincer.

The disintegrating flesh of the beast still wrapped Charles around as he exploded out of the fissure into another whirlpool. The boiling waters ripped off the last of the suckers from his wet suit and sent him bubbling up toward the surface, hurling him toward the air. He found himself thrashing through the spume on the other side of the rocks, making his dead limbs work to get him toward the shore. And there Annette found him, more dead than alive. On his wet suit were great blisters as if the sea had thrown him out because he was diseased.

He recovered quickly. Next day, he was well enough to talk about it.

"I'll never go back," he said. "It's diabolical. You are sucked down, shown the treasure, pulled up, and spit out. Two whirlpools working in reverse directions with a well in the middle. To hell with sunken treasure—I know where mine is!"

So he made love to her that night, searching her naked body minutely, kissing each mole as if it were an ingot, each nipple as if it were a treasure chest, each freckle as if it were a doubloon. He found his final treasure between her thighs, plunging deeper there than into the well of the sea, finding the race of his coming and the wash of her desire their special ocean and reward.

When they lay close together after their lovemaking, he traced his forefinger across the slight swell of her lower belly, fingering the soft red hairs that hid the entrance to her cleft.

"X marks the spot where my treasure lies," he said. "Here are my riches and my greed."

After the treasure hunt, Annette convinced Charles to join the international set in Europe—those thousand people who called themselves "everybody" because they had arranged that there could only be a few of them. He took her to St. Tropez and La Colombe d'Or at St. Paul de Vence, to Monte Carlo and Marbella. He made introductions and he named names. There was Brigitte Bardot, still with the enticing girl's body, with the Lolitos following her like big dogs, hoping to be chosen. Porfirio Rubirosa might be dead on a tree in the Bois de Boulogne, but there were ten coming up to take his place led by Gunter Sachs with the drooping eyes and the sleepy smile, trying to play away his industrial fortune and not even making a dent in it.

Behind him drove the Grand Prix racers, the young men with speed in their veins and death under their wheels. If wealth and the will to spend it was the great aphrodisiac, death and the urge to risk it was a hell of a love potion. Many were to die with their helmets on like Piers Courage and François Cevert, but while they lived they were the new gladiators in the fiercest arena of them all. They had to fight their way to the wheel through the girls and the glitter.

Among them all, Charles walked, tall and aristocratic, with ease, until Annette grew jealous of him again and wished that she had not asked him to take her among the smart ones in their summer places. He had the money and he spent it well; he knew where danger was and he risked it. There was also something uncertain about his reputation so that everyone seemed to know him, but none knew him closely. Everyone accepted him, but not wholly. Everyone wanted his recognition, but not his intimacy. They would gamble with him and hunt with him and go to bed with him, but they would not ask him home.

"One has an encounter with Charles," the old

Princess Isagoni explained to Annette in the Gritti Palace, glowing pink and orange by the Grand Canal in Venice. "One can even have a rendezvous with him or an assignation or an affair. But one does not ask him to a *soirée*. It would be a waste of him—and of the social evening. There is something clandestine about the man. And something thrilling. Whoever asked Bluebeard to dinner? I must say, I admire you for marrying him, but"—here the Princess's faded eyes grew cold as a lizard's—"I suppose only someone of your background could cope with an outsider like that."

"Hot damn right," Annette said.

Irving Page asked them aboard his yacht. He had appeared on KILROY IS HERE many times. He specialized in writing best sellers about the decadent lives of the rich and the notorious, how beautiful they were in public and disgusting in bed. He dealt with last year's scandals and in false names for fear of libel suits. He was a genius at gossip, he always hit below the belt, and the world paid him large royalties for it.

"I bought a yacht on tit," he used to say. "And my old-age pension's going to be paid by pussy."

If his yacht was not as big as the Onassis one, it was brighter. Like Cleopatra's barge, it sparkled on the water, glittering with gold and quartz and mirrors. Red velvet drapes and gilt pilasters turned it into a floating palace that looked more like a sinking brothel. Charles had to laugh when he saw the thirteenth cupid statue with a diamond earring hanging from its tiny prick.

"Irving," he said, "is that a promise or a payment?"

"Fuck me and see," Irving said. "You take it if you earn it."

He soon told them why he had asked them aboard. Over a magnum of Dom Perignon and a kilo of white caviar, he admitted he had no subject for his next book. Perhaps Charles could serve as his hero.

"Tell me your life, Charles," he said. "You're the ultimate mystery man! Do you know, when your back's turned more people talk about you than anyone else. Sure, Jackie Onassis or Princess Margaret get more publicity, but privately everyone—and I mean everyone—talks about you. And such crazy stories—all the juicy stuff, murder, money, high stakes, beautiful broads"—Irving coughed—"like Annette, of course."

"Of course," Annette said.

"I'll give you ten percent," the novelist said. "I've never done that before. Normally I just steal my subject. It's yesterday's news. But you—you've got a lot to tell."

Charles considered the novelist's round pink face, jolly, except for the hard glint of the eyes magnified behind the large spectacles. Of all the ways to make money, the writing of words seemed to him the least interesting. What good did it do, printing a story for money? The good stories were always told by a friend over a bottle of wine. You had to look at the man and judge his character; you had to sift the truth as you heard what he said. The other good stories were what you did yourself and had whispered behind your back. The bad stories were put together later by the scavengers of your legend. These were the lies, the bought lies and the sold lies, the work of art and greed.

"I don't actually remember much about my life, Irving," he said. "I've lived it so far. I don't think about it more than I have to. I don't talk about it at all. Find another man—or invent him. It's cheaper. You don't have to pay royalties on your dreams."

"I can invent a man like you," Irving said, "and pay nothing. But I don't think I'd be able to capture your essence—what's inside of you—"

"I can't," Annette said, "and I'm married to him. So for Pete's sake, Irving, how in hell could you?"

"Maybe there's nothing inside me," Charles said.

He walked over to the ship's rail. The lights on the promenade of Monte Carlo glittered in their necklace that stretched along the bottom of the hill, the last of the strings of luminous beads which fell from the Palace.

"Just tell me the stories of what happened to you," the novelist said, "and I'll tell you about the man behind them."

Charles turned. There was anger in his voice.

"A man's what he does," he said. "Not what is said about him. You people—*everybody,* as you call yourselves—you people do nothing but drift around and talk about each other doing nothing. I do things, Annette does things—and you do things, Irving, when you get around to them. Why waste your time here? You don't have to study the rich and the smart—anyone can imagine how bored they are doing nothing. You don't have to pretend to be idle just to spy on the idle. Anybody can do nothing very well, if they have the money and the contacts—but why report on it? What's interesting about it?" He walked over and took his wife's arm. "Sometimes I don't know where I am or why. Annette, let's go home."

"Right," Annette said. "Tooty de suity."

"I knew you wouldn't accept, but it was worth a kilo of caviar trying," Irving Page said. "I would have enjoyed immortalizing you."

Charles grinned.

"You know how I prefer to go?"

"No."

"Fucking a nude trapeze artist on a high wire over the Grand Canyon."

Annette resumed her program with a newfound energy and was back on top of the ratings.

Her world was becoming more and more a matter of power. Her mass influence soon brought her into politics, and she had begun to dream. The huge audience meant votes for whoever appeared on her program. But it also meant votes for herself, if she were to become a politician.

"Everyone knows me, Charles," she said. "And I'm not going to earn the rent for the networks forever. If you think it's fun sweating it out every day in a goddamn studio, it isn't. But I've got a following and women's lib is coming through. Suppose one day I ran for the Senate—would you say that was mission impossible?"

"No, not at all, the way things are going," Charles said. "But careful—you have a husband. Don't get too busy and have to say—'I had a husband.' "

Annette spent more and more time in Washington. She was moving on the fringes of the power circle around the President. The President's men were friendly to her, and she began to pull her punches for them. The biting questions which had made her famous on her talk show seemed only to bite the disloyal opposition. Her questions for the President and his team were toothless, and she would hear no wrong from them. And in New York State, she became a member of the Republican caucus and sat in at strategy meetings.

"They're short of high-level women," she told Charles, "and I am one of the few there are."

Charles listened to her and tried to advise her. He saw her forgetting to listen and drifting away. She had become drugged on power and politics. She knew the great secrets of state and she hinted at her knowledge. She felt privileged and exclusive being so near the inner workings of the state and the national machine. She went to lunches at the Ford Foundation and to dinner with the Rockefellers. She would not confide what she knew to Charles, sensing that it gave her authority over him. If he told her that power corrupted choice and that dirty deals were dirty deals, even in the White House, she would look at him in a superior way.

"Charles," she would say, "leave that sort of thing to me. It's not your game."

That would begin a row, for Charles hated to be patronized. But the rows were more human, more bearable than their silences and their evasions. Annette was away so much in Washington and upstate Albany as well as at the television studios that weeks would pass without Charles seeing her in their apartment. So he began to stay away himself to see casual girls or keep his body in order.

If making money or playing at politics did not interest him, his physical condition did. There was a certain satisfaction and pleasure in working out well. He would skip till the rope blurred faster than a propeller as it whirled around his head. He would hold his body on stiff arms parallel to the bars for a minute. He would punch and chop the bag until its stuffing burst the canvas sack. He would lift weights until his muscles swelled against his skin. He liked the heady breathlessness of physical effort, then the slow winding down in the sauna and the massage afterward and the final settling into ease in a hard body.

But—for what? Once he had trained his body to kill on reflex or survive in a jungle. But living in Manhattan did not demand that. Outside of the few muggers in the street, it needed a cool nerve and a good digestion and a large bank balance and a serenity to act as a buffer against the petty irritations of living in such a city at all.

There was still sex, of course, all over the city. Charles made a bet with himself that he could have an unpaid girl every day for two weeks. He scored fifteen, a bonus of one. With his money and his looks, it was like puncturing a captive balloon with a pin. He would find them in the Museum of Modern Art and later he would talk to them about Modigliani while he rolled down their pantyhose. They were outside New York University coming from their classes into Washington Square, and he would ask them the way which always happened to be their way until it became his. He would pick them up with the tab in the Singles Bar after two drinks, and he would leave them exhausted and sleeping in their beds before the bars had even closed.

Yet that fortnight of pursuit left him with a sour taste in the mouth. At the end of it, he had proved nothing that he had not known. He could have nearly every woman he wanted. Even Don Juan had ended as a philosopher, having achieved nothing. There were those men who hunted pussies to hang like scalps on their belts, but he saw no fulfillment in the endless pursuit of women. There were at least a billion women in the world who were quite desirable—and he could only screw an infinitesmal number of them all.

He flew back to England and visited the Earl of Aubynne and his son Adam at Clackborough Hall. The child hardly seemed to recognize him for two days, then attached himself to his father's right leg like a dog and would not let him out of sight. The Earl was friendly but reserved. He did not like Charles's intrusion on his ground, nor the sight of the little boy's love for his father. At any time, Charles might decide to take the boy away, especially as Claire had long since left to drift from London to Paris to Rome, not too particular about the company she kept as long as it kept her from thinking of who she was meant to be.

Charles played with Adam and rode him on his shoulders and taught him to kick a football and do all the simple things that small boys find difficult. He felt like kidnapping his son and taking him to Scotland again, to raise him alone among the heather and the mountains. But he was quickly tired by Adam's chatter and eternal questions, and his demands to be played with twelve hours a day. He had no talent for being a father. He was not a domestic creature—or perhaps he was merely selfish. The little boy wept to see him leave, but his feeling of sadness did not last long.

Even another trip to Scotland to go through the ritual of killing the stags on the estate did not assuage his sense of pain. The Earl of Kirtlemuir came over to visit him, bringing along his daughter Catherine. They were not surprised to see him alone, as they had never believed his marriage with Annette could possibly last. But Catherine was plump now and showing her middle age. Her boys were nearly grown.

She did not expect Charles to try and revive their relationship, and he made no move toward her. He killed the necessary stags and left, knowing that he no longer wanted the false roots of a feudal estate telling him who he might be.

VI

There were roots more real in France and Charles left in search of them. He flew to Nice and hired a Citroën and drove toward the small town and village of his childhood. He parked under the trees near the bandstand, which was still there, empty as always and playing no tune. A group of workmen was playing *boules* as workmen always did. One of them was lobbing a metal ball to break up the cluster of them, before rolling the next ball through the dust to bring it close to the mark.

"Smash, then go softly." Charles found the words from his youth in his mouth.

He saw a boy watching the game, as lean and shy as he had once been. Scared by his gaze, the boy ran away as if he could not stop, looking for any escape from that place.

Charles looked back at the men who had finished their game of *boules*. They started another game as if they would go on doing the same thing forever. The silver leaves on the plane trees were as dusty and bright as his memories of them. The only change he could notice in the town square was the garishness of the signs that now hung over the shops. Their orange plastic hurt his eyes.

This time Charles would not tell the *boules* players what to do. He was an older man, not a kid with a gun and a borrowed colonel's uniform. He went back to his car. Driving up to the village was like driving into a stone canyon. The white rocks had spilled and tumbled from the cliffs, and the road wound between boulders larger than hangars. The village had always seemed to grow into the landscape like an outcrop from the mountains, and that had not changed. But the villagers were not the same. They had become summer people from Paris. Young men in faded denim suits with gold St. Christopher medals swinging on chains on their brown chests lounged beside their older male protectors in the bistro, now sporting a vine arbor and called La Mama de Montparnasse. An old lady in a black cloak and large hat stalked the cobbles, pretending to be the ghost of Edith Sitwell or Gertrude Stein.

This was not his village, and yet—Charles could recognize the turns in the road, the shape of the houses. It had been overrun by a plague of artists. It was chic, the ultimate chic which is false simplicity. Its bare stone cottages, in which generations of peasants had slowly withered and starved, had been discovered and made into studios for boulevard Van Goghs, Gauguins à gogo, and café Cézannes.

Charles walked up an alley to get to his farm. Its doors and windows were gone, and a thin dog squatted in the sun on its front step. But its roof had held, so that the squat building looked with blind eyes at the burning mountains. The barn still stood, and he

remembered with an ache the terrible afternoon
when he had found his mother with the sailor there
all those years ago. The faint smell of manure still
clung to the yard—then the sharper scent from the
clothes of the careful man of fifty at his back, a man
with curled blond hair and a beige leisure suit who
had appeared from the cream Mercedes drawn up at
the farmyard gate.

"You wouldn't by any chance happen to know the
owner of this farm?"

"Yes," Charles said, "I happen to be him."

"My goodness, we've been looking for you everywhere. For ages, simply ages! Lucien," he called
across to a sulky youth who was sliding out of the car,
"this is the owner! Mr. Gruex! Forgive us, we've
checked out the title at the *mairie*. It's just so exquisite, we were quite ravished—"

"Exquisite?"

Charles looked at the stony mountains brooding
over the squat house. The only movement in the
wasteland came from the heat, which made the air
tremble with clear flames.

"It's a fairy tale here—I said to Lucien, we simply
have to have it! We'll restore it, dear, won't we? It'll
look just like you remembered it—rafters and old tiles
hand-polished with tender loving care—big jars for
the olive oil and antique brass beds—garlic hanging
on those darling strings and acres of herbs. I promise
you, we'll do it all up with real love, and recreate
that home atmosphere of happy bygone days—"

Charles wanted to laugh. It was too absurd. The
rich playing at peasants like Marie Antoinette with
her milk pails in the palace gardens at Versailles.
What he had survived, others would savor.

"Life wasn't like that here," he said.

"Will you sell?"

As Charles was about to say no, he caught the word on his tongue. What use was the place to him? He had escaped it, and coming back to it, he found it alien. Even the burning-bright force of the sun did not take away its brutal squalor, its arid ugliness. If these urban fools wanted to waste their money in trying to change it into a *bijou* fantasy for interior decorators, that was their affair. They would not be gilding a lily, they would be working on a sow's ear that would never be a silk purse.

"I'll sell," Charles said. "I won't be coming back again."

"It must be horrible—to cut yourself off from your dear childhood days—"

"Ten thousand dollars," Charles said, "and you can have the land too. It grows very good thistles."

He stayed in the local town until the paperwork was done. He tried to find and talk to the comrades of his childhood. Most were gone; some were dead; a few had stayed.

But there was news of his mother. She had escaped from the village with a sailor—no one knew to where.

At first Charles was interested in hearing the old stories but finally he was bored. He had never felt part of any community. He had made his life so completely in another image, and in far places, that he could never come home again.

So he stopped looking for the roots that were meaningless to him. He had been too successful. When he had cut himself free, when he had assumed a new name and a new life, it had been an amputation. He had cut off forever the legs of the boy who had run away from the Provence hills.

Charles took to the sky. He had always liked to watch birds, the gulls skidding sideways along the edge of the wind, the fall of hawks from their high places where they hung in the air, the swallows skimming the bushes when the evenings came. He went to a gliding club and learned to fly the invisible currents of the air. Once the biplane had released his glider, he would soar and swoop above the patchwork map of the earth, finding in the silence of the heavens some of the peace he was seeking. In the flight and glide of the aircraft, he would feel the free motion that had been the one true pattern of his life.

"What do you find up there?" Annette asked him on one of their rare nights together. "Don't tell me it's *God!*"

"You could call it that," Charles said. "I can't believe in the God that most people call God. But I do believe in looking all your life for something that may satisfy your soul—"

"But it's pointless, patrolling empty space. What are you looking at? And what for?"

"I don't know yet. But maybe I'll find it up there." He gave Annette a long cool look. "Would you say I could find what I'm looking for down here?"

Annette looked away, ashamed. That night, she put on her best Halston nightdress in green satin and seduced her husband. The sex between them was as strong as ever, as satisfying, as deep, as complete, her many orgasms jolting her body over and over again like a combination punch, her nostrils drinking down the smell of their bodies that seemed to mix together the most erotic perfume in the world.

"I love you, Charles. We should see more of each other."

"That's up to you. I'm free."

"I'll try to get a week off. I should be able to make it in a couple of months."

"A week wouldn't make any difference to us. It's power which turns you on now—not me."

"You're pretty powerful."

"In bed, you mean."

"Isn't that the best place to be?"

No, the high air was the best place to be, riding the jet stream between the clouds, flying blind through a white powder of air, then breaking above it with the faint whistle of wires into the blaze of the sun, the tops of the clouds lying in their proud blanket beneath the shadow of the glider's wings. Yes, it was best to be lost in a glass capsule in space, the mind lighter than air and rising to the fire above, a feeling that all was possible still and the years did not condemn—and then—

Slow spiral down through the clouds— Break out into gray lower air— Bump across a grass strip before choking back along the highway through the exhaust fumes and the traffic jams— Then the final flop onto the sofa in the empty apartment where no one came.

It could not go on. Charles left for the West Coast and a trial separation. He had heard of a new sport there which he wanted to try. It was literally like walking on air. A man wore a harness attached to a gas balloon filled with helium. Its lifting power was half a pound less than his weight. So when he jumped, he could soar—and come slowly down. He could leap a farmhouse, and with the wind, he could vault a church spire. The danger was a high wind. It could carry the balloon jumper out to sea or into the wilderness. To offset this possibility, the balloon man had a cord control to leak gas from the balloon. He could get himself down in time, if he had the time.

Charles experimented with the new game and added a refinement of his own. He had set into his balloon six small helium booster packs, so that he could recharge the gas if some of it escaped. He could rise after falling and ride the wind.

The day of his long walk was gusty. The breeze was blowing in fits and starts toward the sea cliffs and the Pacific. Once he had launched himself from the dry knoll over the eucalyptus groves, Charles knew that he was not quite in control. It was a good feeling, this element of chance in a life that he had always tried to dominate and direct. With an unpredictable wind, a man never knew exactly where he was going to end.

His first leap carried him over the trees and the creek beyond the grove. Along the bank, two girls were riding their ponies. As Charles flew over them on his balloon, one of the girls caught sight of him and fell off her saddle.

"Jesus!" she shrieked.

The breeze caught the balloon and whirled Charles along the creek, then it blew itself out, dropping him toward a little marsh where the bullfrogs were croaking and waiting for him to splash down in the green slime. He pulled the cord to release one of his booster packs of helium and he rose over the marsh. Then a gust blew and carried him sideways toward a secluded ranch house on the far side of the creek.

The wind took him over the roof, his boots tapping against the chimney, so that he sailed beyond over the pool. Below him, he could see a woman lying naked in the sun, tanning her white breasts and belly to match the rest of her body. She also screamed to see Charles floating above her, and a man came running out of the ranch with a rifle in his hand. The wind took Charles on his way with a couple of bullets buzzing like hornets about his ears.

Again the balloon dipped. Charles began to fall toward the Coast Highway, where the cars and the trucks whizzed past, bumper to bumper at sixty miles an hour. That was no place to drop. Charles pulled his cord again to boost the helium and drifted off toward the coastal strip of houses, landing for a moment on a bungalow roof to see through the sky-light a couple making love below. The woman stared up past the man's heaving shoulders and shouted.

"Harold, there's a flying bear on the roof—*and he's looking at us!*"

Charles kept on his aerial way over the seaside bun-galows. Twice he boosted his balloon so that he could walk up the cliffs behind the housing developments, rising vertically with the rock face. The gusts had be-gun to play with him now, driving him against the cliff and scraping the side of his balloon dangerously, then plucking him out so that he hung dangling in the void, the harness pulling under his armpits. And then, as he rose almost to the cliff's edge, he saw the shadows of three gigantic bats fly over him, the new devils of the air.

He could hardly believe his eyes. Under each of the pairs of wings stretched out on kite frames, a human shape hung dressed in boots and a black jump suit. Painted in red letters on the underside of the cloth of each hang-glider was the legend: LUCIFER'S AN-GELS. The three great bats swooped and hovered about the man under the balloon. They seemed to be attacking him. Charles pulled his release cord and be-gan to drop down to the secluded beach three hundred feet below.

Nearest to him flew a bearded man with a pale and

protruding forehead. He laughed. His long face seemed cut in two as if a sword had slashed it open.

"Hey, balloon man, will you fall with me?"

The bearded man put a hand to his belt and pulled out a knife. He brought his hang-glider over in the wind until he was flying near the top of Charles's balloon. Then he bent forward and struck with the knife, ripping a hole in the fabric. With a hiss of gas, the balloon began to collapse.

"Get down there!" the man shouted. "Get on down!"

Charles fell toward the beach at a speed too fast to live. He pulled the cords that let off the last two packs of gas simultaneously. It saved his life. The balloon inflated enough to cushion his impact—and he knew how to land from his parachute training during the war. He hit the sand with his heels dug in and rolled over. His legs were jarred to the knees, but they were not broken. He picked himself off the beach and looked upward. Above him, the three hang-gliders floated down—Lucifer's Angels descending.

Charles was waiting for the bearded man as he landed on his feet, catlike and dangerous under the shadow of his wings.

"Slip your gear, man," Charles said. "Then I'm going to tear you apart."

The man laughed at the challenge and unbuckled his harness. When he was free, he stretched twice to his full length. Then he jumped into a crouch, his hands far out and ready.

"I'm a black belt," he said, "in judo and karate. And in the other martial arts, I'm an artist— You want to try it?"

It was Charles's turn to laugh. At last he seemed to have an opportunity worthy of the name.

"Watch yourself," he said. "I'm an old-time killer, and names weren't yet invented for what I forgot."

They circled each other warily. Twice the bearded man jumped in with a "Ha!" and a strike. But Charles's reflexes were as quick as ever, and he swayed back each time to avoid the chop. He admired the speed of the other man and noticed out of the corner of his eye that the other two black Angels had come up near him, another tall man and a girl, thin and angular in her jump suit.

"Ha! Ha!"

Twice the bearded man struck, missing Charles with a high kick at the head, but catching him a numbing blow on the forearm with the following chop. Yet as he recovered Charles was in the air with both feet. The bearded man ducked, his reflexes quicker than Charles's jump. But in midair, Charles lashed down with his two hands clenched in one fist, a flying rabbit punch to the neck. The man crouched below him fell, stunned, onto the sand.

As Charles landed on all fours, the other two Angels hit him from either side. One kicked the breath out of his ribs, the other booted him on the jawbone. He blacked out, face on the beach.

He woke twenty minutes later to the sound of breaking glass and the sharp sniff of amyl nitrite in his nose. The lean girl was reviving him. He coughed. She leaned down, her long black hair brushing his cheeks. Then she bit him hard on the lobe of his ear.

"God dammit!" he swore and sat up.

The bearded man was laughing at him, squatting on the sand. He was also staring intently. Two strange bright eyes gleaming from the pallor of his face. It was impossible to look elsewhere. There was something wrong with his eyes. It was not their color or the flecks of quartz glittering in them. The fact was, one of his pupils had broken open so that its black center leaked into the iris.

"Join me!" the bearded man said. "You fight like a fallen angel. You damn near broke my neck."

"You're Lucifer, I suppose," Charles said with some irony.

"Right!" the bearded man said. "That's my name." He howled with laughter. "Come fly with me."

Charles began to laugh helplessly. The amyl nitrate was making his heart race and exploding gases in his mind. He was flying already.

"Where do we touch down?" he asked. "Hell?"

"There's no place like it," the bearded man said.

Hell was in Topanga Canyon. To get there, Lucifer's Angels kept a custom-built camper near the beach. It was decorated with cosmic flames writhing on its sides and damned souls stretching out their arms for mercy.

The house in Topanga Canyon was set back from the road among some eucalyptus trees. As they got out of the infernal camper truck, the bearded man pulled off several layers of leaves and broke them in half and put them under Charles's nose. Their strong odor made him cough.

"They make you high. Have you seen those koala bears at the San Diego Zoo? They're smashed all the time. That's because they live only on eucalyptus leaves. Imagine that—living only on what makes you high!"

The house had been decorated with the same abandon as the truck. Murals ran riot on the walls, flames leaping and coiling in red and yellow paint as they engulfed the caricatures of the great. Then there were large color blowups of Hieronymus Bosch—the tortures of the Garden of Delights and the Hell scenes. There were also magnified Doré engravings from *Paradise Lost* with the winged Lucifer brooding over the hosts of angels thrown down from heaven. Lurid cushions and scatter rugs covered the boards of the floors. One room was draped entirely in black velvet, lightless, timeless, lost.

"That's the womb room," the bearded man explained. "Nothingness. The void. You get put in there to think—or sweat it out. It depends on your karma. What you take in there, you get to see. Heaven or hell, heaven or hell—it's already in your own ribs!"

"I see."

"Do you? Call me Luke. Lukey Lucifer. And your name?"

"Charles de Belmont."

"Belmont. That's the name of a fallen angel! Belmont! Like Behemoth. Beelzebub, Behemoth, and Belmont—what a name for a pop group!"

The other male Angel had come out of the Watts slums by way of Malibu Point, riding the surf on the crests of the breakers like a black avenger coming from the sea. Luke had seen him and had recruited him under the name of Osiris Mark Two, the new Angel of Death.

The girl Angel with the long black hair was called Kali after the Indian goddess of death. She had the shape of a young man, slender and hipless with breasts that seemed traced onto her chest as an afterthought, rather like Michelangelo who added breasts to his statue of Morning after modeling it on a Florentine youth. Kali looked ambiguous and never spoke, so Charles could not tell which sex might claim her voice.

Charles recognized Luke's power, but he laughed at his pretensions. He knew the tricks of a professional California guru. It was an old political method—you pretended your authority derived from a secret source of knowledge to make other people obey you and pay you.

They sat cross-legged on the red cushions that night, and ate nuts and raisins and hash brownies, washed down with California Riesling. Luke did not allow the eating of meat, but he did allow the drinking of the fermented juice of the grape.

"God made grapes," he said, "and Lucifer put the alcohol in them. So drink up! And God made beef, but Lucifer said—leave it on the goddam cow!"

Charles laughed. He liked Luke's style, his stare, his pallor, his beard, his prominent forehead. He was certainly a leader of men, an explorer of the spirit, searching for a way.

"I'll fly with you, but you'll have to count me out of your Angels. I'm not a follower."

So Luke tried to convert him. He told Charles of the ultimate mystery of life, that God and the Devil were the same. Lucifer was the first of the angels, and he was only expelled from heaven because he was superior to God Himself. What men called evil was often better than what they called good, only they were scared of it and gave it a false name. We had wrong ideas about the sacredness of present life, which was nothing compared with the eternity of all living forms.

"California is mission country. It was founded by a chain of Spanish missions—fifteen of them. All good causes and bad causes try to make it here to see whether they'll live or die. I am a Californian, and I have my mission. Hear me!"

"You are an unbeliever in our midst and I should order your destruction," Luke said. Then he grinned. "But you can think and talk, and I like that. The trouble with my Angels is, they can only listen."

So Charles learned to perform one of the ancient dreams of mankind. He walked over cliffs and flew down to the earth below on his own wings, as free in air as a bird. There was a sense of power in soaring and looking down on the sun worshippers sprawling on the beach below, no bigger than pebbles, the roof-tops of the sea bungalows spread out the size of handkerchiefs, the blue lozenges and kidneys of the swimming pools scattered in their turquoise jewelry, the surfers riding the breakers like beetles on tap water, and the cars and trucks on the highways moving along as stupidly as jellybeans. As the air currents pulled him high and as he hovered on his cloth wings, he often did not look beneath him at the petty business of humanity. Instead he looked across the shining shield of the Pacific Ocean toward the west. Sometimes in the burning mist of the horizon, sea and sky merged into one, a mysterious scarf of air and water. If he were to fly out there, it might wrap him around and enfold him in eternity, that confusion of the real and the unreal which the Californians always sought and rarely found.

So Charles would fly alone or swoop down with the Lucifer's Angels. To the beach people, they seemed like supernatural creatures, Draculas or human hawks descending on their prey from the cliff tops. When they landed, they were always surrounded by the young and the curious. Then Luke would preach and the Angels would collect their dues.

Luke preached the Gospel of the Dark.

"Light," he would say, "is the absence of darkness. Day is the failure of night. The secret of the universe is the holes in space, which swallow up everything that goes near them and expand all the time. We too are a universe rushing into a black hole faster and faster. Speed is all. Motion is all. There is no need for a direction, because necessity forces us to do what we have to do. Listen to me and follow! Give—and nothing will be given back to you, because nothing is all we are given."

The other two Angels in their black jump suits would collect money, intimidating the crowd on the beach by their silence and their size. The more beautiful and young and lost were given the address in Topanga Canyon. They could go there of their own free will, if they wished, if necessity and nothingness took them there.

His refusal to join the Angels challenged Luke. Charles was the first admirer he had failed to convert. So he tried to find a weak spot in the older man.

"Youth, Charles, is your hang-up, like it's the hang-up of everyone out here. Come to golden California and find the Fountain of Youth! I call it the Ponce de Leon complex. You think if you surf or you hang-glide or you dye your hair blond, you'll become miraculously young again. Well, you won't and you know it. Charles, you're older than us and that's why you don't want to join us. But believe me, if you become an Angel, you'll find age is another illusion. Come fly with me!"

Charles thought about it. It was true—he was twenty years older than Luke and his gang. Yet there was no sign of it on his lean body, only in his mind and his experience.

"I'm not hung up on being a kid again," he said. "Youth is something to avoid—and survive."

"You don't fool me, Charles de Belmont. You'd give your soul to be young again. Everybody here would."

"I'd hate it," Charles said. "Life begins at forty. I've already committed all the sins, and at last the virtues begin to look quite interesting. Fifty, I hope, will mean an education for me. Sixty is certainly the start of wisdom. By seventy, I should have learned how to be happy. And by eighty, I'll know enough to be able to say to you, 'come die with me!' "

"I'll get you, Charles," Luke said. "You've learned to talk well, but I don't believe a word you say. You're hipped on the youth kick. Everybody is. We've got it in our hands, and we're going to turn the whole thing inside out. We're where it's at."

As he drove around Los Angeles, Charles did not disbelieve Luke. The older people did seem to be giving up before the assaults of the young. It was not only the displays for the youth market—the psychedelic posters and the pop T-shirts, the neon beach buggies and the blaring rock records, the wild hair and the bare feet. It was the fact that the middle-aged had begun to imitate the young instead of being copied by them. Matrons would waddle along in cutoff jeans fraying around their ample thighs. Curlers were thrown away for windswept permanent waves. Old bosoms sagged braless under see-through shirts where teen-age breasts bounced back. Aging playboys stumbled along in sneakers stolen from their sons. It was called the pursuit of health, but it was actually a desperate grab for another chance at youth before second childhood.

There were no standards left in California because of the love of never growing up. Once Charles would have liked this total risk and commitment to new experiments. But in his forties, he had begun to trust his instinctive judgments. He did not call his justifications of what he did either good or bad. Those kinds of words did not suit him. But he reckoned that there was a basic code of conduct that everyone knew in their bones—and if that code was giving up, God help the thin glue that held society together. California seemed to him all bits and pieces, settling like dice wherever they were thrown.

Sometimes he would visit the house in Topanga Canyon, and he would be surprised at the pilgrims he found there. Luke's band of Angels was growing. His two lieutenants, Osiris Mark Two and Kali, each had five followers. These were all teen-agers, eight girls and two boys at the shrine of Lucifer. Their devotion was total. If Luke said a word, they would run on an errand. The cult of nothingness was everything to them. Luke did not have to explain. What he said, they did at once. They had been looking for certainty in their disordered lives and they had found it.

"You're breeding zombies, Luke," Charles warned. "You're stealing the minds of those kids."

"The great Hasan al-sabah, he also worked with young men. He called them *Hashishin*, the Assassins. He warned the powers of his world, the Muslim Princes and the Crusaders, to obey his orders, as he knew the future and the mysteries of the heavens and the earth. When they did not obey him, he sent the Hashishin out to kill them."

"And you?"

"I am a Californian in the twentieth century, not a holy prophet in the twelfth century. I know the law."

"But you do not believe in it."

"I do not believe in it. I do not fear it. But I am well aware of the time I live in."

The quality of some of the pilgrims to Topanga Canyon puzzled Charles. There were film producers from Malibu, searching for some secret of togetherness and community in Lucifer's Angels.

"Sharing," one of the Malibu men told Charles. "Sharing. That's what these kids have got. They share everything. We've lost that."

"They share nothing here," Charles said, "except Luke's authority. Sure, dictatorships are a sort of sharing—you all get the same orders and you all eat the same sort of shit."

"He *knows*," an interior decorator said to Charles, fingering his turquoise-and-silver worry beads. "You can feel he knows. I mean, like, you know, he doesn't get his power from simply *anywhere*. It must come from somewhere. And if it comes from Satan, I guess he must be right. That's just another name for God."

The smart people of the beaches and the hills began to double-park their BMWs outside the house under the eucalyptus trees.

Luke knew just how to use them. He was as expert a fund-raiser as a Senator from Texas or an Israeli government bond salesman. He would preach his thing—all acts were necessary; the only true gift needed no receipt; money was meaningless in the sight of the ultimate nothing. Then his lieutenants and young Angels would kneel in pairs on either side of the sitting donor until they had collected from him. These were not thanks offerings to Luke so much as tribute to his will and his power.

Charles gave Luke nothing. He became more and more worried by the expressions he saw on the faces of the visitors to Topanga. They arrived with a smile and a sneer, ready to disbelieve. But after the silences and the drugs and Luke's sermon on evil in the place of good and destruction as the basis of creation, the superiority would dissolve from the faces of the listeners. They would show only uncertainty and confusion and a desperate wish to have faith in anything at all.

They were standing on the edge of a cliff, strapped into their wings, sworn to a combat of free fall. The first man to earth was the victor, alive or dead.

"I'll collect on your soul," Luke said with his gash of a smile. "That's the sort of thing Lucifer knows how to do."

Charles dived over the cliff, cutting down the surface of his wings so that the hang-glider was almost a tail behind him, a long streamer. The previous night he had strengthened the fabric and double-checked the wire controls. He was not going to die for lack of care. That cut the risk.

His sudden plunge took Luke by surprise. The bearded man launched himself off in a swallow dive, then had to bank and slip down after the hurtling Charles. He was too late with his maneuvers and too slow. A hundred feet above the stony beach, Charles opened his wings with a slapping of air and a jerking at his armpits that wrenched his shoulders half out of their sockets. The reinforced fabric held and he stepped down onto the beach in a long glide, landing like a pelican on the water, watching his adversary come down a full minute later.

"I can fall faster than you, Lucifer," he said. "So don't *you* try to teach me evil!"

Annette came out to visit him twice in his cabin in the Malibu hills. She was disturbed by him and did not understand.

"Charles, you've got that thing men get when they turn forty. They want to be young again—do all the things they missed in life—"

"But I missed nothing. I did all the things I wanted to do."

"Obviously not. Or you wouldn't be flying a kite with yourself hooked on it."

"It's more important than that. I'm searching—"

"What for?"

"I used to live by taking risks and making money. I was on my own, except when there was a woman with me—"

"Thanks for the Oscar."

"But that wasn't enough. You can call it age, if you like. If I look back now, all I can see is preparation— the trap of preparation. I've been preparing myself to do something well all my life. Now I'm prepared and experienced—but for what?"

"Get a cause. Get politics. Use it like I do. The President said to me last Thursday—"

"I'm not interested, Annette. You can't just get a cause like that to fill a gap in your life. You have to feel it—and I don't. I suppose I'm still preparing myself up there in the sky, but I feel I'm closer to being whole—nearer the sun or something—"

"You're talking crap. Mystical crap. I never thought I'd hear that sort of shit from you." Annette gave a hard laugh. *"Nearer the sun!"*

"Don't laugh, Annette. I want to feel whole. And that for me isn't the mind escaping the body—it's the mind and the body feeling one with the earth and the sea and the sky. There's a moment, I think—of illumination maybe—when I'll know what all this long preparation was for."

"Hot damn, California!" Annette sighed. "That's where people go soft in the heads before they die."

Their lovemaking was mechanical, the end of their marriage. Charles went through the manual and Annette went through the motions. He took a long time and he had to fantasize a gang rape, where a young faceless girl was stripped and abused by a horde of Lucifer's Angels, pushing into her two or three at a time. Annette felt little, staring at the ceiling above her, knowing that their long affair was over.

"We can't go on with this," she said at the end of her second visit. It was midnight. Charles had rolled off her and she had lit a cigarette. "There's no magic in it anymore."

"Magic," Charles said. "Isn't that the kind of word you find idiotic?"

"We had some magic going for us. Now it's gone."

"You're right."

Charles put out a hand and cupped one of Annette's breasts, usually so firm in his palm. It was slack now, unresponsive to his touch. He let his hand lie there, then took it away. There was nothing to be said.

When he drove her to the airport the next day, she would not speak until the last minute. As he took out her bags and gave them to the redcap, she turned to him and kissed him, pressing her body against his chest.

"When you know what you are preparing for," she said, "come back to me."

"Will you be waiting?"

"I'll try."

VII

The ritual murders began the next Thursday. Two young male hitchhikers were found naked and broken at the bottom of a cliff. Their ankles and wrists had been wired together. Two bat's wings had been cut onto their shoulderblades with a knife, the skin flayed off in two strips. They had been thrown off the cliff top so that their bodies and faces had been badly smashed. There were no clues.

A week later, a mansion on Sunset Boulevard was attacked at midnight. A high security wall was scaled, a guard dog killed with a rifle bullet. A professional Hollywood divorcée who dated the male stars and pretended she was paid for public relations was knifed to death with her teen-age daughter. Again the pair of bat's wings were cut into their backs and their skin peeled away from the bloody marks. Again they were thrown off the roof of the house to break their bodies on the patio. The police could find no clue except in the skill of the flaying. It seemed to have been by a butcher or a medical student.

Charles had his strong suspicions. He drove up to the house in Topanga Canyon. The Mercedes, BMWs, and Jaguars were parked two deep outside the door. Two Angel guards knew him and let him enter. There was a touch-therapy session in progress in the main room—or a group feelie, whichever way you took it. Six of the young Angels, dressed only in open kimonos, were stroking and being stroked by five of the Malibu and Stone Canyon people. Their fresh skins were catering to well-preserved decay like Bathsheba did to King David or the Indian virgins did to Gandhi. In the background, a *mantra* was being intoned on a tape—to give a holy touch.

"Where's Luke," Charles asked Kali, tall and ambiguous as ever.

She caught his arm and began to squeeze his neck with the strong fingers of her other hand.

"He told me to look after you if you came."

"Another time. Where is he?"

"In the womb room. Not to be disturbed."

"He has to be."

As he walked toward the room that was soundproofed and lightless and draped in black velvet, Kali chopped at him but he was too quick for her. He caught her wrist and landed her on a floor cushion with the force of her own movement. Then he was through the door before she could follow. As it closed behind him, he could catch a brief glimpse of Luke sitting cross-legged on the floor, wearing black silk pajamas and some sort of metal talisman around his neck. Then there was blackness and nothingness.

"I have been expecting you," Luke's voice said out of the total darkness.

"You know why?"

"You have no proof."

"I do not need it. I know."

"You know nothing."

There was a long silence. Charles listened in the blackness and heard nothing. The soft quilt on the floor would make no sound, if Luke were creeping forward, ready to kill. So Charles felt for a corner of the room and squatted there, waiting for the attack.

"You have moved away, Charles," Luke's voice said from the nothing. "You fear me."

The voice was as near as it was before. When Charles had moved, Luke must have moved toward him. Yet Luke had made no noise and could not see him.

"I don't fear you," Charles said. "I may have to defend myself from you."

"How can you?" Luke asked. Then he laughed. "I can see you. You cannot see me."

"You cannot see me."

There was another silence. Then Charles felt a light blow on his cheek. He struck out with the edge of his hand—and hit nothing at all.

"I can see you," Luke said. "You can see nothing. You cannot defend yourself from me."

"That was sheer luck."

There was another pause. Then Charles felt a bruising chop on his wrist. Again he struck back, again he hit only the black air.

"I told you I could see," the voice said. "You must believe me."

"There's a trick to it."

"No. I have the power of the inward eye. That is more powerful than the outward eye. I am Lucifer and I can see you in the dark."

"There's a trick to it."

"Power. That is all."

"I do not believe in your power, Luke. I believe you are dangerous. You are a murderer. Or if you are not, you are sending out your fallen Angels to murder for you."

"Why should I? What would my motive be?"

"Power to prove you have power. That is the worst side of power, when it's aimless—futile—merely for kicks."

There was another silence. Charles was hit a sudden blow across the face that knocked him sideways. He rolled across the padded floor along the wall. Then he rose in a fighting crouch and waited.

When Luke spoke, his voice was still the same distance away.

"Do not insult me, Charles, or you will die for it. If I let you live, it is only because I still intend you to be my chief disciple."

Charles knew he was powerless in the black nothingness of the room. He could not find the door—and his enemy could see in the dark and kill him. He would have to wait for his chance.

"I do not insult you, Luke. But I do not fear you and I will not follow you. I think you have read too much about your dead guru Hasan al-Sabah. Do you think he is reincarnated in you? Are you sending out your teen-age Hashishin to put the fear of the Devil into the whole of Los Angeles, so you can then put in your demands on them?"

"It's a good scenario," Luke said. "I wish I had thought of it."

"I think you have. I think you have done it."

Charles began to dance and slash the air, making a moving target of himself, until he heard the mocking laughter of Luke nearer him.

"You look like you're having an epileptic fit,

Charles. You'll wear yourself out. You won't escape me. How in hell—"

Charles threw himself through the darkness at the sound of his voice. He connected. He grabbed a leg in its silk pajamas and used it as a pivot to swing Luke around onto his belly and face against the quilt. Then Charles bent the leg back until the bones began to crack in his hands.

"Break it," Luke said. "I don't have to walk." He laughed queer and high. "I fly!"

Charles shifted his grip slightly, twisting the leg bones in their sockets. The pain must have been terrible. Luke groaned.

"Let me out, Luke."

"Bastard—"

"I'll snap the bones and keep on twisting. The splinters will come out of your skin. You'll never walk again."

"All right."

Mysteriously, the door of the womb room started to open. As the crack of light began to illuminate the black velvet interior, Charles could see that Luke had a control mechanism in his hand—and the talisman around his neck was an infra-red night-sight.

"That's not magic, you seeing in the dark," Charles said. "That's technology."

"Which is modern magic," Luke said. "Now let me go, you pig."

Charles changed his grip slightly, turning the leg over so that Luke rolled sideways. Before his enemy could recover himself, Charles was through the door. He ran past the touch-therapy session in the main room, which seemed to have become a general get-together in the flesh—the eleven bodies were entwined with each other like a knot of vipers.

When the two Angel guards at the door tried to check him, Charles hit them each one blow, the first in the neck, the second in the balls. He drove away in his car before any pursuit could be mounted. But he knew he was no longer safe. Lucifer's Angels would come on the wing in his wake.

As Charles drove back to his cabin in the hills, he considered his options. He could go to the police, but he had no real evidence which was not circumstantial. Anyway, he had never gone to the police in his life before executing his own kind of judgment. He felt the adrenalin of danger already shooting up his veins, and he was younger for it. Yet if he left Luke and his Angels on the loose, other people might die because of his silence. There was a chance of that—but it was more likely that Luke would deal with him first. There should be no more murders until the informer was dead.

Charles trip-wired the approaches to his cabin, the door and the window. He slept on the edge of waking, and when the little tin plates jingled, he was instantly alert and ready for the attack. Only one shape came into the cabin alone, outlined sticklike against the bright dark outside.

"You want me?"

"Yes."

"You are alone?"

"Yes."

It was Kali, the tall lieutenant with the male body and breasts and black long hair. Her voice was deep with a break in it that could be suddenly shrill.

"My instructions are," she said, "to give you anything you desire."

"Love? Or death?"

"Whichever."

Charles laughed.

"Luke does have a sense of the dramatic. Does he swear you come alone?"

"He swears it," Kali said. "He is a man of his word."

"I know that."

Charles looked at the tall figure by the door, slim-hipped, hard-breasted, with her sunken cheeks and full-blooded mouth. It had been a long time since he had had a strange woman. His couplings with Annette on her two visits had not satisfied him in any way.

"Love," he said. "We'll take care of death later."

Her naked body was as strange as it seemed. It was completely hairless even at the crotch. The legs were muscled like a sprinter's, the hips like a boy's without the pelvic triangle of a woman. Yet her small breasts were firm and natural, while her vagina was tight and deep and satisfying. In his wolfish want of a woman, Charles came quickly without stopping to please Kali. Yet she sighed beneath him and clasped his body to her own in a tremble of desire.

Only when he was feeling her after the lovemaking did Charles find that she was missing something between her legs.

"That's odd," he said. "I can't find it."

"What?"

"Your clitoris."

Kali laughed in her hoarse, shrill way.

"They're putting it in next month," she said. "Then I will be complete."

"What?"

"You want to know?"

"I always want to know."

Lying with her head on his shoulder, holding him for her comfort, Kali told him her story. She had been a young man; she was a transsexual. Luke had paid for her to have the operation she needed to become the woman she wanted to be. As a boy, she had stolen clothes from her sister to wear. As a young man, she had haunted Hollywood Boulevard in drag until Luke had found her and had paid for her to change her sex. It had been terrible, the castration, and then the making of the labia and the vagina from her scrotum. But the estrogens that had built up her breasts and womanized her had been like a slow entering into a dream through her flesh. Now she only needed a cosmetic clitoris to become a full woman. She could make love like a woman already.

"Was it satisfactory, Charles?"

"Yes, Kali."

A few years previous, Charles would have reacted terribly from such a deception. It would have revolted him, he who had given up vice with his divorce from Claire. But now, after his initial feeling of repulsion, Charles felt only compassion. Kali had been given what she deeply desired. He had wanted her as a woman—and as a woman she had pleased him. Who was he to judge?

"Is that the secret of Luke's power?" he asked her. "Does he give you all that you want?"

"I am instructed not to talk about Lucifer to anyone. It is our rule."

"I think that is why he is so dangerous. He understands people's hidden obsessions—and he caters to them. But often those dreams of flying or sexual gratification are nightmares of sadism or slaughter. You can't work everything out of your system."

"Nothing is oneness," Kali said. "Nothingness is all. God is evil. You know our rule."

"I know it," Charles said. "And I hate it."

When Kali had gone next morning, Charles found that he had been duped. Another ritual murder had taken place. One of the Malibu film producers had been caught at his beach house. Again, his ankles and his wrists had been wired together, again the bat's wings of skin had been cut out of his shoulderblades. But this time there were new markings on the broken body found in the surf below the rocks. The brand of a cloven hoof had been burned into each of the man's buttocks, as if the Devil had stepped upon him for his sins.

Before he went back to the house in Topanga Canyon, Charles taped a hunting knife to his ankle, its hilt on the side of his shoe. He did not expect Luke to use guns on him. His identification with Lucifer would make him challenge Charles in a fight to the death.

The Angel guards surrounded Charles at the entrance and searched him thoroughly, missing the knife taped to his leg. They took him in to see their master, who was sitting on a black cushion, his wrenched leg stuck out in front of him.

"I knew you would visit again, Charles. You can't stay away, can you?"

"Do you think I like risking it too much?"

"No. It is necessity which brings you here."

"I *have* to see you?"

"Yes. You are compelled. As you would say now, the print-out of your fate is programmed within your forehead."

"You are already dead," Charles said. "At a certain moment, you will make a mistake. And then—the police will have you. They are probably watching you already. Then it's life for you on death row in San Quentin. No great drama like the Inferno—just a tedious and endless prison sentence."

"No one will destroy me," Luke said. "I am neither innocent nor guilty—such words have no meaning for me. What I must do is conquer my adversary. And you are the one! We must see what fate has already chosen for us."

"When and how?"

"Tonight. On the cliffs. You have lamed me, so we must fly. It would be appropriate. We will fly linked by a chain. We will each have a knife. You accept?"

Charles considered the dozen Angels surrounding him, their eyes glancing and glittering, the drugged fanatics of the soul.

"I really have no choice, Luke."

"That is what I have always said."

The two of them stood on the edge of the cliff under the full moon. A thin steel chain fifteen yards long handcuffed them both together by their left wrists. Their black hang-gliders were erect above them, swelling and subsiding in the gusts and lulls of the wind. Four Angels stood behind them, while another ten of them patrolled the rocks and pebbles of the lonely beach far below.

"Well, Lucifer minor, shall we fly?"

"It is time."

They ran to the cliff's edge and launched themselves into space together. A gust caught Charles's wings of fabric and blew them to the side, until a sudden yank from the handcuff on the chain stopped him in midair. Using the impetus, Luke was diving down, his long knife glinting in the moonlight. Like a bird of the night, he was dropping to hack at the cloth and struts of Charles's glider.

Charles tried to work himself to the side, but the controls were sluggish. And Luke was gathering up the chain with his left hand, closing the gap on Charles's dead weight below. He suddenly fell and struck, dropping like a hawk with his knife as his claws, slashing at Charles's right arm and cutting through the skin on the back of his enemy's hand. The blood spurted out and Charles dropped his knife, which plunged down to the beach beneath them.

The wind took Charles's glider and puffed him out to the full length of the steel chain. The two gliders were slowly falling down the face of the cliff, but there was a way to go before they could reach the rocks and the sea. Linked in their flight and their death, the two men shouted at each other.

"I shall kill you now, Charles! It is decreed!"

"I'll kill you, Luke!"

Luke came at him again sideways as they dropped through the air. He pulled himself along the chain, taking up the slack. He thought Charles was defenseless, the bright blood spilling from the back of his empty right hand. But Charles jackknifed his body and tore the hunting blade free from the tape on his ankle. Although his hand was bleeding and cut, his fingers were still working.

As he righted himself, he saw the flying Luke swing in with the knife at his head. He jerked up his left hand, taking the knife point on his handcuff. The point skidded and caught in a link of the chain. It snapped off short. At the same moment, Charles drove upward with his hidden knife and put it easily up to the hilt in Luke's belly.

The body of his enemy fell through the air, dragging him down on the chain.

They drifted toward the beach, linked and wounded. Charles could see the ten Angels waiting to finish the game of death which he had begun with Luke. He knew he could not survive that last attack. Yes, Luke was right. Necessity had spoken, and his life was due to end before he knew its purpose, in nothing at all.

Yet no more than twenty yards above the beach, the wind blew again, carrying the pair of gliders over the rocks on their black wings. The gust lasted until they were out above the breakers and beyond the reach of the Angels waiting for their revenge.

The waves were high when Charles hit the sea. He struggled in his harness, but he managed to slip it before he drowned. Luke seemed to be dead, either from the wound in his belly or suffocated by the weight of his glider pressing his face below the waves. The Angels were swimming out from the shore, bringing retribution with them. And Charles was chained to their dead leader without hope of salvation.

So Charles prepared to die. Then the sky spoke. With the noise of thunder, the engines of helicopters hammered in the dark. Searchlights dropped their beams from heaven. Megaphones blared out the voices of authority. The Angels turned back toward the shore to escape, but there was no escape. Two choppers landed on the beach, spilling out the men in blue with their revolvers drawn, while the third chopper dropped its cable to gather in Charles and the body chained to him, the living witness and the human Lucifer, fallen from grace into death itself.

VIII

The trial of the Lucifer's Angels brought Charles a
dreadful prominence. Day after day, he faced the ordeal in court on the witness stand and the cross-exam-
ination of the defense attorneys. None of the Angels
would testify against their dead leader except for
Kali, who turned state's evidence. So she came under
fierce attack as a transsexual to discredit her testimony, while Charles's whole life-style was put in question.

"Mr. de Belmont, you have lived a life which could
justly be called—sensational?"

"No, sir. It was my own. I did not broadcast it."

"Through your stepdaughter, you were involved in
a sensational criminal case. Was that a coincidence?"

"I was asked by her mother to find her. I did. I saw
her killed. I found the murderer."

"You seem to enforce the law in your own way—is
that not a danger to society?"

Charles had to think before he could answer the
question.

"I do not refuse a challenge."

"Isn't that rather primitive, Mr. de Belmont? You have admitted that you grievously wounded the leader of Lucifer's Angels during a knife fight in midair, after he had challenged you. Would you say that was the act of a responsible and mature member of society?"

"I did not see any alternative. I was forced into the duel by the threats of the Angels."

"But you voluntarily returned to the house in Topanga Canyon without informing the police. You felt that you had to deal with the matter *personally*. That is where you were antisocial and primitive, Mr. de Belmont. And I may add, irresponsible. Do you agree?"

"I have always acted on my own. I do not intend to change."

"Then it is time you learned to change. Your plea of self-defense is hardly adequate for the aggressive stance you have taken in your testimony. Can't you leave the law to take its course? Must you interfere?"

"I do what I feel is right at the time."

Worse than the inquisition of the defense attorneys was the attack of the news and television reporters. Charles's past life was investigated from his exploits in the war through his two marriages in Brazil and England to his present relationship with Annette Kilroy. Their separation became a public matter, confirmed by her. She was angry at his notoriety, which harmed her new political image.

"They're correct, Charles," she said to him on the telephone. "You never grew up. It was all right playing Batman on your hang-glider—that was adolescent. But to play Batman literally and try to right wrongs yourself—that's greasy kid's stuff! You never grew up."

"And you, Annette, never grew in understanding."

After three months the trial ended with the conviction of three of the Angels for second degree murder and the rest of the Angels as accessories. Because of her cooperation with the authorities, Kali's sentence was reduced to one to five years. Charles's plea of self-defense was accepted by the court, although the judge admonished him for his failure to warn the authorities of his suspicions.

"The Wild West is over, Mr. de Belmont," the judge said. "The law will look unfavorably upon you for taking it into your own hands, if you ever appear before the courts in California again."

To escape from the criticism of the authorities—and from the hero worship of the millions who still admired the brave lone man—Charles took his hang-glider up to the canyons on the Colorado River. He backpacked his equipment for two days to reach the high bluffs before the Grand Canyon—and the total solitude of the sandstone cliffs. On the long hike there, he felt a weakness and a trembling in his legs, but he put the failure of his muscles down to an adverse reaction from the past months of persecution. The body also grew disgusted when the spirit had had enough.

When he woke at sunrise in his bedroll on the edge of the great canyon, he found he could hardly move. His muscles seemed to have set with the cold of the night air. It took him half an hour to massage life into his legs, and another hour of lying on his back bicycling in the air to feel restored. The sun had risen now, making great scallop shells of red rock among the black overhangs of the canyon walls.

Slowly Charles strapped himself into his glider harness. Perhaps it was the high air that was weakening him. Perhaps. As it was, he took three times longer than usual to put the wings on his back. Then he walked forward to the canyon rim on legs that would hardly support him. They didn't give him pain—he could hardly feel them at all. But the wind was already pulling the wings on his shoulders and the space was empty beneath him, all the thousands of yards down to the coiling serpent of the Colorado River. He launched himself into the air toward the sun.

He floated slowly down, circling and rising and swooping and falling, the sun blurring his weeping eyes so that the whole of the red wilderness was misty bright paradise to his vision. The numbness of his limbs had extended over his whole body, so that he felt he was an eye, nothing more, floating free in the universe, a part of all the air about him and the land below him, at peace, in joy, received again into the nature he had so long denied.

For him, the long drift down lasted an eternity. Time stretched out infinite. There was no end to his illumination, his beatitude. His whole life had brought him to this rare vision of his oneness with the earth and the atmosphere. It was enough for a man to have seen that once. It was enough.

When he came down on a sandstone bluff near the Colorado River, he put out his legs to cushion the shock, but they would not obey him. They buckled and flopped so that he fell against the rock and was dragged by the glider to a stone outcrop. His hands were still working, so that he could undo his harness over the next half hour. He lay there in sight of the rapids on the river, the sun in his face, his body shaken from the intensity of his vision in the high air, his eyes wet. He knew his legs were paralyzed, but he did not care. He had seen his God, such as it was for him.

A rubber raft shooting the whitewaters of the Colorado River found Charles and took him to the hospital in Flagstaff. The diagnosis was that he had polio, and he was flown back to New York and Annette. A series of tests confirmed the preliminary diagnosis. Charles had been struck down by an unknown virus, perhaps dormant since his long suffering on the Amazon. The effect was a partial paralysis, which could spread.

Reduced to a wheelchair and dependent for the first time since his childhood on another human being, Charles found his life acceptable—even easy. His illumination on his last flight seemed to have changed his nature. If he was not born again, he had seen his way again. He praised Annette for her care of him and her love of him, and she responded to his praise. His need of her won her back. She was ambitious and wanted to be dominant—and now the one man she loved had lost his independence and power to walk out of her life. She could control his movements, if not his mind. She could arrange his life, if not his thoughts.

"Charles, I love you in your wheelchair."

"Why? Does it make me more powerful and charismatic, like Franklin Roosevelt?"

"It makes you more human. You can't do everything yourself now. You need me—and no woman can really love a man until she knows she's needed."

"So it takes being a cripple for me to recognize I'm part of the human race?"

"Not that. It takes your polio to make you see that we would all be able to love you more if you were less on your own."

Charles retained his pride by having rails fitted everywhere in the apartment in the Hotel Pierre. He could look after himself in the bathroom—that he insisted upon, dragging himself from basin to toilet to bath on the chrome bars set into the tiles. His arms and chest developed an amazing strength, while his legs withered away.

Sexually, he was not active. From time to time, Annette made love to him, and they both enjoyed the experience. But it was the lovemaking of shared emotion and experience, a glow rather than a fire, a nostalgia rather than a hope. Their passion was sublimated into an admiration for each other. They could see the qualities they shared in common—a toughness, a resilience, good humor, and an endurance through the years. They would stay together now.

The Watergate scandal broke and ended Annette's political ambitions. Her friends in Washington were on their way to indictment and jail. Even the President left with a pardon from his successor.

"Well," Annette said, "I'm not too sorry. If I've lost a seat in the Senate, I've found a husband."

"We'll go to California one day," Charles said. "There's someone with a long way to go there, the new governor, Jerry Brown. A kid who likes living somewhere between the sacred and the profane. Head in the clouds, feet deep in the earth. You'd better get close to him. He might take you to a White House which didn't get dirty in the rain."

But Charles was Annette's ambition now, to make him better—and closer to her. She insisted on massaging his legs daily, working the wasted muscles, forcing the toes to move. At least the disease did not spread, keeping to the thighs and below.

"It was strange," Annette said, "the affliction hitting you on your flight into the sun. Do you think it could be psychological?"

Charles looked at his shrunken legs and grinned.

"Yes, there's a connection between mind and body, especially in a man like me. Perhaps that illumination up there was a warning, too—to detach myself from all that physical stuff, and reach—"

"For the sun?"

"For love—here and now."

He took her in his arms. He had found her again.

Part Five

CLOSING THE BOOK

England, 1977

The Fourth of June at Eton had not changed much ever since King George the Third had lost the American colonies and declared an annual holiday at the old school. The elegant fathers of the schoolboys wandered around the meadows by the Thames in their gray top hats and coats, flattening the daisies with their polished black boots. The Ascot races coincided with the Fourth, and it was better to dress correctly for both occasions.

The wives and daughters fluttered and frothed in their light summer dresses and large hats or loose long hair, their voices wheeling like the swallows through the immemorial trees. Their sons were all but ignored in their black tailcoats and white ties and striped pants, little dinosaurs left over from a golden age long gone.

Adam had been elected to Pop, the society of prefects who ruled the other boys. He was waiting for his father and Annette, wearing his colored purple vest, his sponge-bag pants and his red carnation in the buttonhole of his tailcoat. He had asked Charles to bring down a gray frock coat and gray pants and top hat for him. Evidently, he wanted to slip away to the races at Ascot, although the Eton boys were forbidden to go there. But who was Charles to disapprove of his son at the races?

Annette wheeled him out of the back of the custom-built Rolls-Royce down its special ramp to the ground. Adam was waiting for him by the wrought-iron lamp which the boys called the Burning Bush. He looked lean and tall and handsome with a crooked smile that Charles recognized as his own. He bent to kiss his father in his wheelchair.

"Sorry about what happened to you," Adam said.

"I feel better already seeing you again," Charles said.

"You've brought the gear?"

"For Ascot? Yes, it's in the car. You're just like me. You can't keep away from the races."

Charles had also ordered the traditional picnic lunch in a hamper from Fortnum and Mason's. In the wicker basket was cold pheasant, caviar, potted shrimps, smoked salmon, and strawberries and a pot of thick cream. They spread it out on a white cloth in the fields—the same playing fields where the Duke of Wellington once said he had won the battle of Waterloo, forgetting that he had had a few soldiers there too.

Around the edge of the cricket field, most of London society walked in two circles going opposite ways. They could see and be seen—which was what society was all about. Those who did not actually have a son at Eton adopted one for the day. Most of the boys seemed to have suddenly acquired five sets of parents and ten pretty sisters. Of course, given the divorce rate of the Dukes, five sets of genuine parents was perfectly possible.

"Good to see you again, Charles." The Earl of Aubynne came up with his friend, the Earl of Kirtlemuir. The two aristocrats were tall and distinguished in their light gray frock coats. They both carried leather cases for their racing binoculars.

"And good to see you," Charles said. "Do you know my wife Annette?"

After the introductions, the noblemen joined them for lunch. They showed none of the pity toward Charles which he could not tolerate in other people. He might as well have been sitting on the rugs on the grass with the others instead of in his wheelchair. His guests were natural and interested in what he had been doing.

When Adam went off to change into the clothes which his father had brought him, the talk changed to the subject of the boy.

"He's turning out very well, Charles," his grandfather Aubynne said. "He's bright, he's athletic, he gets on with everyone. If anything, he's too good at everything. He'll find it hard to choose later."

"He must have some weakness."

"Only that. He will really have anything he wants in life." Aubynne smiled. "As his father did."

Charles smiled, then shrugged, holding the arms of his wheelchair.

"I'm a bit limited now."

"Come up to Scotland again," Kirtlemuir said. "You're the best shot I've ever seen. You can shoot perfectly well sitting down. You know, Aubynne, he knocks down those wild grouse like sitting rabbits. He's a killer."

"I can't stalk deer anymore."

"Nonsense. A bit of Scotch air and you'll be running around the fields in no time at all."

The sun shone through the leaves on the tall oaks on the edge of the field, lighting up a scene that had ruled the old world for centuries. There was a calm there, an assumption of power, an easy arrogance that allowed the great to relax and sprawl on the grass. They were so sure of their place in the world that they could be very simple. And Charles, too, was sure of the place he had earned in the world. He had felt great love; he had flown near the sun; he was guarded now by the sympathy of perfect companionship.

He took Annette's hand.

"I never got everything I wanted," he said. "Although Annette's nearly everything."

"What didn't you get?" Aubynne asked.

"You know. That membership in the Jockey Club."

Aubynne smiled and nodded toward the path through the trees. Adam was walking toward them, dressed in his gray Ascot clothes. The top hat on his head made him look more elegant and older—the image of the young Charles de Belmont. His father could see himself again talking to the Queen after his horse had won the Gold Cup. His voice caught in his throat. He said nothing.

"With some of the money you gave him, Charles, he bought a few good horses. They have been very successful, so successful that—"

Adam bent and kissed his father's cheek and held him close. As Charles's face pressed against the beating heart of his son, he could see from the corner of his eye the Jockey Club insignia on the binocular strap hanging on Adam's arm.

"I am the youngest member of the Jockey Club,"

Adam said. "Grandfather put me in—with a little help from his friends. He said it was because of you."

As his son walked away with the two Earls to catch the last races at Ascot, Charles could see a handsome woman waiting for them tactfully under the trees. She was quiet, mature, perfectly dressed, an ornament to the scene. It was Lady Claire, his second wife, so much a part of the occasion that he had hardly noticed her. She had not come up to greet him because he was with Annette, but he knew that Claire would soon come to see him, alone. The wild days would be forgotten as though they had never been. He would only meet again the mother of his son, who had rebelled against her true place in the world before taking it for her defense.

Charles turned to Annette. He looked into her green eyes and smiled at her. It was stupid to have cared so much about something which was nearly irrelevant now, but things like the Jockey Club had mattered to him. Now he had a son who would go on to do easily what had been hard for his father. Adam would win without much effort where Charles himself had struggled often and sometimes lost when the odds were against him.

"Annette," he said, "give me your hand."

"Yes, my love."

He took Annette's hand and pulled himself upright, holding onto her. He nearly fell over, but he willed himself to stand straight.

"I'll walk again," he said. "All is possible. All begins."

THE END

★ ★ ★ ★ ★ ★ ★ ★ ★ ★ ★ ★ ★ ★ ★ ★ ★ ★ ★

PEARL

A NOVEL
by Stirling Silliphant

★ ★ ★ ★ ★ ★ ★ ★ ★ ★ ★ ★ ★ ★ ★ ★ ★ ★ ★

In December of 1941, the Hawaiian island of Oahu seemed as close to Eden as any place, until the massive military destruction in the tropical paradise shook the world! PEARL focuses on six people who are permanently scarred by the event: a U.S. Army colonel and his wife; a woman obstetrician and an Army captain; and a Japanese-American girl and a young Navy flier. It is a novel of shattered lives, dreams and innocence, in one of the most crushing events in U.S. history—the bombing of Pearl Harbor!

Now a Spectacular ABC-TV movie!

A Dell Book • $2.50

At your local bookstore or use this handy coupon for ordering:

Dell Bestsellers

A young boy in the Catskills develops into a
famous and breathtakingly skillful magician—
with something to hide. His attempt to keep his
secret from the public draws him onto a bizarre
course that subtly leads into thrilling and
psychologically terrifying regions.

MAGIC

A dazzling psychological thriller
by **William Goldman**
author of *Marathon Man*

"Eerie . . . psychic . . . startling. The goose bumps
grow a little further in your arms as predictable
events somehow become unpredictable."
—*Chicago Book World*

"This dazzling psychological thriller cannot be
put down." —*St. Louis Post-Dispatch*

"A brilliantly alarming novel." —*Cosmopolitan*

A DELL BOOK $1.95

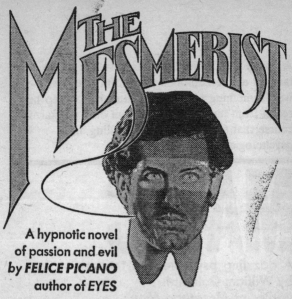

THE MESMERIST

A hypnotic novel
of passion and evil
by **FELICE PICANO**
author of *EYES*

In the Spring of 1899, a stranger came to Center City.
He was young and handsome—but his dazzling smile and
diamond-hard stare concealed a dark and deadly power!
Too soon, Center City was in his debt; too late, it was in his
power. Terror gripped Center City like pain, and only the
mesmerist knew how it all would end—and why ...

"Compelling!"—*Chicago Tribune*

"The reader is pulled into the horror of minds in jeopardy.
A gripping, well-written tale!"—Mary Higgins Clark,
author of *Where Are The Children?*

A Dell Book $2.25